Sacrifice for Love

Vicki Green

What would you do for the one you love?

Vicki Green

Distributed by Createspace

Editor: Kathy Krick @K2 Editing:
https://www.facebook.com/K2Editing

Cover Design by Cover to Cover Designs:
https://www.facebook.com/CoverToCoverDesigns

Published by Entertwine Publishing:
https://www.facebook.com/Entertwinepub?ref=br_tf

Brittany and Leland Hertig on cover:
Brittany:
https://www.facebook.com/BrittanyAufderheidesModelPage
Leland: https://www.facebook.com/LelandHertigModel

Photography of Brittany and Leland by Leland Hertig

Due to strong language and sexual content, this book is not intended for readers under the age of 18+.

This is dedicated to all those who have that special person in their lives

or those that long for one.

Sacrifice For Love (Beyond Love series #1)

By

Vicki Green

It's not hard to sacrifice for the one you love,
Once you find the one to sacrifice everything for.

From the depths of their love comes misery, despair and heartache. For he loves her like no other and she loves him the same, except they are told that their love can never be.

Brock and Taren's love was as innocent as their childhoods. As they grew into adulthood so did their love. Their families were far from friends. Brock from the 'Blue Collar' side of the track. Taren grew up in wealth and privilege. However, that didn't matter to them as they were oblivious to anything but their friendship.

Brock's determination causes him to devise a plan to have what is his. What was always meant to be but, will it be the end for him and Taren? Will his sacrifice cost too much?

A Modern day 'Romeo and Juliet' with a twist.

Prologue

Taren

I remember all the times my parents hated me for going over there, forbidding me to and telling me how wrong it was. They'd tried to ground me, take away my more than generous allowance, and scream at me, but they were not able to stop me. They'd said I needed to stay away from them, from *him*. But I couldn't. We grew up together, spending all of our time together, playing out in the field overgrown with tall grass and weeds. Laying for countless hours watching the stars, sharing his beat up blanket. How can you stay away from the one you love? The only one that loves you unconditionally. How can you shut off feelings inside you when you don't want them to, when just the air you breathe when you're with him is the only thing that helps you want to live?

My parents think that it's a phase that I'll get over and that I'll conform to how they want me to be. Yeah, right. Where they are proper, prestigious and stuffy, I've always been a tomboy. I've wanted nothing more than to wear my tank tops, sneakers and capris or yoga pants, play in the field, throw a ball or climb the big dirt mounds at the constructions sites. I love getting filthy and not having to wear fancy dresses. Many times I got home after dark with dirt clumped in my long black hair and under my fingernails that were too long to have fun the way I wanted, just to have the nanny help me wash my hair in the bathtub. Too many times to count. But God. I just wanted to be me. Why couldn't they understand that? Why couldn't they love me for what I am and not someone they wanted me to be? Infuriating!

Then there's Brock. I've spent so much of my time dreaming about him, fantasizing about us taking off together, making a life for ourselves and being together always. My heart is never still when I think of him. My feelings for him always overwhelm me, and I can't wait until I see him the next time. Every day this occurs and every day I'm planning on how to get out of the house to meet him at our secret place at the far end of the field. I feel like we're stuck in some modern day *Romeo and Juliet* movie. The Capulet's and Montague's (except it's the Mills and Evans') are striving to keep us apart, our love forbidden. And according to my parents, it is very forbidden.

However, as life gives us happiness, it also has a way to take it away. Secrets are kept that I can't even tell Brock, for fear that our love will shatter. That is something I will not, cannot, allow happen. I would cease to exist, and I'm afraid of what he'd do if he ever found out.

My almost happy existence slowly evaporated several months ago, the moment everything crashed down on me and would never be the same again. Brock's parents own a small bar. It's a comfortable place filled with laughter, love and friendship. His dad and brother also own a construction business and between the two businesses they make more than enough to have a good life.

However, my parents are on the "wealthy" side and don't condone me hanging around them even though they are more like my family than my own. My brother, Sebastian, was on their construction crew. He worked hard and loved what he did. Even though my parents didn't think it was good enough for him, that he could do better, they were proud he was one of their crew leaders. He strived for excellence and could do no wrong in their eyes. Then that fatal day. It was the day my world stopped. The day an accident at the site took my brother's life. It was the day my parents tried to sue the company but failed, and the day that I was forbidden to ever see Brock again. Not only did I lose my brother, and the only one in my family that loved me for me, but I lost the love of my life. The one that was going to take me away from my horrible existence, protect me, take care of me and love me forever.

I shiver as I remember the last nine months, the last time I left my room, or ate a good meal. The last time I saw Brock. It's time to give my big girl panties a yank and start to live my life again, even though it's not the life I want.

Chapter One

Taren

"Taren. Come on, girl. You need to eat and get cleaned up. I swear. You're wastin' away in here and look at you. All skin on those bones and no life in those eyes. What you need is a bath and some good food." I watch as Mimi flutters around the room, opening drawers, then walking into my deep closet and reappearing with a dress and heels. She's been my nanny since I was born but has become more like a mother to me than my own. "You know your parents are entertaining tonight. You must keep up appearances." She stops as she sets my dress down on the foot of the bed, the shoes on the floor beneath and looks at me. Sighing, she walks around and sits down next to me and takes my hand, the other one patting the top. "Girl, I know you're hurting but Sebastian wouldn't want you to go on this way. He'd want you to get out there and see Brock, be with him and have the fun you always had. He wouldn't want you to stop living, honey." Her words make me cringe and shake. I haven't heard Sebastian's name spoken since the day we buried him. My heart flutters with the mention of Brock's name. No one is allowed to utter his name in this house. I laugh internally at the thought of living how I want to, defying my parents again and sneaking out of the house to see Brock. However, with the added security they've installed and my cell phone confiscated along with my computer, I have no way to be successful at any attempt. I feel her pat my hand again, bringing me out of my thoughts and focus on her. "You know I'd help you any way I can, child. I've always helped you but they've made it so much harder now. Come. Let's get you cleaned up and get something in your tummy and you'll feel better."

Will I? Will I ever feel better again? Giving up, I allow her to help me off the bed and follow silently into my bathroom. Even the hot water with my favorite lilac bubble bath doesn't help my mood but the feeling of her massaging my scalp as she washes my hair does feel nice. I close my eyes and think about how much of a bitch fate is. I know in my heart that it was fate that brought Brock and me together. Then why is it we're apart? Why was Sebastian taken from me? So young. So much life ahead of him. How can I live without them both? Cruel. Fate is cruel and a bitch.

"I have a surprise for you when we're done." Her eyebrows raise and her eyes widen and I blink fast to clear my head. "There now. Get dried off and dressed and I'll be waiting with your surprise in your room."

A surprise? I wonder what it could be. She leaves and I quickly climb out of the tub, dry off and get dressed. This is the most energy I've had in months, but still my heart is heavy. I brush my teeth, put on makeup and brush out the snarls in my hair. When I enter my room, she's sitting patiently on the bed, and my eyes snap down to a piece of paper she's holding. My heart begins to race with all the thoughts swarming in my head of what it could be. She pats the mattress next to her and I pull my dress up around me as I sit down. "I know this has been difficult for you, honey, and I know this isn't what you want for your life but I think it's for the best." She sighs and pushes some of my damp hair behind my ear. "You know I'd do anything for you. I think sometimes life gives us things to make us stronger even though at the time you think you'll never be able to live again. But I also think fate jumps in at times and throws us more curve balls, adding to the dismay or maybe even making things better for a bit. Either way, we must remain strong. I don't know what fate has in store for you, my darling, but I do know that this...." She holds up the paper, and my eyes follow. "This is meant to be. I don't know how long it will take for this to happen but I truly believe it will, someday. You must stay strong, obey your parents and get back into their good graces. You have to do this even when it's so hard to do, even when you don't want to. It will all be for the greater good later. Trust me."

I practically tear it as I grab it from her hand. She stands and kisses the top of my head and my eyes scan the letter. I look up, deciding I need to slow down to take it all in, and watch her leave the room. Pushing myself back on the bed until my back hits the headboard, I get comfortable and then begin to read, my heart choking me.

Taren,

Fuck, I miss you. I know why they won't let me see you or let me near you. But shit, I want to hold you in my arms so badly, touch your sweet soft skin and tell you that everything will be ok. I went crazy after the accident and wanted to go to the funeral but Pop wouldn't let me. He told me I needed to stay away but all I really wanted to do was come to you and comfort you. I'm so sorry, baby. You know it was an accident and that there's no way Pop would have wanted anything bad to happen to Bast or anyone else for that matter. God, Taren, I'm so sorry about Bast. I know you two were close, and you know I loved him like a brother. Fuck! I want you in my arms right now, run my fingers through your soft hair and hold you tight. I want to be there for you, take care of you. I love you so much, baby. Promise me you'll stay strong. Promise me you'll take care of yourself until we can be together again. You must do what your parents want, for now, get them back on your side then I will take you away, far away. We'll always be together. We were meant to be together. Promise me. I'll try to get another letter to Mimi soon. Stay strong for me. Please take care of yourself until I can take care of you. I love you so much!

Yours always,
Brock

Tears leave my eyes as I crush the letter to my chest, my eyes closing making them fall down my face. With renewed strength, I wipe the tears away and open the drawer on my night stand, hiding the letter under my notebook and push the drawer closed. Hope. A glimmer of hope. He's out there, waiting for me, and I need to do whatever it takes to get to him to be together again.

My stomach turns as I walk down the stairs and head towards the formal living room. When I enter, panic hits me hard as I look at the couple sitting on the couch across from my parents and a young man sitting on the chair between them. He's not a bad looking guy, actually rather good looking, with dark green eyes, dark hair, short and well-kept and a strong jaw. I know what my parents are trying to do. They've wanted nothing but to find me what they call a "proper young man" to marry me, combining our family's wealth. All I can think about in that moment is Brock's face, his eyes pleading to do anything for us to be together. I play my part well, smile and nod at each of them and take a seat in the chair opposite the young man. I feel like I'm on display, probably because I am. My body heats. I feel stifled, panicked, strained.

My eyes snap to my dad when he begins, "Darlene, Grant, Jeffrey. May I introduce you to our daughter? Taren." I shift in my chair when his eyes meet mine, his brows lowering over them.

"Very pleased to meet you, Taren. This is our son, Jeffrey," Grant states with his hand out to the young man. I would say that

Jeffrey is as uncomfortable as I am, however, he gives me a look with hunger in his eyes and my unease just tripled.

"Nice to meet you all," I reply to Grant, ignoring Jeffrey completely.

"Well, now. Grant, how about I refresh your drink. Dinner should be ready soon." They begin to talk all at once since the pleasantries are done. I take a chance to look at Jeffrey, who hasn't moved and is still looking at me. His eyes looking like he wants me for dinner instead of food. "Taren?" My head turns swiftly to my dad to await my orders. "Why don't you take Jeffrey out to the deck and show him the scenery." *Oh, yes. Throw me to the wolves in an isolated spot.*

"Very well. Jeffrey?" I don't bother to look at him as I rise, and we walk down the hallway towards the back deck. I feel the heat of his hand on my lower back and stiffen. We walk out onto our elaborate deck, and I walk until I place my hands on the railing overlooking our huge well-manicured backyard. Since I haven't been out of the house in so long I lean up on my tiptoes and gaze across the vastness knowing I can't see where I want to in the dusk of the day. Through the high trees, over a small road and then beyond at the back of our field is the small shack Brock and I built. We laughed and sweated as we built it together. It's not much, but a place that we could go to be together without prying eyes.

"Taren?" My feet hit the floor when I hear him speak my name and put my fake smile back on as I turn my head to him.

"Okay, so we know this is more than awkward. Nothing like our parents trying to set us up and I can tell you don't want this anymore than I do but…." *Why do I feel like he's going to make me a deal and why do I want to hear it so badly?* I look into his eyes, a smirk on his face and shiver. "Look. I say we let them hitch us. You can have your boyfriend on the side and me my whores. It's a win-win." *Just as I suspected. He's an asshole. An arrogant asshole.*

I smile sweetly and turn to him fully. "I have no intention of marrying you or anyone else my parents try to hook me up with for that matter. However, I wouldn't be against pretending that we *plan* on marrying yet defer once it gets closer. I'm sure Daddy will want a long engagement to fully exploit us being together. In the meantime, I'm sure your father will be more than willing to join partnership with Daddy, thinking we'll soon be family."

His grin broadens as he cocks his head. "I like the way you think, Tare. I think we may be able to work something out."

I walk over, my long fingernail pressing against his starched white shirt, his head lowers as his eyes watch it move up until I reach the bare skin on his neck and he swallows hard. "Just so we're clear. My name is Taren and there are no side benefits, strictly appearances. That's my final offer."

He looks up into my eyes as he smiles, showing his gleaming white teeth. "Like I said. I like the way you think. Even though…." His hand grasps mine, pulling my fingernail away from his skin, and he brings it up to his lips, kissing the top of my hand. "I'd love side benefits with you." My body stiffens once again with the thought of him touching me in any sexual way then his eyes widen. "Oh, don't worry, Taren. I will keep my end of the deal. Trust me?" *Not with an inch of my life.* I nod slightly and relax just a bit. "Good. We have a deal. Shall we?" He releases my hand, placing it in the crook of his arm, and as we walk back inside for dinner the only thing I can think of is how soon I can be with Brock.

Brock

"Hey, Brock! Time for a cold one!" My head turns with the sound of Kane's voice and cold one. Thank God for my brother. He's the only one, well besides my mom that kept me from making a huge mistake and going over to storm Taren's house to get her. And I mean he actually hit me, knocking me down at my parent's bar and right in front of everyone. But I know he did it out of love for Taren and me. I give him a quick nod and finish unloading the skid of wood. Between working construction for Pop, with Kane as foreman, and also working part time at his bar, I've been plenty busy, but I still think of her constantly. What she must be going through. She's basically being held captive in her own house, dealing with the death of her brother and no one is letting me near to comfort her. All I can think about is holding her in my arms, sitting with her in our shack, or staring up at the stars at night while laying on our old beat up blanket. Then again, she's all I think about from when I first open my eyes every morning until I close them at night, it is then that I dream of her.

"Brock! Shit, man! Let's go!" I throw the last piece of wood on the pile then cover it up with the heavy tarp and remove my gloves as I walk towards my bike. After straddling the seat, then starting it up, I follow Kane's truck out of the site. The cool breeze feels great against my overheated skin as we drive down the familiar street until we reach the bar and park it in my normal spot on the side of the building.

It's always like a family affair at Pops Bar since my parents own it and we've spent most of our lives in it. Several pats on our backs and arms as we walk in, people all around speaking at once, then we head straight for the counter. Kane has his normal stool at the end and mine next to it. The two men sitting there take one look at us and smile as they stand, taking their drinks and walking away to find another place to sit. I straddle the stool and notice Irish, sliding two beer bottles down the counter. "Thanks, Irish!" I yell as I pick up my bottle and take a drink as I hand the other to Kane. Irish has been a bartender/waitress here for a couple of years now and grew up down the street from us, her family close friends with ours. She's quite the looker with her long, dark brown hair that reaches down to the middle of her back, but normally pulled up in a high ponytail. She has brilliant dark brown eyes and yes, I'm a guy, so of course I noticed her more than ample breasts as they grew over the years, but she's like a sister to me so uh, no. Just ewww. She and Taren became fast friends and whenever I wasn't with Taren, the two of them were inseparable. Of course her parents hated that too.

"'Bout time your foreman let you off work. Slave driver," Pop smirks as he pats my shoulder on his way by me. I watch him walk to the side, smiling at me and then at Kane as he enters the back of the counter and leans against it in front of us. "Mac! Two hamburgers with all the fixin's." My stomach grumbles at the mention of food, especially the hamburgers here. Even though this is a small bar in one of the oldest neighborhoods around, it has the best food ever. "Kane, you're gonna work yourself and your brother into the ground. Take off at a normal time. I won't be losing my sons and digging their graves early just because of work."

Kane slams his bottle down on the counter and people who don't know him would think he was angry until his wide grin appears. He's always had a tough exterior. His left arm has a tattoo of a Celtic knot around his bicep. Whereas his right side is covered in Polynesian tribal designs that go from around his nipple into the chest plate, then up and over his shoulder and down his arm a quarter of the way. He also has a large back piece that's a black tribal design and it goes from shoulder to shoulder. His body is lean and mean with the workout he gets daily at work and then at the gym on his off hours. I try to join him to work out as much as I can. He normally keeps his face unshaven but trimmed and when he's not wearing his construction hat he usually wears a cap of some kind over his short, black hair. I'm more of the clean shaven baby face, as Ma calls it, with my dark brown hair cut short and sticking up all over the place on top, probably from my fingers running through it constantly. We both have brown eyes.

"Pop, you taught me to own up and meet deadlines, keep it real, work hard and make it work. I'm only followin' in your footsteps and tryin' to bestow your good ethics on your baby boy here." I watch him take a big swig of his beer as he winks at me then reaches over and rubs his hand over my head. I chuckle and push his large hand away.

"Yeah, yeah. Don't give me that crap, boy. Both my sons are hard workers but that doesn't mean work yourself into an early grave. Lighten up. Hey, Brock! You up to working here a little after you eat and rest up? I could use the help tonight."

I know what he's trying to do. I know my family too well and am thankful they're trying to help me keep my mind off of Taren. "Yeah, Pop. Sure." He gives me a smile then leans over and pats my shoulder. Irish brings us our plates, the old fashioned grilled burgers stacked and the plate having an overabundance of fries. "Hey, uh…." Irish smiles as she walks back, smacking the counter with the mustard and ketchup bottles then gives me a wink. "Oh, thanks, Irish."

"Don't mention it. Not like I don't know what you like," she yells as she walks back down along the counter. Again, another great supporter and one that I have really good talks about Taren with, not like Ma who can sympathize but out of her love for her son. Irish actually helps keep me grounded, stops me from making stupid mistakes. Well, most of the time.

I have a great time and practically wolf down my food. Then Kane leaves to go workout and I head back into the kitchen to help out. I'll never understand how he can fill his stomach and then workout, but he says then he can work it off. I think I'd puke. Once the bar closes and we get everything clean, I get on my bike and make the short journey down the dirt road behind the building to my small two bedroom apartment. It's not much to look at from the outside, but Ma helped me when I moved in to make it look and feel homey inside. I park my bike on the side, hidden behind a large tree and walk around to the front, letting myself in the door of the building, and check the mailbox slot on the right. Bills, normal, and a letter that makes my heart skip a beat. As I unlock my front door the feeling of needing a hot shower to wash away all the dirt and grime from the day almost overwhelms me, but instead I sit down on my couch and rip open the envelope with shaky hands. This is the first time I've heard from her since the accident and am wondering how she managed to get a letter mailed.

Brock,
My love. I miss you so much my heart is breaking. I received your letter and I read it several times a day, almost hearing your voice. God, I want to feel your strong arms around me so badly, feel your

skin and look into your beautiful eyes. Soon, my love, soon. Meet me in our special place as soon as I can signal you. I can't wait to taste your lips, lay my head against your warm chest and feel you laying close to me. Don't worry about me so much, I know you are. I'm fine and we'll be together soon. Wait for me.

Yours always,
Taren

I read it a few times, stroking the paper with my calloused finger like I could feel her words. In my mind I'm picturing her sitting on her bed and chewing on the end of her pen as she thought of the right words to write. Soon. I wonder what she has planned. Fuck! I can't wait to see her again, hold her in my arms and kiss her full lips. I've never been inside her. We got close several times, but it never felt right, never the right moment, although I would give anything to be inside her right now. I've dreamt so many times of being with her that way, making love into the night and then holding her in my arms afterwards, her skin aglow in her post-coital state. Damn, my cock is hard just thinking about it.

Turning off all the lights, I walk into my room, placing her letter under my pillow and strip as I walk to the bathroom. I turn on the water in the shower as hot as I can stand it, and as I step under the spray, the water stings my already warmed skin from the sun. I take the soap and get a good lather, spreading it all over my body, the smell of freshness infiltrating my senses. My cock jumps when I grasp it and begin squeezing, stroking up and down its wide girth. "Fuck, Taren!" I yell out as I close my eyes, imagining it's her small hand on me instead of mine. It doesn't take long for my balls to tighten, my release imminent. "Damn!" My scream echoes in the small area as I release all I have, my liquid meshing with the water and swirling down the drain. Feeling a bit better, in more ways than one, I dry off, brush my teeth and run my fingers through my wet hair, then turn off the lights and crawl into bed. I move my arm under my head and stare up at the ceiling wondering what Taren is doing. Is she asleep? Is she laying in her bed thinking of me? Finally, my eyes grow heavy and close.

Chapter Two

Taren

Another day of playing my part. Another day of longing for Brock. I need to find the chance to get free of my parents. I'm hoping they will return my cell phone and laptop to me soon. I need to see Brock, so desperately, hear his low gruff voice and feel his touch. I'm being taken out to dinner by Jeffrey to some chic restaurant. Time to form a plan. I have a hard time dressing, not wanting to get all dolled up. I'd much rather be in my yoga pants, t-shirt, and meet Brock at our special place. I dab on the last bit of mascara when the doorbell rings downstairs and sigh. Time to play my part.

We get to the restaurant and I zone out, feeling numb and not my normal self. "Miss Mills," Jeffrey says in a sweet and somewhat sexy voice as he pulls my chair out for me. Grabbing my dress, I fold it under me as I sit and cross my legs under the table. My eyes focus in on the look Jeffrey is giving the hostess and her cleavage and I try to resist rolling them.

"Your waitress will be right with you, sir."

He winks and smiles at her, and then she walks away flustered. Removing my napkin from the silver ring, I unfold it and place it across my lap, then take a roll from the basket in the middle of the table and spread some butter on it. "Quite a lovely dress, Taren. You look beautiful tonight." He takes a sip of his water, looking into my eyes and I want to reach across the table and smack the smirk off his mouth. If I wasn't so in love with Brock, and if I was a total pretentious bitch, I could totally go for this guy except for the fact that he's an asshole and a total man whore.

"Really, Jeffrey, thank you, but there's no need to be so formal. This is just an arrangement, a deal. You remember that, right?" He sets his glass down and opens his mouth to speak when we're interrupted.

"Good evening. I'm your waitress, Sylvia. Are you ready to order or do you need a few more minutes?"

Sylvia is wearing a tight shirt, showing her ample breasts that are smooshed together by a very skimpy shirt, while staring right into his eyes, ignoring me completely. He's staring right at her breasts, not even looking at her face at all. *Not obvious.* "Ah, yes, Sylvia. We'll have the Bourbon steak, medium rare, asparagus with hollandaise sauce, a dinner salad with Italian dressing and for an appetizer, the oysters on the half shell. Oh, and two gin and tonics. Thank you." My anger starts to boil, and then I watch as he hands the menus to the Sylvia but before she can grasp them, he lets them slip and fall to the floor. "Oh, I do beg your pardon." She bends over to retrieve them, and as he leans down to help I hear him whispering, his eyes still trained directly on her now almost falling out breasts, but I can't hear what he's saying. When Sylvia rises, her cheeks are flushed. She winks at him and then turns and walks away. *Serious, man whore.*

"While I appreciate your kindness, I would have rather ordered for myself. I don't care for half of what you ordered," I tell him, trying to keep my angered voice down.

He reaches across the table and takes my hand, bringing it up to his lips and kisses the top. I yank it back and put it in my lap, quickly. "Now, Tare. It's my job as the man to order for you and I promise you will learn to like whatever I order. As far as our arrangement? Why don't we proceed with the marriage and have our side benefits. I think it would work well for us. Don't you?" His voice causes shivers to run through me.

Another waitress brings over our drinks and appetizer and sets them on the table.

I'm really trying hard to keep my anger at bay, but I'm not sure how much longer I can contain it. As soon as she leaves I lean over the table, trying to keep my voice down. "The name is Taren and we had a deal. If you can't keep your end of it, I can just call everything off. I have no issues with doing that. So, which is it?"

He takes a bite of his buttered roll and then wipes the corners of his mouth with his napkin. I want to wipe the smirk off his fucking face. "Now, now. No need to get your dander up, princess. We still have a deal but you can't blame me for trying. Everything is a sacrifice, everything we do. I just hope yours is worth it."

My sacrifice? Yes, it's worth it. It's worth everything. I will sacrifice whatever it takes for my love. "Oh, it's worth it. What I need is…." The slinky waitress chooses that moment to bring us our food, setting everything down from her large tray in front of us. I about lose the bile that's in my throat from the smell and quickly drink some water.

"I hope you enjoy. Will that be all?" She asks directly at Jeffrey.

"Another of these," he says holding up his empty gin and tonic glass. "And then yes. For now." He winks at her and she saunters away and I pray to God I don't vomit all over the table. He begins to cut his steak and stops, mid cut, and looks at me. "You were saying?" He raises his fork with a piece of steak and sticks it in his mouth. *That's not all I'd like to stick there.*

"Yes, well. I need my cell phone and laptop back from my parents. I need you to talk with my father and suggest it so you can be in touch with me." I look around at the food in front of me and decide I can at least stomach the salad.

"Very well," he says in boredom. "But then you must allow me to take you out again, soon." *Asshole!*

I look up at him, chew and swallow. "Okay, but then you need to let me use you as an alibi one night. Deal?" He laughs. *Laughs.* Not a chuckle either, a full out belly laugh.

"Deals, deals, deals." He leans forward, his arms on the table and looks me square in the eyes, making me feel uncomfortable when I see the hunger in them. "Then you must act more like a true date when we go out. I expect your arm around me, touching me fondly, like you're really in love with me." He sits back and clasps his hands together in front of him. Pride shows on his face like he's getting what he wants. "We are to look like we're to be married, right?" *Okay, this may just kill me, but I'm determined and will get what I want and what I need too.*

"Okay, deal." I sigh, reluctantly.

"Good. Now eat up. I don't care for my women to be too skinny." I watch as he cuts another piece of steak, my appetite leaving with his words, but I manage to get through my salad.

After dinner, he takes me home, walking me to the front door and proceeds to put his arms around me. I stiffen immediately. "Relax, princess," he whispers, his mouth inches from mine. "Audience." My eyes move slowly to the front window and then snap back to Jeffrey when I see the drapes pulled to the side slightly. Reflexively, I swallow hard when his lips touch mine, his hand pressing against my lower back, pulling me closer to him and then his tongue forces its way into my mouth. Right when I push back to slap him, the front door opens stopping me.

He releases my mouth and then leans back, his eyes giving me the creeps, looking as if he wants to devour me. "Ah, Jeffrey. Taren. Good evening. I hope your dinner was enjoyable?" My dad's boisterous voice seeps out into the darkness. We turn to face him and Jeffrey grasps my hand and threads his fingers through mine. *I'm gonna have to scald that hand in hot water as well as my mouth and tongue.*

"Mr. Mills. I was just telling Taren what a lovely evening it has been. Thank you for allowing me to take her out and…." He turns to me, looking all the great actor he isn't and smiles. "Thank you, my dear, for the complete enjoyment of your company tonight." He brings my hand up to his lips, kissing the top lightly but doesn't release it when done. "I look forward to another night very soon. Perhaps Friday night, some dinner, a movie and even a little dancing?" I peek over at Dad who's standing there gloating and then back at Jeffrey.

"That would be lovely, Jeffrey. Thank you for dinner tonight. I look forward to Friday." He kisses my hand again, and then I tug it free, secretly gritting my teeth and trying to disguise the fact that I want to hurl. I walk inside, passed Daddy, and stop when I hear them whispering. *Damn, I can't make out what they're saying.* Running upstairs, I jog to my room and after closing the door, I strip on the way to the shower and set it as hot as I can stand it. After a much needed scrubbing, I get the rest of my nightly duties done and slip on my favorite sleep tank and panties. Once I've settled into bed I lay there, staring at the ceiling and hoping that all of this will be worth it in the end. It has to be. Brock's stunning face enters my mind, his brown eyes that I love so much, and his full lips that I long to kiss and my heart rate increases. I can see him sitting on his motorcycle with his black leather jacket on, even though the heat of the day is burning. His broad chest reveals his wifebeater beneath it, calling to me to run my hand over his soft skin. Sleep doesn't come easy tonight, but as I roll over and place my hands beneath my cheek all I can think about is him.

I awaken with the sun shining and a renewed feeling of determination. A beeping and vibrating sound alerts me to a....TEXT! Oh, my God! I quickly sit up and look at my nightstand, grabbing my phone and scrolling through all the texts and voicemails. Wow, I can't believe I have my phone back! Brock left most of them but there are a few from Irish as well. I listened to all the voicemails, tears falling when I hear Brock's voice, sounding concerned and worried, and I save those. Then I read through all the texts and quickly send a text to Brock, my heart beating so fast in anticipation.

Me: Brock! I miss you!

Almost instantly I get a text back.

Brock: U got ur phone back! Thank fuck! I miss u 2!
Me: Fri nite. Secret place
Brock: Can't wait! Fuck I miss u so much!
Brock: I love u!
Me: I luv u 2!

My smile is huge and I can't wait until Friday.

Brock

Thank God, she's okay. Friday night. Two nights from now.
Fuck! "What's got you all bouncy, Brock?" I turn and see Kane
standing there, with his beefy arms crossed over his chest and giving
me his cocky grin. I could trust him, tell him that I'm gonna see
Taren, but I don't want to put him in the middle, again. Even though
he's always been there for me, watched over me, it's time I stand on
my own two feet. I don't want any of my family getting mixed up in
this again.

"Nothing. Just got stuff on my mind. Things to do, ya
know?" He nods and winks, like he knows something's up. I could
never hide anything from him, but I think this time it would be for
the best.

It was a long day and so was the next. Tonight I'm meeting
Taren and of course the day went slower than hell. After work, I
raced over to the store and bought everything I need for tonight.
Definitely gonna have to take my truck. No way will it all go on my
bike. I decide after my shower to go over there early and get
everything set up. Fuck, I can't wait to see her and hold her in my
arms.

Once I've loaded my truck, I drive the familiar streets to our special place. I look up to my left as I drive on the dirt road, knowing I can't see her house from here as it stands high on a hill, the high trees masking it anyway from my vision. Dusk is fading fast, as I drive. The trees are thick around this area and as far as I know, only Taren and I know the way to the field and our shack. I pull off the road, driving deep into the woods until I get to a small area on the left. It's the only place where a vehicle can park. I grab all the bags, thinking how smart I was to get the big shopping bags with the handles since I also have the cooler to carry too. I stumble across the giant slippery rocks in the creek, thanking God the water isn't high since it hasn't rained much lately and once I get to the other side, I begin the trek to the field.

Taren and I discovered this area one day when we were hanging out and decided to go exploring. I think we were about fifteen. I remember her smile and her giggles as I chased her through the woods, then lost her at one point, and I thought I'd go mad trying to find her. I was running so fast and stopped dead in my tracks when I cleared the trees and ran smack dab into a large overgrown field. My head snapped to the left when I heard her giggle, and I quietly crept towards the sounds of her voice. I had to be careful because the ground made so much noise with the snapping of twigs and the rustle of tall blades of grass. My smile grew when I spotted her purple top. She was looking the other way, her hand covering her mouth. I bend down low as I get closer until I'm right behind her and grab her around the waist. She shrieks and then laughs as I lift her into the air. I turn her in my arms, our breathing heavy, and her mouth changing from a smile to one of awe as her body slides down mine. I think right then is when I knew I loved her. It was like slow motion, like in a movie, when our mouths started getting closer and closer until I couldn't take it anymore and pressed mine against hers, hard. I never did have a lot of patience. Her arms moved around my neck. Her fingers twisted in my hair as my hand moved up her back until it wrapped around the back of her neck. She moaned, and I swear my cock stood straight up against my jeans, pressing against her. Sexiest thing I've ever heard. She pulled away and smiled, but I wanted more. So much more, the horny teenager that I was. But I only wanted one girl, one sweet, beautiful girl who I wasn't allowed to have.

We spent almost every day or night there, as often as we could. I had this brilliant idea to build a cabin, which turned into a small shack, beyond the field. I got wood scraps from Pop's construction sites when he said I could have them. I dodged his and Kane's questions about what I was building and after a while they gave up asking. I thought it was "cute" when Taren wanted to help, and she did, some. She handed me what I needed when I asked, and I let her help decorate inside, and she also helped me paint the outside and inside walls. It took us several months to get it done, but once it was, it was ours. Our secret place.

It was small and intimate but enough room for us to move around, and it was hidden by the tall grass of the field and the tall trees that surrounded it. By the time we were eighteen, I had made it even better. Working in the kitchen at the bar afforded me to buy a double cot, blankets and pillows, a small table with two chairs, and later I even bought a futon that we used as a couch. I got most things from Goodwill, and they were in great condition. We made one small window, putting the small table and chairs underneath, and we had kerosene lamps. I also brought a cooler filled with drinks, eats and ice when we'd go there. I built a small table and bought a used small TV and a DVD player. Of course, there was no running water and no electricity or plumbing. I bought a small generator for those and a small place out back to use as a bathroom. Wasn't like what we were used to, but at least it gave privacy, and we didn't have to go out in the woods. I'd also found an old tub at the dump yard. That wasn't fun to get all the way out here but worth it in the end. Takes a bit to boil enough water for a bath, but we didn't use it often.

I'm shaken from my thoughts as I see the shack coming into view and push away the tall blades of grass. My muscles hurt from working all day and then hefting everything here but so worth it. I set everything down that's in my right hand, so I can open the door and pry it open with a piece of wood to let some fresh air in the stuffy confinements. I walk in and grab the box of matches from the counter, lighting one then open the small door to one of the lamps. A soft glow emanates then I turn it up lighting up the small room. I knew it would be dusty and dirty, so I brought some cleaning supplies as well. I walk straight over to the small window and lift the pane. A cross breeze blows from it to the door and back again giving some relief. When I turn, I see the light flickering and move the lamp out of the breeze. I then light the other one, setting it on the other side of the room and retrieve the bags I left outside. I smile as I spot the old battery operated radio, walk over and turn it on, the sounds of music filling up the quiet area nicely as I begin to get busy cleaning.

When I'm done, I look around feeling pretty pleased with myself at the way everything looks. Fresh flowers set in a vase in the middle of the table on a new tablecloth, giving it a nice feel. Assorted goodies on a plate next to the flowers, music playing, beers chilling in a bucket on the small table next to the futon, candles and kerosene lamps lit causing a soft glow around the room. I check my watch. She should be here any minute. I hope she doesn't get caught or have any trouble on the way here. Maybe I should…. I hear a soft gasp and turn quickly. There she is. Her hands are covering her mouth and her beautiful blue eyes wide, sparkling in the dim light. She's stunning and takes my breath away. Always.

"When? How? This is beautiful, Brock." She doesn't hesitate to run to me, throwing her arms around my neck. Her mouth is on mine as my arms wrap around her tightly. I missed this. Missed *her*. She's everything. I push her back, needing to look at her. It's been too long.

"God, you look amazing. Did you have any problems getting here?" I ask, a bit breathless from our kiss. She smiles and shakes her head and then my mouth finds hers again. I can't help it. I love her.

After some long overdue kissing, we sit at the table, and I get us two beers. "The flowers are gorgeous, Brock. I have to tell you, this place never looked better. You cleaned!" She looks around the room, and I chuckle as I set the beers down and sit across from her. My eyebrows lower as I see her smile turn into a frown as she looks down at her beer, her hands around the bottle. "I didn't think I'd ever get outta there." She looks up, and I see the glimmer of wetness in her eyes. "After…. After the accident, it's like I was held prisoner. Dad took my phone, my computer. I thought I would go crazy and almost did so many times."

"What changed, Taren? Why the change of heart? I know your dad and something had to give. He hates my family and me. Always has but its deeper now." I reach across and take her hand. "I'm so sorry about Bast. You know it was an accident, right? It was horrible what happened but no one caused it, Taren. I swear!" She squeezes my hand, and I watch a lone tear fall down her sweet face. We never got to talk after it happened. I never got to tell her how sorry I was, how he was my friend too.

"I know, Brock. He's always had it out for you and your family. This just made it worse. I know it wasn't the site's fault. I tried to talk to him, tell him but he wouldn't listen. And Mom, well, she just does what he says. She's no help." She stops and looks up at the ceiling. "God! I wish I knew what to do." Her eyes move back to mine, and she sighs. "I'll be twenty one next month. Maybe I can figure out a way to move out, get a place of my own then he can't stop me from being with you, doing what I want but…." She looks down, her hand leaving mine, and then she places both hands in her lap. *Something's up, something's not right. I can feel it.*

"What, Taren. What are you afraid to tell me? You know I'll stand by you no matter what and I'll do anything I can. You can always move in with me. I know Ma and Pop would help you too. You know they love you. And Kane! He'd help as well as Irish. You have tons of people who love you and would be willing to help. Just tell me what to do," I plead.

She stands and walks across the room, her arms hugging her waist, and I know whatever this is can't be good, but I'll do whatever I can to help her. I hear her take a deep breath and turn around, her hands resting behind her on the counter I built so long ago. "You know Pop doesn't like us being together either, well not as bad as my parents, but still." She chews on the inside of her cheek. "I'm supposed to marry Jeffrey Stratton," bursts from her mouth. I stiffen, my hands clenching into fists. "I've told Jeffrey there's no way I would marry him but we made a deal, for appearances only. We pretended we're going to marry so Dad will let me leave the house once again. Maybe I can even get him to give me the money he's been promising for my twenty first birthday early, like for a wedding gift. Then I can leave. Be free of him." I look down, blinking rapidly as my anger boils, then look up as she kneels down between my legs, her hands covering my tight fists. "I had to, Brock. It was the only way I could see you again. Don't you understand? Until I can move out, get away from him, there's no way I can ever be with you." Tears fall as her eyes plead at me, searching for me to understand. But how can I? Jeffrey Stratton and his family remind me once again that I'm from the poor side of town. That I'm not good enough in her family's eyes and would never be. "Please, say something. Tell me this will work, that we can be together. Help me find a way for us to be together always. Tell me you still want me." Her chin quivers and my heart breaks at her sadness.

My fists unclench and I grab her waist, lifting her onto my lap as my mouth latches onto hers. My tongue wastes no time diving in, tasting her sweetness as my hand fists her long hair. I feel like I can't get close enough, never enough. I feel the warmth of her fingers in my hair, and that just makes me press against her mouth harder. The need to breathe causes me to pull away, but I rest my forehead against hers. "God, Taren. I'll always want you. I never want to let you go."

Her breathing comes out in pants as her eyes look into mine. "Then take me, Brock. Please. Please, take me. Make me yours forever. Show me how much you love me." I swallow, adrenaline rushing through me, overwhelming me, the ache of wanting to be inside her so badly, and touching every inch of her soft, velvety skin.

"Fuck, Taren. Are you sure? You know I'll wait, as long as you...."

Her hand moves up and cups my face, her thumb rubbing against my jaw and the look on her face telling me she's more than ready. "I've never wanted anything more. Please?"

Chapter Three

Taren

He lifts me with ease, carrying me the few steps over to the cot and carefully lays me down. His mouth finds mine again as he pulls up on the hem of my silky shirt, his calloused fingers feeling rough on my skin, sending chills through my body. God, I love it. I love him. I raise up as he lifts it off my head and stare into his eyes. He reaches behind me, and I feel my breasts spring free when he unclasps my bra. Slowly, he slides each strap over my shoulders and then down my arms, all the while our eyes never leaving contact. Then for a moment he looks down at my breasts. I should feel shy, even though he's seen them before, but something about the intenseness of the moment, everything that's happened making me bold and carefree. I smile as I lift up his shirt, watching the plains of his flat stomach appear, the tightness of his abs and his broad chest. He helps to remove it, grasping it from his back and pulling it over his head. His skin has a bronze glow, kissed from the sun, and soft to my touch. His peck twitches as I trace around his nipple with my finger. I've always thought he was good looking growing up, gorgeous and sexy, my heart skipping a beat every time I saw him. But now? He's beyond that. He's so much more.

He pushes me down, gently, until my head is laying on the pillow. My eyes close halfway in anxiousness as his fingers trace my skin down to my stomach and then under the waistband of my shorts. Wetness has already begun to pool in the area I long for him to be, aching for him. His eyes stay on mine as he starts pulling down my yoga pants, taking my panties with them, until he has to move back a bit in order to remove them completely. He stands on the floor at the foot of the cot and scans my body. My heart beats wildly in anticipation as he unbuttons his jeans. I watch his muscles flex as he bends, pushing them down and steps out of them. When he stands back up, my eyes zone right onto his very hard cock, standing thick and erect. I swallow hard. I've felt it through his jeans before, but I had no idea just how large it was. Until now.

He crawls onto the cot, his eyes full of desire, and I'm eager for his hunger as I feel the same. He settles in between my legs. His mouth claims mine. My hands quickly move around his neck, and my fingers run through his soft hair that I love so much. He stops. Fear and anxiety fills me that maybe he's having second thoughts. "This is gonna hurt a little, baby. I'll try to be careful." I can feel him press against me, and my legs spread wider. I can't feel any pain as he moves inside, only pleasure until he pushes further, and it's like there's something stopping him from going deeper. I search his eyes and then he thrusts hard and swift. I close my eyes tight as some pain hits me. It's not horrible but that pleasure I had felt is gone. "Are you okay?" I wish I could answer, but I'm holding my breath. "Try to relax, Taren. Breathe." I open my eyes, a tear sliding down into my hair, and I take a shallow breath. His hand cups the side of my face, his thumb moving over my cheek, and he smiles. "That's my girl. Any better?" I nod slightly and take a deep breath. The pain has subsided and now all I feel is him.

He begins moving slowly, deeper until I am full of him. It feels incredible, indescribable. He feels amazing. I've thought about this day, dreamt about it, as I'm sure most girls do, but I never thought it would literally take my breath away. A rhythm starts and suddenly my hips are meeting each movement. This is the best feeling I've ever had, so sensual, and as I look down at where we're joined, heat begins to rise inside me, fluttering up my body. So much love being shared, so tender, gentle and caring. His body starts to shudder, and the look on his face is the most beautiful thing I've ever seen in my life. I never thought he could look more gorgeous, but he does. His brows are lowered. His forehead creased as if pleasure is overtaking him. His lips part and the muscles in his arms tense as he holds himself above me. I can feel something enter me, a little at first and then more. He cries out my name and then collapses half on me, half on the cot. His breathing is heavy, and my heart beats so fast I feel as if it's lodge at the base of my throat.

His head turns to me, and he smiles, but then it turns quickly into a frown. "You didn't have an orgasm." I chuckle, then giggle and laugh. The puzzling look on his face is priceless as I turn on my side, facing him. His cock pulls out of me, and then he turns on his side too. His arm is stretched across my hip, his chest close to mine and our faces are but a breath away. "Well, I wanted you to cum with me. Was it not good? Did I hurt you?" Now his face is sad, and it breaks my heart. I don't want anything but happiness from what we just shared, not sadness.

I brush my finger over the creases on his forehead and smile. "Oh, my darling. I've read it's uncommon for a woman to have an orgasm on her first time. It was amazing. You're amazing. It was something we shared that I will never ever forget. I love you so much."

He leans into me, kissing me sweetly and then moves back, looking into my eyes with such love. "Fuck! I didn't even ask if you were protected. I'm so stupid, I...."

I place two fingers over his lips and he kisses them. "I've been on the pill for my irregular cycle for a few years. It's okay. Don't worry and you're not stupid."

The corner of his mouth turns up into a grin as he lifts and moves over me. I turn onto my back and my arms move around him as he presses his mouth against mine. "Well, good then. In that case, I'm ready to have more of you. And we'll just have to keep trying until you have an orgasm." A giggle escapes me, but when he plunges into me, my head tilts back and a moan leaves me from deep within. "God, Taren. I can't get enough of you. I'll never have enough. You feel so good. Fuck!" My hips are moving in his fast rhythm, and then he touches me where no one has ever touched me before. When he rubs my swollen clit, my hips buck wildly. "I want you to cum this time, baby. I want you to feel what I feel when I'm inside you, when I fall into ecstasy."

My head lowers, and I look into his eyes. I look lower until I see his finger rubbing and circling. My breathing accelerates as I watch his cock pull out almost fully and then thrust back inside me. *So hot!* I begin to feel a foreign sensation brewing in my stomach. The tingles I felt before move through me, but they're more extreme, and then that heat begins again. He starts to move faster, and I try to keep up as best as I can. I hear panting above the low music and realize it's us. As his finger increases its speed and presses down, the flame of the heat intensifies and starts moving all the way up my body quickly. A sudden rush of what I can only describe as adrenaline hits me hard and I cry out. "Brock!" My eyes feel out of focus as the sensations flowing through me are so incredible, strong and overpowering. I feel high, weightless, like I'm almost floating, but yet I can feel the heaviness of his body on mine. It's so weird, strange and amazing all at the same time. This time when he leaves me, I actually whimper from the loss. I feel a pulsing, where he was, and I'm tender but God, it feels heavenly.

I watch as he walks over to the bucket of water on the counter, taking a cloth and dipping it in. He returns and smiles down at me. "This is gonna be…."

"COLD!" I yell as he brushes the cloth against my sensitive area.

"Sorry," he whispers.

He cleans me, and I watch him clean himself, which makes me horny again, then he throws the cloth into a small basket in the corner. He climbs back onto the cot beside me, brings the blanket up over us and I roll over until I'm in his arms, my head laying on his strong chest, feeling his heart racing beneath. I close my eyes as I feel his lips kiss the top of my head and then his warm breath as he speaks. "That was incredible, Taren. God, I love you. So much. We need to get you out of your parents' house and move in with me. You're an adult. You could do it, you know? Move in with me. I swear I'll take care of you. It might be hard on you though, maybe you shouldn't. You wouldn't have the money you're accustomed to and…."

My head raises as my hand moves up the warm skin of his chest until I place a finger over those luscious lips. "Stop. Let me follow through with this plan. When I turn twenty one I'll receive the large sum of money. That will be the time to leave there, move in with you and we can start our lives together. Trust me?" He sighs and then smiles, nodding. "I know it seems like a long time and I want nothing more than to be with you, you know that, but the money will help us begin in a better way. I'll have more time to find a job and help out with everything."

"I don't want you to work. I can take care of you, baby."
He's so sweet.

"I know, babe. You work so hard and I appreciate it but what would I do all day? I'd have too much time to sit around the house and long for you to get home. It would make me crazy." My head moves with his deep laugh. I rise, resting my head in my hand, and he does the same. We stare into each other's eyes for a few minutes, his finger tracing my skin at the base of my neck, and I feel so loved, so comfortable. "I'm going to apply this week at the newspapers in town, try to put my writing degree to use. Are you ready to do this next month? I mean…." I look down and take his hand, tangling my fingers with his. "Do your parents know that we want to be together? I mean, I know they know about us but do they realize…."

He releases my hand, and my eyes look up into his as he raises my head with his hand on the side of my face, his fingers weaving into my hair. "Baby, my parents know how I feel about you. They may not like your parents after everything that happened with…. Well, you know. But they've always known my love for you is strong and that we want to be together. I'll talk to Ma, on the side. She understands better than anyone. Now, c'mere."

My heart swells and my smile rises as I move back into his arms. I lay my arm across his slim waist, feeling the bulges of his tight abs, and squeeze with all the love I'm feeling. I look up at him and see him watching me. "You can say his name. It's okay. Sebastian was your friend." He smiles and I watch his throat constrict as he swallows. We never had the chance to talk about the accident and I really don't want to spoil our time together by doing it now but he needs to understand that I don't want to ever forget my brother. Bast understood what Brock meant to me, means to me. Bast, Irish, and Brock's family have always been a part of Brock's and my lives, even when my parents wouldn't condone it. I lay my head down on his chest and can hear his fast heartbeat and right now, I'm already home.

We laid in bed for an hour, talking and planning how things will be once I move in with him. He said I could redecorate his apartment, make the spare bedroom my office, if I wanted. He talked about how he would take care of me, worship, and protect me, and how one day he would marry me. With a heavy heart and much reluctance, we cleaned up the shack, turned off the lamps and I helped him carry things back to his truck. He held my hand the entire way, making sure I didn't fall along the way or slip off the rocks while we cross the creek.

"Do you have everything? Uh, you might want to put on a little, uh, makeup and brush your hair. You look like you just had sex." He smirks as we reach his truck.

"I did have sex." I smile as I reach into my purse, grab my brush and start running it through my long tangled hair. He winks and smiles as he lifts the bags into the bed of his truck, and I watch his strong muscles flex which each movement. After he's loaded everything and I've managed to make myself look presentable, his hands grasp my waist, lifting me into the passenger seat of his tall truck, and I watch him walk around the front as I buckle my seatbelt.

He decided to drive me back to the dirt road, so I wouldn't have to walk as far.

As he starts the truck, I look at the clock on the dashboard. A little after midnight. With any luck, Daddy would have gone to bed thinking Jeffrey and I would be home late from our date. With my luck? He's probably still sitting up in the living room reading one of his history books. I hold onto the door handle as the truck bumps over the uneven terrain. The trees looking a bit scary in the darkness, but I've been through here so many times over the years that I'm not afraid. He finally pulls out onto the dirt road and drives for a little bit then pulls over off to the side. Once he puts it in park and leans towards me, I follow until our mouths meet. Our hands are all over each other, and our kissing starts heating up my body, from the inside out. "Fuck, I don't want you to go. I wish…. I wish you were coming home with me now, never leaving again. A month is gonna be an eternity." We press our foreheads together, our heavy breathing the only sound in the truck. I don't want to leave either. I want to go to bed with him, lay in his arms, feel him inside me again and sleep with him tangled up together all night.

"I don't want to go." His eyes widen, and I feel bad because I know he's thinking I've changed my mind. "But I have to, my love. A month isn't so long, not after the last several months we've been apart. At least now I can sneek away and meet you again at our special place. We can at least look forward to those nights until we can be together forever." His eyes sadden, but he nods. I kiss him one more time, grab my purse and bag from the floor, put the strap over my shoulder then kiss the tips of my fingers and place them on his swollen lips. "I'll text you. Soon, darling. Soon." With a heavy heart, I open the door and climb down, shutting it and look at him through the window. I mouth "I love you" and smile as he mouths it back to me. I turn and look up the hill, dreading the long walk back.

I get about halfway up when I hear the engine of his truck and turn, watching it begin to move up the road, but it's hard to make out in the distance and darkness. I touch my lips, still feeling the warmth of his and smile. I continue to walk and before long I see the back deck coming into view. Finally, I walk up the steps and to the back door, slowly sliding it open, so I don't make any noise. I head straight into the huge pantry closet, set my bag down, open it and dig for my sleep clothes. Quietly, I change and stuff my clothes in the bag, zipping it back up slowly and pushing it under the last shelf. My parents never come in here, only Mimi and the maid, so I'm sure this will go unnoticed until the morning when I can retrieve it and take it to my room. I close the door to the pantry and walk over to the cabinet, getting a glass and then to the sink, filling it halfway with water and then walk out of the kitchen and towards the stairs. Just as I thought, Daddy's sitting in his big leather chair, a book in his hand, and from the side view, I see his reading glasses low on his nose.

I try to calm my racing heart and take a deep breath. "Daddy?" His head turns to me, his eyebrows raising high. "You should go to bed. It's late."

"Oh! When did you get home?" his voice rough and hoarse from reading. He clears it and smiles. "I didn't hear you come in? How was your date with Jeffrey?" Relief flows through me along with calmness as I walk into the room and sit down across from him, taking a drink of my water.

"It was nice. I didn't want to disturb your reading so I went directly upstairs. I got thirsty and came down for a glass of water." He smiles again and removes his glasses, rubbing his eyes with his finger and thumb, marking his place in his book then closes it.

"That was nice. Yes, I'm getting quite tired. I think I'll head up to bed." He rises and takes the few steps to me, kissing the top of my head and walks out of the room.

I follow, turning off his reading light and then upstairs until I'm safely in my room. I lean against the door as I close it, releasing the breath I'd been holding for so long, blowing some strands of long hair away from my face. I did it! I can't believe it worked. Quickly, I take my phone from the waistband of my panties and walk across to my bed, sitting down and then send off two texts.

Me: Made it! It worked! Can't wait 2 c u again

Brock: Thank fuck! Me too! When?

Me: Let me check. Will let u know

Brock: God. I hope it's soon! Love u

Me: Love u 2!

I smile, kiss my finger and touch the screen then send off the next one.

Me: It worked. Thank u

Jeffrey: Good. U owe me

Me: I know

Jeffrey: Tomorrow night. Date

Me: k

Ugh! I lay down, my back bouncing on the mattress and sigh. I guess I have to take the bad with the good. I just hope I can keep him from trying anything, or I'll need to change my plan. I sit back up, plugging my phone into the charger, setting it on my nightstand, pulling back the covers and settle into bed. Staring up at the ceiling, all I can think of is Brock, how he touched me, made love to me and how I'm no longer a virgin. I feel different. I wonder if anyone will be able to tell. Brock's right, it is gonna be a long month. Finally, I close my eyes and let sleep take me.

Brock

I think I got about two hours of sleep. I worried about her until I got her text that she was home safely. I wish she would stop thinking about the money and just leave. I won't lie. The money would be great and would really help out, but I don't care about it. I can provide for us. If she got a job at one of the papers that would help too, however, I really want to take care of her. Ma's always worked, and I know my parents struggled until the business at the bar and construction company picked up. We can do that too, I don't mind. I'd do anything for her. Anything to have her with me always.

I finally get up, take a quick shower and head over to my parents. Ma makes the best breakfast, and I'm starving! She always takes the mornings off as Pop gets the bar ready. Kane and I always meet up over there, stuffin' our pie holes with her awesome food. They only live down the road from me in the small house that we grew up in but one filled with care and love. Pops had a really hard time when he and his business was accused of killing Sebastian from Taren's dad. I saw it happen and there's no way the construction site had anything to do with it. Kane and I had to go testify in court, and it was one of the longest days of my life. It was the only time I got to see Taren. She was so pale, so shaken up. I just wanted to hold her, comfort her, but I wasn't allowed anywhere near. Her dad hated me anyway, thought I wasn't good enough for her, then after the accident, he blamed my whole family, and I was considered even lower than dirt in his eyes. Now, Pop hates him, hates what he put our family through. He told me right after court I shouldn't be around Taren anymore, that nothing good could come from that family. Ma understood though. She knows Taren and I love each other, and that we're meant to be together. She told me to give it some time and that Pop would come around. I'm not so sure.

"Ma! I'm starving!" I yell then stop dead in my tracks when I get to the kitchen doorway. There sits Taren's mom. What the fuck? I look over at Kane sitting at the table eating. He looks up at me with sympathy and confusion, shrugging his shoulders.

Ma turns around in her chair and smiles. "Brock, you remember Mrs. Mills?" I nod slightly, my stance stiff. "She came by to talk with you." She turns to Mrs. Mills. "Betty, you all can go in the living room for some privacy." I watch Mrs. Mills smile, stand then walk past me into the living room. I begin to turn when I feel Ma's hand on my arm and look at her. "Brock, dear. Be nice and listen to what she has to say. Not everyone is against you and Taren." I raise my eyebrows with this news. She pats my arm, her smile giving me the encouragement to go and see what Mrs. Mills wants.

When I walk into the room, Mrs. Mills is sitting on the couch. She looks at me and smiles as I walk over to a chair and sit. "I won't lie, Mrs. Mills. I'm a bit surprised to see you here." Then my thoughts are all over the place, my heart beginning to beat faster. "Is Taren okay? Did something happen?"

She sits up straight as her eyes widen. "Oh, no, dear. It's nothing like that. I just wanted to chat with your mom and also tell you that you and Taren have some support." She looks down at her hand, holding a tissue, and frowns. "I never thought it was your father's construction site or your family that had anything to do with Sebastian's accident." She looks up at me with pleading eyes. "I tried to tell Tom but of course he's too stubborn to listen, too eager to blame someone. You have to understand, he only wants what's best for Taren but something inside him died when we lost our son. I know he's never been very civil to you or your family and I'm sorry for that. I guess he's set in his ways from his upbringing and he may never change. But…. I know what young love is and I will do what I can but know that I am limited. He doesn't listen to anyone when he gets his mind set."

This has to be the oddest conversation but yet I feel a little hope, having her and Ma on our side. "Does Taren know? Does she know she has your support? I'm more concerned with her than myself."

She smiles and relaxes. "I'll tell her. She was out rather late last night." I stiffen and swallow. "She seems a little different this morning. Happier. Would you know anything about that?" She tilts her head and smiles. *Shit, what do I tell her? Do I tell her where she really was? Fuck! I don't know what to do.* "Oh, never mind. I'm sure she'll tell me, if there's something to tell. We've not been very close and I'll always regret that. I'll talk with her when I get home."

I relax and feel like I'm sweating bullets. She stands so I do too. "Please, tell your mom thank you for the tea and we'll chat again soon." I nod as she turns and walk towards the front door, but then she stops and turns to me. "Just do me one favor? Don't make me a grandmother before my time." My heart stops as she turns and walks out the door. *Fuck! She knows.*

"It was very nice of Betty to come here, don't you think?" I jump at the sound of Ma's voice, like a jump start to my heart. I turn around to find her smiling. "I have to agree with her. Don't make me a grandma before my time."

"How does she know? How do you?" I whisper.

She walks to me and takes my hand as her smile broadens. "Oh, we mother's know. We can tell, at least with a daughter. Sons are a little harder to figure out but daughters? We can see it in their eyes, their skin and how their mood changes with their happiness." *Damn!* "Brock, you both are adults and I know it's been hard on you, the accident, her dad and just the circumstances but know that I will always stand by you, support you in everything. It seems Betty will too but I think it's more difficult for her. I'm not making excuses for Tom. God knows he's always needed a swift kick in the…." I grin and try to hold in my chuckle. "But losing a son. Well, I just can't imagine. Losing a child would do something to you. I know he's never really liked you, because of us, because of how we live, but that probably drove him over the edge." She stops and shakes her head. "If you all decide to have a life together, I'm sure it will be hard on her without her father in her life because I'm not so sure he will ever condone it." She releases my hand and grasps my upper arms with her hands. "Just know you all have support, you have other family that will be there for you both."

I swallow hard again almost choking on my feelings. "Pop?"

She pats my arm. "Give him some time. You know he's always liked Taren, been there for you and Kane, even Irish. He loves his family. Time will heal things. Now, go eat. I'm sure everything's cold now."

She leaves and walks upstairs so I walk to the kitchen. I take the plate of food set out for me and stick it in the microwave. "So, you and Taren finally did it, huh?" I freeze at Kane's words.

Chapter Four

Taren

Standing in front of the mirror, I touch the skin on my cheek. Do I look different? I feel different. I feel like a woman. A woman in love. A woman who had *sex* with the man she loves. My hand moves down my flat stomach as I remember Brock's gentle touch. The little bit of soreness I feel reminding me where he'd been. A knock on my bedroom door interrupts my thoughts and I slip on my robe, almost skipping there. I open it quickly. "Mom."

She smiles, carrying in a tray. I watch as she takes it over to my nightstand, setting it down and then sits down on the end of my bed. "Good afternoon. I brought you a sandwich and some tea. Thought you might be hungry." She pats the mattress and smiles. "Come. Sit with me for a few minutes."

I walk in confusion to my bed, sitting down by my pillow. I wonder what she's up to. She and I have never had that close of a relationship, although I've always wanted one. But she's always stood behind Daddy, whatever he wants or says. I don't know whether to be happy about her being here or worried. I pick up the cup of tea and take a sip. That actually tastes really good and the warm feeling of the liquid flowing through me.

She looks at my dresser, stands and walks over, picking up the picture of me and Sebastian. It was taken on the beach. I think I was about five and Bast was seven. We always had such a great time when they would take us there.

"This is one of my favorite pictures of you and Sebastian." She traces over Bast's image with her finger, like she could feel him. "You're too young to know what it's like to lose a child and I hope that you never know this feeling, this loss." She turns to me, still holding the picture and I can see the glimmer of tears in her eyes. "I know you feel the loss of losing a brother, that's equally as hard but bringing a child into the world, nurturing them, teaching them, watching them grow into adulthood and then to be taken away is the hardest thing I think a mother can bear." She wipes away a fallen tear, sets the picture back down, and turns to me with a sad smile. I watch her walk over and sit down next to me, folding her hands on her lap. I take a sip of my tea and set the cup back down on the tray. "I'm sorry I haven't been there for you like I should." My head snaps to her. "It's no excuse, really, but with your father and my upbringing, there wasn't much family closeness. It was more support the man of the house, his decisions, his actions. I should have been there for you regardless." She looks down at her hands. "I've made so many mistakes. I…."

I place my hand on top of hers. "No, Mom."

Her head rises and she looks at me. "Yes, I should have. A mother's love should be unconditional. A mother should support everyone in the family no matter what."

"You've been there most of the time, Mom. You have," I plead.

She pats my hand and smiles. "Well, I just want you to know that I've missed too much with you and Sebastian. It's too late for me to make it up to him but not you. Now, tell me all about Brock. I know you two have been together since you were little but I think things have changed." *Oh, my God! She knows! Nah, she couldn't. Could she?*

"I…. I don't know what you mean. I don't know what you want to hear, Mom. I mean, yes, we are very close but Daddy…."

"Tut. I know what your father wants but I don't want you to have to live with someone that doesn't make you happy. Someone you don't love. I want better for you than what I've been through." My eyes widen in shock. "Oh, don't get me wrong. At one time, when we were young and first starting out, I loved him." She looks up at the ceiling like she's remembering. "He was my world." She looks back at me. "Still is. But he's changed over the years. I've stood behind him but with you, I will do my best to support you as much as I am able."

I lean into her, her arm moves around me and over my shoulder. "He's everything, Mom. I love him so much."

I feel her run her fingers through my long strands of hair, and I feel something inside that I haven't felt since I was younger. A mother's love. "Just be responsible, Taren." My eyes go wide, and my heart begins to race. "What are you going to do about Jeffrey?"

I sit up slowly and look down at my lap. "I'm not sure yet. I...." *God, what do I tell her?* I can't lie to her, not now, not after our talk. I look up at her and take a deep breath. "Jeffrey doesn't really want me either, Mom. Right now, we're just going out for appearances but.... I know it's not the right thing to do but I...."

"It's okay. I won't meddle but just know there are feelings involved in any decision you make. Remember that." She kisses my cheek and then stands, walks to the door and closes it behind her, leaving me with a lot to think about.

By early evening I get ready for my so called date with Jeffrey. He told me to dress comfortable so I put on a pair of black jeans, a nice silk blouse and my nice black sandals. I'm dreading this so much and almost want to fake a headache but then when I want to meet Brock again I won't have an alibi without Jeffrey covering for me. Ugh! I hate this! Why can't life be simple? Why can't Brock and I just be together and live happily ever after? Living a life of wealth is not what people make it out to be. If they only knew. My phone vibrates on the dresser and I all but run to get there to pick it up.

Brock: When do I see u? Fuck I miss u!
Me: Soon baby. I'll let u know.

Brock: Hurry. I want u in my arms.

Me: Me 2!

The doorbell rings and my heart drops. I look at my reflection in the dresser mirror and take a deep breath. Time to get my big girl panties on! I grab my purse, throw my phone in it, and walk out of my room and down the stairs. Jeffrey's smile is huge as I approach him and so is Daddy's. Jeffrey takes my hand and kisses me on the cheek and then looks at Daddy, Mom standing beside him. "Well, sir. We may be out a bit late tonight, with your permission." *Suck up.*

"That's fine, son." *Son?* "Just take care of my little girl." *His little girl? Sheesh!*

He takes my hand and pulls my arm through his, patting my hand. "Yes, let's go, Jeffrey. I'm famished." I lean forward and kiss my mom on her cheek, and then we turn and walk out the front door. I notice it doesn't shut behind us, so I can only imagine Daddy watching his prodigal son leaving. He opens the car door for me and then closes it once I sit down, and he's quickly in his seat and backing out of the driveway.

"Great performance, Tare. Award winning." *God, he's suck a jerk.* "How was last night? Did you get some?" He asks smugly.

I look straight, not giving in to the urge of wanting to smack him. "It was nice, thank you."

I see him staring at me from my peripheral but I don't look at him. "Oh, come on now, baby. I know you got some. It's written all over your face. I'm surprised good ole daddy didn't say anything. He must be a stupid fuck."

I feel the heat rise in my face as I turn to him. "Look. Thank you for helping me but don't call my daddy names. You have no right! And what I do when I'm not with you is none of your business. That was not part of the deal." *God, I want to punch something, mainly him.*

"Oh! Don't get your dander up, girl. I was just playin'," he responds dryly.

The silence is thick as he drives us to our destination. He takes me to a nice little diner, not too crowed and clean. After ogling the waitress, he places our orders, not letting me decide what I want to order, again. "So, can you cover for me again tomorrow night, please," I ask sweetly.

He sets down his drink and wipes the corners of his mouth, and I cringe internally. "Well, what's in it for me? I'd love to help you out but…. I scratch your back, you scratch mine, so to speak." *I want to scratch his eyes out.* I need to think of something that won't get me in trouble and won't make me want to kill him. "I know! We can go away for a weekend. Somewhere cold, like skiing." *What? Oh, no, no, no, no, no, no!*

Then a brilliant idea hits. "Well, an entire weekend? Hmmm. I think that would take a few times covering for me first, don't you?

That's only fair." I take a bite of my roll and internally high five myself. If I can play this right, it would be a month before our so called weekend trip, I would turn twenty one and move out and right into Brock's arms.

"Hmm, I don't know, Tare." My heart is beating so fast and I suddenly feel ill. "Well, maybe we can work something out. I'll cover tomorrow night, then we'll talk. But for now? You're mine tonight. Ah, here's our dinner." I breathe a sigh of relief and hope I can get through the night unscathed. *God, I fucking hate when he calls me that.*

Brock

"What's got you so quiet tonight, Brock?" Kane disrupts my internal monologue and I take a drawl of my beer then look at him. He sighs. "Hey, I'm sure she's fine. She's a strong girl. Give her some credit." He takes a drink and winks. We're so opposite. I worry about everything and he's cocky, sure, and confident. My hair is brown and cut short but his is black and keeps it closely shaven. Ma says I have a baby face, always kept clean shaven where he has a scruff of black hair on his. Sometimes I wonder if we are really blood related.

Pops Bar is really crowded tonight. Sounds of laughter, talking, and pool balls being struck, rolling over the green felt of the pool tables, are all around. The dart machine rings as people score and the TV's arranged all over the place are on different channels. The atmosphere is full of life. I imagine some are relaxing after a long day of work, others just hanging out with friends and maybe some are on a date.

"I know you're worried about her, it's natural when you're in love but I think she can take care of herself." I glare at him, feeling uncomfortable. "What?" The confusion on his face would be comical yet it's not.

I lean closer, gritting my teeth. "Will you lower your voice, Kane? Fuck. Did you not hear anything I said this morning?" Rolling my eyes I move back and bring my beer up to my mouth, draining the bottle.

"I heard you. So you both had sex for the first time, doesn't mean you need to babysit her. And no one can hear us over all this racket," he laughs. I smack his arm, irritated.

A beer bottle slams down in front of me causing both Kane and I to jump. I look up into the eyes of Irish, whose face is filled with anger. "No one can hear, huh?" I sneer at him. He leans to the side, laughing, as I try to hit him again.

"Why am I just now hearing about this? Her best friend. What the fuck, Brock?" Anger radiates from her, foam rises from the top of the bottle and spews over, running down onto her hand.

I slide my empty bottle across the counter towards her and grasp the full one, tugging a little but she's got a firm hold on it. "Look, Irish. I'm sure she'll tell you, she's just…."

"I'm her best friend. We've always shared everything that happens to us with each other," she growls. *And I mean growls.*

"Come on, Irish. Give the girl a break. After everything that's happened lately, have some patience," Kane speaks and her eyes snap to him. I take advantage and reach over and pry her fingers loose then snatch the beer. *Girl has a firm grip.*

"YO, IRISH!" Her head whips the other way when Pop calls her. *Thank God.*

She starts to walk off but snarls my way. "I'll have a little patience but I better be hearing from her by tomorrow." She continues to mumble as she walks down behind the counter to a customer.

"Damn, that girl can be wicked. Good thing she likes us," Kane says, smiling over the top of his bottle. A laugh escapes me and damn it feels good. He slaps me on my shoulder and chuckles. "Everything will work out, bro. I really believe that you are meant to be together. I know it's not the best circumstances, her dad being a jerk and all, but I have faith it'll work out. Now, be a good little brother and go around the bar and get me another beer. I'm dying of thirst here." Rolling my eyes, I get up and walk around the counter, bend over the ice chest and set a beer down in front of him then walk back around and sit down.

"Hey, Kane! Wanna play some pool? I got some money to back me up tonight!" I look over my right shoulder and see Greg, one of the guys on our crew, standing there with a pool cue.

The guys in our crews are a tight knit bunch. Kane hangs around them when he's not off with a woman. Kane's always been there for me, had my back, gave me a job and listened when I needed an ear to tell my troubles to. I couldn't ask for a better brother. Now, if only he could find a woman to tame his womanizing ways, that would be a miracle.

"Hey, stranger," a sexy voice rings from over my shoulder. I turn my head to see one of Kane's many women bent down over his shoulder, her arms around his front and hands rubbing across his chest.

His hand grasps her arm as he turns his head slightly. "Ah, Bambi. Where ya been, girl?" He looks over at Greg, shakes his head and smiles. "Sorry, man. Another time. I think I just became busy." I roll my eyes as he stands, turning until his arms are wrapped around Bambi, his mouth takes hers and I swear I heard her moan. "Catch ya later, bro," he says while staring at her then tosses a couple of bills on the counter. I watch them walk towards the front door, arm in arm.

"Too bad for me but great for him. Wanna play, Brock?"

I watch Kane leave the bar and slowly turn to Greg. "Sure, why not? Haven't got anything else to do." I grab my beer as I stand and turn. He claps me on my shoulder and laughs.

"I hear ya, man. I hear ya."

I walk alongside him and watch as he racks up the pool balls. It's gonna be another long night.

About midway through our third game, I switched to water so I could help clean up once the bar closes. Now, I'm back in the kitchen mopping and trying to finish up so I can get home. I haven't heard from Taren, except once, telling me she loved me and that she can meet me tomorrow night. I'm excited and yet frustrated, wishing we didn't have to sneek around, that we could just be together. I'd love to be able to take her out, walk hand in hand, kissing her when I want and lay with her in my arms at night. Maybe someday.

"Hey, Brock!" I look up just in time to release the mop handle and catch the keys Pop throws at me. "Lock up, will ya?" I just nod and stow them in my front pocket as he turns to leave. It takes me no time to finish mopping then clean off all the counters in the kitchen and turn off the lights as I walk back into the bar area. I see Irish cleaning the bar counter and nod at her when she looks up.

"Hurry up, Irish. I'm ready to go home," I yell as I walk down along the counter, pushing stools in as I go.

"Keep your pants on. Almost done," she yells back, not looking up.

I chuckle as I sit down on the last stool, in Kane's place, and watch her. "You know, she would have told you sooner but she's had so much going on. You know that, right? Besides, she just got her phone back from being confiscated from her dad." She looks up at me and then puts the rag down below the counter and walks over, resting her arms on the cleaned surface.

"I know. It's just…. Well, you know I only have you and your family as friends besides her." She sighs. "I feel so bad for her. After her dad made her a prisoner in her own house, I was so mad I had to punch out the bag at the gym. I couldn't text her or talk to her online and was ready to go over and tell her dad just what I thought about him. If it hadn't been for Kane, the voice of reason, I would have." *Ah! I know that feeling too well.*

I smile. She's such a good friend and I know she'd do anything for Taren. "I hear ya. I about did the same thing. Kane can be a dickhead sometimes but he is pretty smart. Don't tell him I said that." I chuckle.

She laughs and then holds out her hand, giving me her famous smirk. "Gimmee the keys. I'll lock up. I have a couple more things to do to get ready for tomorrow." I dig the keys out of my pocket and place them in her hand.

"Thanks, Irish. I owe you." I get up, pushing in the stool and start walking to the front door.

"Again!" she yells out. "You owe me, again!"

I laugh as I unlock the door, then turn and wink at her, closing it behind me. I stand there in the night's slight breeze and start to walk towards my bike, hearing the automatic lock of the door click behind me. I get to the edge of the building when someone grabs my upper arm, pulling me around the corner. I let out a groan when I'm pushed against the building, a strong hand around my throat. Searing pain rocks me as I feel a fist connect with my cheek, the feeling of metal cutting my skin and warm liquid sliding down my face. My vision is clouded for a moment as I struggle, my hand pushes against a firm chest, the other pulling on the arm pinning me.

"'Bout fucking time you came out. I was getting rather impatient," a low voice sneers. My vision starts to return, and I look into the dark eyes of Jeffrey Stratton. "Just wanted to give you a few reminders, asshole." I cringe when his fist rams into my ribs, my breathing accelerating but his hand around my throat tightens making it hard to take a breath. "Leave Taren alone." My eyes close as pain flows through me and then reopen to see the anger in his eyes. Something shiny catches my eye from the small overhead light at the end of the building and I see what cut me. A big ring on his finger, a wide band and large diamonds surrounding it. "She's gonna marry me, joining our families and we'll be rich. Something you can't give her." I bite my lip keeping my groan muffled when his fist connects with my cheek again, the metal of his ring slicing into my skin again. Another jab to my ribs and I start to feel dizzy. When he release his hold, I fall to the ground gasping.

My arm immediately moves around my stomach, my other hand pressing on the ground in front of me, trying to stop me from collapsing completely. "HEY!" Irish's loud voice bellows in the night.

"Next time, I won't be so nice, asshole," he sneers, kicking me in the ribs as he starts to walk away then shortly after footsteps come running towards me.

Irish is on her knees beside me, her hand on my back. "Geez, Brock. What happened?"

I look up at her, one eye swelling quickly and blood running down my face. "Just some friendly reminders," I choke.

She puts her arm around my waist and struggles to stand me up. "Shit! I'd like to give some friendly reminders not to touch my friends. Come on, let's get you home and clean you up. Should we call Dean?" She half drags me to her truck, and I look over at my bike next to it. "No way, slugger. You can get it tomorrow. Come on." She opens her passenger door and helps me inside. My head lulls back onto the head rest, my eyes close, and I wince. "You look like shit, man." She speaks as I hear her door shut and the truck starting.

"You should see the other guy," I laugh and then grimace as pain shoots in my side. "No calling. I'll deal with it."

"Oh, good. So you got him a couple of times?" Her voice sarcastic, as usual.

The truck bounces on the dirt road, my hold tightening around my waist. "Fuck, no! I wish. He had me pinned against the building, caught me off guard then kept hitting me too fucking fast."

The truck stops abruptly, and I open one eye, the other already swollen shut, to see my apartment building. *Thank fuck! I just want to crawl in bed.* She gets out, runs around and opens my door, helping me out. She keeps her arm around my waist as we walk up the two steps, into the building and take a right to my door. I fumble with the keys in my pocket until she pulls them out and unlocks the door, half carrying me in. She kicks the door closed behind us and then straight down the small hall into my half bathroom, flipping on the light. I push away the pain as I manage to sit up on the counter and turn to look in the mirror. "Fuck." Blood is thick over the right side of my face, my eye lid swollen and turning a deep purple. *Hmmm. I look kinda tough.*

She bends down under the counter and grabs a wash cloth, wets it in the sink and I turn to her as she starts cleaning my face. "Damn, man. You're gonna need stitches on this one. I can do that for you with your kit."

I stare at her, wincing every now and then, watching the look of concentration on her face. My mouth turns into a grin. "Why is it we never hooked up, Irish?"

She laughs. "Shit. You've been in love with Taren since I can remember and Kane, well, he's always been too much of a womanizer. Besides, you all are like brothers to me and I can't think of you in *that* way. And you're too young for me."

I chuckle at the thought, same as I had the other day. "Hey, I'm only a year younger. Why don't you ever go out on dates, find someone you can be with? Seems like your always working, always alone. Doesn't seem fair, pretty girl like you." It's true. I've never seen her go out with anyone or even really talk about a guy in the many years I've known her. I've always wondered why. She's a beautiful woman and any man would be lucky to know her.

"Hmm, haven't found any one I want to grace my presence with." She laughs and then moves back a bit. "Okay, this top cut is gonna have to have stitches or I can use your butterfly tape to close it. Either way, I think you're gonna have a scar. I recommend when it heals to apply vitamin E oil on it to lessen the scarring."

I turn my head and look in the mirror. One large cut on my cheek and one smaller one underneath it. My cheek is swollen, turning purple and even though I let him get the best of me, I do look tough. "Butterfly tape. I hate needles."

"Ha, wimp."

She finished doctoring me up, gets me a baggie full of ice wrapped in a hand towel and leaves me sitting on my couch, kissing my other cheek, then leaves. I sit here staring at the TV nothing really on at three in the morning and hold my make shift ice pack against my swollen eye. I've got a lot of explaining to do to Ma in the morning.

Chapter Five

Taren

Brock: Can you get out today? I'm off.
Me: Let me see what I can do

Me: I need to go out all day. Cover?
Jeffrey: I suppose
Me: Thx

Me: Meet u at 2?
Brock: Fuck! Can't wait! C u then

I run around packing a small bag full of things to munch on and a change of clothes, along with my bikini. The small pond we had found so long ago beyond the field would feel amazing in today's heat. I sit down at my desk and boot up my laptop, tapping my fingers against the wood impatiently. Finally, it's up and immediately the IM chat box pops up showing Irish's name. Ut, oh. Shit! I haven't talked to her yet. She's gotta be pissed.

Irish: What the fuck, Taren! Why didn't you tell me you did the dirty deed with Brock? Why am I the last to know?

Me: The last to know? Who the hell else knows?

Irish: Well, Kane. He knows everything everyone does. How are you, sweetie? I've missed you.

Me: I'm rolling my eyes right now. I'm ok, hanging in there. We need to get together soon. I've missed you too.

Irish: Find out a day/time and we'll go hang out at the mall. Make it soon!

Me: Definitely! I'll let you know soon!

How the hell does everyone seem to know that Brock and I had sex? I'm so freaking embarrassed. I sign off as it gets closer to the time to leave when I hear my door open. Mimi walks in with a stack of folded clothes, looking at me as she puts them away in my dresser and then walks over to me. "You're going to meet him, aren't you?" I nod slowly, unsure if she is going to tell on me or not. "Good. Just make sure you get home safely and protect yourself. Are you sure you're doing the right thing, keeping this from your parents? I know your dad is rough on you but maybe it's time to tell him the truth." My heart races because deep down I know she's wrong. It's not time. It may never be time until I can move out.

I shake my head and swallow hard. "No, Mimi. He's not ready to hear about me and Brock, he may never be. Mom knows though." She smiles. "I'm so relieved but terrified all at the same time. I have to be careful." I stand and face her, taking her hands in mine. "You can't tell a soul, Mimi. I'm planning on moving out as soon as I turn twenty one next month. I'll get the money Daddy promised and Brock and I can be together, out in the open, like a real couple. That's what will make me happy."

She releases my hands and takes me in her arms. "I know it will, honey. I will help in any way I can. Everyone deserves happiness, especially you."

I lean in and kiss her cheek. She's always been so good to me. "Thank you, Mimi. I've got to go but I promise I won't be too late and I'll be careful."

"Good. Your dad is out of the house running some errands. Now would be a good time to leave. I'll let him know when he returns that you're out on a date. I just won't say with whom. It won't be a total lie that way." She winks. *God, I'm so fortunate to have her.*

I grab my bag, smiling and start towards the door. "Thanks! Love you!" She calls back her love to me as I walk out the door and run down the stairs.

I have a hard time lugging my bag without falling down the long hill to the dirt road but finally manage to get there. After walking across the road and into the thick wooded trees, I make it to the creek and see Brock's truck already parked in the same place it normally is when we meet here, but he's not in it. I slip twice as I make my way across the big rocks in the creek, cold water splashing over my tennis shoes and legs then start the trek through the clearing and across the field. The gentle breeze blows the overgrown grass and also making my long hair whip around me and into my face. I didn't want to tie it back today, wanting his fingers to tangle in it, just how I love. The shack is in my sight, hidden behind the growth, and my heart beats wildly in anticipation. I always feel this way when I get to see him. He's the most handsome, strong but yet gentle man I've ever known. I chuckle to myself as I remember how scrawny he was when we were younger, how he would try to flex his muscles telling me he'd been working out with Kane. God, I miss those times.

I open the door to the shack, the hinge creaking, and step into the small room. The lamps are lit, a nice breeze flowing in from the raised window, fresh flowers in a vase on the table and the bucket chilling some drinks by the futon. I look over at Brock, laying on the cot, and gasp. My hands fly over my mouth as I drop my bag with a thud and run over to him. I sit down next to him and reach over to touch his swollen cheek. "Oh, my God! Brock! What happened?" His eye is swollen shut. A small bandage runs along his cheek and there's another one underneath it. It is all swollen, purple and red. I'm afraid to touch his injuries, so I quickly get up and run to the cooler on the floor, open it and grab a cloth. I practically throw ice into it, wrap it up and run it back over to him, gently laying it against his swollen eye. He winces and so do I.

"It's nothing, Taren. Not a big deal." He winces again.

I concentrate on what I'm doing but my anger begins to steam. "Nothing? Brock, have you seen your face?" He captures my wrist, pulling me down until his mouth is pressed against mine. I'm having a hard time staying mad at him when his touch travels all the way down my body, but I am still concerned and don't want to hurt him. "Brock. Mmmm," I moan and then kiss him harder. His hand weaves underneath my long hair. His fingers tangle into the strands, and I can't think straight anymore. *What was I gonna say?* He releases my wrist. His hand touches my throat, sliding down my chest and then cups my breast. I raise my hand, placing it over the side of his face, my thumb starting to rub his jaw when he winces, his mouth snapping shut, muffling his groan. "Oh, shit!" I yell as I sit up straight. My heart is beating so fast. Partly due to my desire but mostly due to hurting him.

He struggles to sit up and I'm afraid to touch him anymore. "I'm ok, Taren. Really. It looks worse than it feels." He winces again, his hand moving to this side. "Okay, it does hurt a little but really I'm fine. Can you get me a beer, please?"

I stand, grab him and me both a beer and bring one to him, sit back down on the bed and suddenly feel like I could cry. He looks at me, takes my beer and twist off the cap then hands it back to me. "Don't cry, baby. I'm really ok. It's all on the surface. They'll heal. Come here." He holds out his hand, and I place mine in it then move over until I'm sitting next to his good side. His arm wraps around my shoulders and squeezes. "See? I still have a good side left that I can cuddle with."

A sob escapes me intermingled with a laugh and his hold tightens. "Who did this, Brock?" I look over at him and by the sound of his silence I know he's not going to tell me. "Brock, please. Was it because of me?" He's always been so strong, so tough. I have to know or it will drive me crazy. Who would do this? Deep down, I have a feeling I know.

He turns his head, looks me in the eye and frowns. "Taren, you need to change your plan and stay away from Stratton. He's no good and I don't trust him. You shouldn't trust him." Anger swells within me. That's exactly who I thought it was.

"He did this to you?" My voice raises an octave and my hand clenches into a fist.

He winces as he reaches across me, laying his warm hand against my face. It's so hard to look at his battered face as only one of his eyes searches mine. "Baby, just promise me you'll call off the deal and stay away from him. We'll figure out another way to be together. I don't want anything to happen to you. I'd die first." I swallow hard and lay my head on his shoulder. His fingers brush away my fallen hair as he kisses my forehead.

"I want to hit him back, make him pay for doing that to you," I respond, my eyes looking up at him. "Why? Why would he do this to you? I don't understand."

"It was a warning, Taren, to stay away from you." I gasp, not able to stop my reaction. "We'll find a way to be together, baby. We don't need your money. We can have everything we need just being together. Don't you understand that? Did you know your mom came to see mine?" I rise up, my mouth opening in shock and realization hits me. "Yeah, it was kind of awkward since I was there but she was really cool about everything. She's on our side, Taren." He smiles as he pushes some of my hair behind my ear, leaving his hand there. "I'm sure she'd help us and Ma too. We have support, Taren. We can make this work. Even Irish and Kane would be there for us."

"And you're dad? Is he behind us?" I whisper.

His face scrunches, and I know the answer. "Doesn't matter. We have everyone else. If you keep your plan, something bad's gonna happen. I don't want you to get hurt or lose you, baby. Please say you'll call it off. We'll make a new plan, one that will finally let us be together. Talk to your mom. Tell her what's happened and what Stratton is really like. I'm sure if she knew she wouldn't want you to be with him. I bet Mimi would help too. You know she has a soft spot for me." He smiles, but it seems one sided with his swollen face so it turns into a lopsided smirk.

I laugh and run my fingers over his bare chest under his half opened shirt. "That's true. I think she does have a crush on you." The lights flicker and I turn to the window to see it's darkened outside, a heavy gust of air blows through the shack. Thunder rumbles in the distance. "A storm's brewing." I turn back to Brock and smile. "Okay. We'll figure something out. I didn't care about the money other than it would really help us start out but I trust you. I trust us." I lean down, my mouth covers his and all I can think about is his lips and nothing else matters.

Brock

We end up sitting in each other's arms for about three hours, talking, kissing, munching, and kissing some more and making plans. She gets up, and I watch her cute ass sway in her shorts as she walks to her bag. When she bends over to pick it up, I want to run over and bring her back to bed. Sadly, I'm not very fast right now with my injuries. Fucking Stratton. She has to get away from him. I meant what I told her.

Thunder roars again outside, and the rain begins to pelt against the window. She walks over to it, lowers it until only a crack is open and then walks back across the room, doing something on the counter that I can't make out. I look at my watch. It's only five thirty, and it looks like it's nighttime from the darkness of the storm. I reach over and turn the radio on. Music flows in the small area. She turns her head, smiling at me and my heart flutters. She really is the most beautiful creature on earth. She turns and walks back to me, climbing onto the cot with a bowl of assorted fruit and cheeses and snuggles close as my arm wraps around her. I don't think I can ever get close enough to her.

"We may need to leave a little early or ride out the storm. I want you to be able to get home safely."

She answers by putting a grape up to my mouth, and I pull it in, and then suck on her fingers. "I say we ride it out," she whispers. Her eyes deepen with lust, her voice low and sexy.

I take the bowl of goodies from her lap, wanting some other kind of sweetness as quickly as possible. I turn to my left, wincing as I set it down on the small table and then turn back to my girl. My hand moves underneath her long soft hair, wrapping around the back of her neck, urging her to lean in and my mouth is on hers instantly. "I think…. There's a lot we can do…. to occupy our time," I whisper as I kiss her lips in between.

"Mmmmm," she moans as my tongue moves into her luscious mouth, tasting grapes, and her sweetness intermingled.

I slowly slide down, my other hand grasping her upper arm, and I try to hide the pain as she moves on top of me. Her hands move up and into my hair. Even though I keep it fairly short, there's enough there for her fingers to tangle and tug. I'm not sure which is worse at this point, the pain from my injuries or my hardened cock. Her lips release mine, and I'm about to protest until her body moves down mine. Her mouth trails hot kisses on my chest. Her hands leave my hair and unbutton my shirt along the way. *Fuck! She's killing me here!* Once my shirt is completely open, she rises, sitting back on my thighs, pulling my shirt aside. I move up, biting my lip from the pain, and watch her remove it. As I lay back down, she unbuttons my jeans, sliding the zipper down slowly all the while staring into my eyes, hers full of desire. *God, she's fucking sexy!* She moves backwards, stands on the floor at the end of the cot as she pulls my jeans off completely. I think by the widening of her eyes she's a little shocked to find I'm commando.

Before I start begging her to come back to me, she starts unbuttoning her blouse. Slowly. My heart beats frantically as she removes it off one shoulder, then the other, dropping it on the floor, giving me my own private teasing. She's wearing a baby pink bra, lace around the top and a little bow in the middle. She turns, reaches behind her, and unclasps the hook. I swallow hard as she removes it completely, turning back around facing me. My cock is embarrassingly hard and standing at attention. Not like it's the first time, definitely won't be the last. My body always reacts this way around her. But this? Fuck! She's so pure and unknowingly sexy. Only been touched by me.

I can't stop my hand from reaching down, grasping my more than aching cock and begin stroking as she unbuttons her jean shorts. She looks down, watching me, and licks her lips as she shimmies out of them. I watch as she slides her matching panties down her long legs and I stroke a little harder as she steps out of them. She's killing me.

She crawls on the cot in between my outstretched legs, and when she pushes my hand away, she puts her fuck hot mouth over the top of my cock and I about lose it right then. *Hottest thing ever!* This is something I've always wanted her to do but never prompted, always waited until she felt comfortable enough. But I always prayed she would. Shit, what guy doesn't? I look at her full lips wrapped around my cock as she sucks. A loud guttural moan leaves my mouth. She releases me, licks the tip and I grab her upper arms quickly. "Baby, I'm about to lose it and want to be inside you." She puts her knees on the mattress on either side of my legs as I keep my hold of her arms and she takes my cock in her small hand. Aiming for her entrance as she slowly sits down, making me go so deep inside her.

"Ugh!" She moans as I fill her full. "God, so deep, so good."

She begins to rock and I move in and out, each time she gasps and moans. Those beautiful, sexy noises she's making just spurs me on that much more. I thrust harder each time until I feel her muscles clamp around my cock as well as her legs squeezing mine, and I know she's close. Her legs begin to shake, and I watch her beautiful face as she comes undone. "BROCK!" she screams and collapses on top of me. I pump into her a few more times, my own release surging through me.

"Taren!" My voice is hoarse as my entire body shudders, and I release everything I have into her. She shivers and I manage to bring her to my side, struggling to pull the covers over us as she cuddles into me. The pain I feel doesn't come close to the ecstasy that's filled me as I hold her close, brushing her long hair back with my hand and kiss her damp forehead. "That was the hottest thing I've ever seen," I whisper against her warm skin.

She looks up at me through her long lashes and smiles. "That was amazing and so hot."

I smile back and kiss her nose. "It was sexy as hell."

She giggles, rubbing her nose against my lips. "I think you've worn me out, Mr. Evans."

I lay my head back down as she snuggles back into me. "Then sleep, my love."

I close the only eye that's open and soon I fall into a deep sleep, comfortable with her in my arms.

My arm moves up, and I can barely make out the time on my watch. I reach over and shake Taren, who had rolled over onto her other side and was still sleeping. "Taren? Baby, it's after eleven thirty. Let's get you home." Thunder roars as a large boom sounds, the rain extremely loud outside. She rolls halfway, turning her head, and looks at me sleepily then her eyes widen, and she jumps out of bed.

"Oh, my God!" she yells running around and getting dressed. "I'm so gonna get caught! Shit!" She's so fucking cute. I'd laugh but it hurts too much.

After securing the shack, we fight our way to my truck in the downpour. We both slip on the rocks getting across the creek and by the time we get buckled into my truck, we are soaking messes. "Let me drive you home. You shouldn't be dragging your bag and catching your death getting up that damn hill."

She looks over at me, shivering, her hair dripping water everywhere and frowns. "You know I can't let you, Brock. He might be waiting up for me and it'll be hard enough to explain why I'm soaked." Her hand grasps mine in the seat between us and squeezes. "I know you only want to take care of me but we can't take the risk. I'll be fine. I'll hurry, I promise."

She's so fucking stubborn but I guess that's one thing that attracted me to her, well that and her sexy body. Hey, I am a man. I finally manage to get the truck through the thick trees and onto the dirt road, which is now mud, then drive to the spot she normally takes to head up the hill, pull over and park. I turn to her, rubbing my thumb over the soft skin of her hand and frown, my eyebrows lowering. "I wish you'd let me take you home. I know you're strong, Taren, but it's such a bad storm. It's not right. I'll worry."

She leans into me, the coolness of her wet lips pressed against mine, her fingers thread through my drenched hair as I lay my hand against the side of her face. She moves back, her eyes searching mine and smiles. "I know, babe, and I love you for it." She grabs her bag from the floor and pulls on the door handle then turns her head at me. "I'll text you as soon as I can." She leans over again, kissing my lips quickly and then opens the door and gets out.

I sit there for a bit until I can't see her through the darkness and rain anymore and head home. I have the weirdest feeling.

Chapter Six

Taren

I slipped so many times I've lost track. My knees hurt from hitting the ground, and I think my ankle is cut from slipping off a rock when we were crossing the creek. I'm cold, shivering and can hardly see where I'm going in the dark and pouring rain. Finally, I get up the hill far enough that I can see the deck lights. They glow like a beacon. Thank God. A few minutes later, I'm trying to be quiet as I walk up the steps, the back door is locked so I dig out the keys from my purse. Finally, I get in the door and tiptoe across the wood floor of the kitchen, water dripping off me leaving a trail. As soon as I get changed I'm gonna have to come back down with a towel and clean this up. Evidence.

"Where have you been, Taren?" I jump at Dad's voice in the dark. It scares the shit outta me. I gasp and drop my bag with a heavy thud, my back hits the breakfast bar hard as I turn. So much for quiet.

"Uh, Dad. I couldn't get in the front door for some reason so I tried the back." My heart is beating so fast and I feel ill. I know there's no way he's buying this.

Thunder booms and lightning flashes briefly brightening up the room from the back door momentarily. I see him sitting at the kitchen table, his hand around a high ball glass, a small amount of amber liquid still in it. He raises it, drinking down the rest. I try to swallow but the lump in my throat won't go down. "That's interesting. How was your date with Jeffrey? Did you have a good time?" *Crap, crap, crap!*

"Um, yes. It was, uh, nice." My wet hands are clamped on the edge of the counter behind me, holding me up, as my legs begin to feel weak and unstable. Fear radiates through me, along with shivering from my soaked clothes and my heart is beating so hard I can feel it in my chest. Is this what it's like to have a heart attack? Maybe I'm having a panic attack. I wouldn't doubt it at this point.

"Hmmmm, that's very strange since I ran into him at the golf course earlier," he mumbles. *Oh, no! No! What am I going to do? How in the hell am I going to get outta this*? He sets the glass down and turns fully towards me, an almost sad look on his face but then it turns into anger. "You know, I've never asked much of you. Given you everything you've ever wanted, not asking much in return and yet, you lie to me. You hang out with the one person I forbid you to, the person that shouldn't be allowed to walk the earth. He and his family are nothing but trouble, blue collar trash the lot of them."

Now, my anger has swelled from within. "You have no right to talk about them that way. They didn't kill Sebastian, Daddy. They…."

He slams his fist down on the table, and I jump. "Don't you ever talk about your brother like that! If he hadn't been there working with those people he'd still be alive!" He rises and stares me down. "Go to your room." He points to the doorway but continues his angry stare into my eyes. "I will have your cell phone, you will marry Jeffrey and that's the end of it."

I release my death grip from the counter and stand tall, raising my chin in defiance. "No, Daddy. I won't. I won't marry someone like a business deal. I will marry someone I love, not so that you can make a mockery of me and a sacred vow like marriage. I won't do it, Daddy." Both of our chests are heaving rapidly in anger. I can't believe how he's acting. "What happened to you? Do you think you're the only one that lost someone they loved? I loved Sebastian too. He was my brother!" I scream, my entire body shaking, my fists clenched at my sides.

"GO! I won't hear any more of this!" He yells back, his face red and his body shaking.

"I won't do it. I'll leave first!" My chest is heaving, my stomach in knots and I'm not sure if I'm shaking from the cold or anger. Most likely both.

"Fine! Then get OUT! Go! Go to your lover!" He takes two steps towards me, getting right in my face, but I hold firm. "You don't think I don't know your sleeping with him? How could you do that to Jeffrey?"

"I DON'T LOVE JEFFREY!" My head begins to pound, and I'm shaking so badly.

We both stand there staring each other down and finally he turns and starts to walk towards the doorway. "You have ten minutes to get out of my house." Tears form in my eyes as I watch him walk away. "I no longer have a daughter," he says quietly and walks out.

My tears intermingle with the rain on my face. I feel like I can't move. I look over at the clock on the wall, and two minutes have passed since he left. The floor is slippery as I walk to the doorway. He's nowhere in sight as I turn to the left and walk up the stairs. When I enter my room, I stop dead when I see Mom sitting on my bed, crying. She stands and runs over to me. Her arms wrap me in a hug, and yet I just stay still looking straight ahead in shock. "Oh, Taren. I'm so sorry. He's gone mad. I'm sure of it." She moves back, keeping her hold on me and looks at me. "What will you do? Where will you go?"

My eyes focus in on her wet face, tears streaming down her cheeks, and I don't hesitate with my answer. "I'm going to go to Brock's. He loves me. He'll know what to do." I free myself from her arms and walk to my closet, grab the other duffel bag and start throwing clothes into it. I don't touch anything nice or fancy, just grab my t-shirts, tank tops, and the silky blouses I like to wear. I walk out and into my bathroom and find Mom in there with my small cosmetic bag, helping to pack up all my necessities. I turn and walk to my dresser and begin filling my bag with all my bras, panties, shorts, yoga pants, and sleepwear. Then I go to my desk, grabbing my journal, my laptop and various papers, stuffing them on top of my clothes. Pulling the strap of my purse up my shoulder, I turn as Mom comes out of my bathroom and hands me my small bag.

"Call me when you get there. I will come as soon as I can and help in any way possible." She sniffs and wipes her nose with a tissue.

I set both bags down on the floor, call a cab and then throw my arms around her. "I know, Mom." We stand there for a couple of minutes and just hold each other. I move back and pick up my bags and look at her. "I don't know how you can stand to live with him. I really don't. I'll call you soon."

She starts crying harder as I walk out the door. I head down the stairs, looking straight ahead and once I get the front door open, I turn and look around one last time. I hold my head up high, take a deep breath and walk out, shutting the door behind me. Closing the door on my old life.

I had told the cab service to have one meet me down the street. I knew it would take five minutes or so to get there. The rain was still coming down hard. Thunder and lightning is loud and lighting up the sky. We haven't had a hard rain like this in a long time. Figures it would pick tonight to come. When the cab arrived, I open the passenger door, lugging in both bags and sit, then closing the door and staring ahead. I give the cab driver Brock's address. My hands are folded in my lap, and I sit there numbly. I feel sick to my stomach as we drive and hope I don't have to ask him to pull over on the side of the street. All I can think about is how can a father just kick his daughter out of the house? Do I mean so little to him? And how can Mom stay there? I'm angry, hurt, freezing and my knees and ankle hurt. I jolt when the car stops and look out the front window at Brock's building. Taking money from my purse, I lean forward and hand it to him and grab my bags. Once out in the pelting rain, I walk up the two steps and open the door. At least it's warmer and dry in here. I walk the few steps to the right and set my bags down, raise my fist and knock.

Silence. I'm sure he's asleep. Just when I raise my fist again the door opens. "Taren?" A sob escapes me before I can stop it, and I'm in his arms. "Baby, what's wrong?" I bury my face into his warm chest and sob. I feel him move me into the room. One of his strong arms leaves me, but then it's back again shortly, and I hear the door close behind us. "Come. Let's get you dry." He leads me through the apartment and into his bedroom. My right arm is around his waist, the other glued around his stomach, and my hands are fisting his t-shirt. I squint when he turns on the light in his bathroom and then finally look at him as he grabs my waist, lifting me onto the counter. I just sit there, shaking, tears streaming as he pulls up my soaked shirt. I lift my arms, allowing him to remove it and then he reaches behind me and unclasps my soaked bra. He pulls down my shorts and panties, lifting me with one arm around my waist until he gets them off. I watch his concentrated face as he pulls off my shoes, then my wet socks, and he frowns when he looks at my skinned and bruised knees and the blood from the cut on my ankle.

He works in silence as he takes out his medicine kit from the cabinet beneath me. Then leaves the room, quickly to return with one of his t-shirts, pulling it down over my head. I help by pushing my arms through the sleeves. He proceeds to clean up my knees and my ankle, covering the cuts with Band-Aids as I breathe in his smell from his shirt. I take a deep breath as he takes a towel from his linen closet, next to the counter, and starts drying my long hair that I know by morning will be a tangled mess, but I don't care. He stands there for a minute looking into my tear filled eyes, placing his hand against the side of my face, his warmth flowing through me and making me shiver with his touch.

He quietly places his one arm around me, the other under my legs, lifting me into his arms. My arms instinctively move around his neck, my head resting on his shoulder as he carries me into his bedroom, then lays me down in his bed. He begins to stand back but my arms tighten their hold, not wanting to let go. "I'm just going to get in next to you, baby. I'm not going anywhere," he whispers. I release him and watch him walk around the bed, my eyes adjusting to the darkness. He crawls in beside me, pulling me against him as I roll over. My arm lays across his flat stomach as his wraps around me, his other hand pulling up the covers and making sure I'm completely warm then holding onto my arm. He kisses the top of my head, my hair still a little damp, and I sigh into his chest. "I'll never leave you. I'll always be here for you, my love. We'll talk in the morning. Sleep now."

I lay there, comforted in his arms, my head racing with everything that happened. The look on Daddy's face, his eyes and his horrible words. I'm not sure how long I laid there replaying everything over and over again but notice Brock's light breathing, the relaxing of his arm around my shoulder and his hand on my arm. I start to think about things I need to do tomorrow. Go to the bank and withdraw money, call Mom, and find a job. I know Brock will take care of me, but I'm still scared. I've never been out on my own before, never had to know how to survive, budget money, buy groceries or any of the other tasks in day to day life. Guess now's the time I need to learn.

Brock

I'm not much of a cook, but I'll do anything for Taren. She was so distraught last night. She didn't say a word, but I tried to comfort her as best I could. My thoughts are that her dad found out and kicked her out. I just don't know how bad it was, but I can imagine. She was pretty devastated. I'm trying to make her pancakes and bacon. Well, the bacon didn't come out too bad. I have everything just about done when she walks into the kitchen. I look over and my heart just stops. Her long dark hair is a tangled mess, fanned out all around. Her beautiful eyes are half open in that "I'm not quite awake" state. She looks so sexy in my t-shirt and my eyes scan down to her long silky legs, and I want to pick her up, throw her over my shoulder and take her to my bed. *Our bed.* Or tackle her right here, right now and smother her with love.

"What? Do I look that bad?" she asks making me blink out of my lust filled mind. She raises her hand up to her wild hair. I take the few steps over to her, wrap my arms around her as my hand sweeps her hair over one shoulder. My mouth is on her neck as my nose breathes her in. "Oh, do I smell bad too?" Her voice is a little lighter, a little more breathy, so I keep on with my admiration of her lovely skin and breathing in her unique smell. My nose rubs up and down the side of her neck, her face, then back again as my lips kiss and nip along the way. "Wait! Do I smell bacon?" I freeze and she lets out a small laugh, so I stop and move back then wave my arm to the table.

"After you, madam." I bow, and she smiles as she walks by and sits down on a chair.

I walk back to the stove, put the pancakes on a plate and then grab the plate with the bacon and carry them over, setting them on the table. I had managed to set the table earlier with orange juice in our glasses, syrup, butter, napkins, and silverware. What I wasn't able to do yet is pick up my apartment. Clothes are everywhere, dirty dishes in the sink and on the coffee table in the living room, my hamper in my closet is overflowing and I have to leave for work in about thirty minutes. I dread having to leave her after everything she went through. I'm sure it's gonna be weird for her being here and I have to leave. I sit down across from her, everything taking almost the entire table top. With just me, this apartment has been the perfect size. The small table and three chairs fit nicely under the front window in the kitchen, the living room is small but holds my couch, two end tables, coffee table, and my oversized recliner with a fairly decent sized TV hanging from the wall across from them. The two bedrooms are small but I have the small laundry room at the end of the hall, a bathroom in the middle of the rooms and another bathroom in my bedroom. Until now, I've loved living here but with Taren it may get a little cramped. I'm sure she isn't used to being in such a small amount of space.

"Soooo, you work today?" she asks and then takes a bite of her pancake. She doesn't make a face so I figure it must not be too bad.

I take a couple of big gulps of juice and set the glass down. "Yeah, bad timing huh? I'm sorry." She shrugs and takes another bite. "I can check with Kane and see about taking off today. I'm owed days off." Her eyes move up to mine with a look of hope in them but then she shrugs again and sets her fork down on her plate.

"Nah, wait and use those when we can go somewhere or just spend some time alone." She smiles. "I'm just gonna call Irish and see if she wants to hang. Do you mind if she comes over here?" She looks around the kitchen and then into the living room and back at me.

I chuckle. "Sure. Hey…." I reach over and take her hand, threading my fingers through hers. "This is your place now too. You can do whatever you want."

Her smile grows bigger. "Can I…. um…." She bites the corner of her lower lip like she's shy and afraid to ask me something. *So cute.*

"What? Go on." My smile broadens with playfulness.

"Well, do you mind if I do some decorating? I mean, it's not like this place isn't nice or anything but, uh…."

Now I full out laugh and release her hand, sitting back in my chair. "Oh, you don't like the yellowing white walls and the bachelor pad look?"

She laughs and it sounds so good. "Well, yeah, ha! I could fix it up, not girly or anything but just make it a little nicer than it already is."

I reach out for her hand again, pulling her up from her chair and around the table until she's on my lap, my arms wrap around her tight as my nose buries in her long matted hair. "Baby, you do whatever you want." Her head turns to me, and I reach up, caressing the soft skin on her cheek with my thumb. "I don't know what happened last night but I can imagine. When you're ready to talk to me about it, I'm ready to listen. I won't ever pressure you to say or do anything you don't want to. Know that. Trust that." She leans in, her mouth presses against mine and breakfast gets cold.

After we reheat and eat our breakfast, I head back to take my shower and shave. The whole time I'm washing I'm thinking how awesome it is that she's here, that we can finally start our lives together, but I wish it was under better circumstances. Deep down though I always had a feeling when we'd be together that our families wouldn't be happy about it, especially her dad. I just wish she hadn't been so hurt. It makes me want to go straight over and tell her father off, but I know that will just makes things worse. By the time I get dried off, brush my teeth and run my fingers through my wet hair, I put on a semi clean wifebeater and jeans thinking I really need to do laundry soon. I feel a little better since the warm water helped to open my swollen eye a bit, but I still look like shit. I walk out of the bedroom and turn the corner and see she's been cleaning the kitchen. Shit, it looks better than the day I moved in here. She turns around and smiles, leaning her hands on the counter behind her, holding onto a sponge. "I just thought I'd start in here." She beams. I take the few steps to her and put my arms around her waist.

"Looks great, baby. What else are you gonna do today?" I kiss her lips quickly.

"Well, I'm gonna need a new cell phone. I'm sure Daddy will shut mine off, if he hasn't already, and I thought Irish and I could do a little shopping. I don't want to spend too much money although I have quite a bit in my bank account but I want to help out around here." I had a feeling this would come up but I thought it would be later.

"I don't want you to worry about money, Taren. I make enough to pay for the apartment, utilities and food. You just spend it on yourself. I want you to relax and feel like this is your place also but I'm the bread winner around here." I laugh and she does too, but then she begins to play with an imaginary piece of lint on my shirt.

Her eyes are bright as she looks up at me. "Well, that's very caveman of you." I laugh, and her smile widens.

"Sweetheart, do what you want to *our* apartment and here…." I reach into my front pocket as she steps back, pulling out my cell phone, turning her hand over and putting it in her palm. "Take this until you get your own. If I need to call or text you, I'll use Kane's."

"But…."

"No, take it. I don't want you out there anywhere or here without a way to get ahold of me. Call or text me anytime and I'll let Kane know." Her lips squish into the most adorable pout. "Do it for me. It'll make me feel better."

She signs and nods. "Okay. But I'll get a new one when I'm out today with Irish. I love you," she whispers as she leans up against me and kisses my mouth.

God, she's making it hard to leave. I wish I could stay and hold her in my arms all day, cuddle in bed and make sweet love to her. I hate leaving her after what she went through last night. I kiss her back and then turn to walk to the front door. "I'll talk to you later."

"Have a good day, babe," she hollers as I shut the door.

Damn! I love having her here but I hate leaving on her first day. It's gonna be a long ass fucking day.

Chapter Seven

Taren

After Brock left I turn around and look at the living room. It's definitely been a bachelor pad. Before I start to clean I decide to start a load of laundry and get my cell phone. I grab a load of his colored clothes, put them in the washer, add soap and turn it on then go back into his room, *our room*, and dig for my phone in my purse. Even though our laundry was always done by Mimi, I watched and learned. I figured someday I would be out on my own and would need to know how. Of course I'm not surprised when I turn on my cell phone to find the number has been shut off. Daddy really works fast. I grab Brock's phone and scroll through his contacts, feeling like I'm invading his privacy and find Irish then hit call.

"God, Brock! This better be good at this hour and on my fucking day off," she growls in the phone. I stifle my laugh. She never was a morning person even when she didn't work late at night into the morning hours.

"Irish. It's me. Taren." I wait and hear shuffling in my ear.

"Taren? What the hell you doin' using Brock's phone?" She yawns and now I feel bad that I woke her. More shuffling and then another yawn. "What's wrong, bestie?"

"Well, I kind of moved in with Brock, last night, um, really late and I…."

"Whoa, whoa, girl! You moved in? Last night?" She all but yells in my ear.

"Should I call back later? Are you not awake enough to talk because you keep repeating…."

More shuffling and more yawning. "No! I'm mostly awake. Give me fifteen minutes to take a shower, dress and I'll be over. Hang tight."

"But…." The line goes dead and I quickly get up to run around the place and at least pick up. Shit! She can get ready faster than any girl I know and make it look like she spent hours on herself.

Between Kane, Brock, Irish and me, we are all stair-stepped in age, each just about a year apart from the other. We always hung out together growing up and had so much fun. When Irish started working for Pops a couple of years ago I thought we'd never get to hang out much anymore. She worked most afternoons, most weekends, and into the late hours of the night, but she said she needed the money and liked to work. On her off times, she's always working out at the gym. I swear she could be a nun as little as she dates. But she just tells me she'll know when the right guy comes along. I just hope he comes along before she's old and gray.

A knock comes on the door in exactly fifteen minutes. How does she do that? I look around as I walk, checking out my quick cleaning effort, and open the door. "Hey, chica!" She passes me and goes right into the living room and sits down on the couch. I close the door and walk there, sitting down in the oversized recliner. "So, what's been going on? Your dad kicked you out, didn't he? That motherfuc…." I put my hands up and cringe. "Sorry. I guess he is your old man."

"Yes, he did. It was horrible but I knew it was coming, at some point. The main thing is now, I need to get a new cell phone. He's already shut mine down." I can see her anger boiling. Her fists clench as her face turns a light red.

She stands and starts pacing the floor. "That asshat! God, he doesn't care about anyone but himself. What about your mom? Is she standing behind him on this?"

"Actually, I'm not sure but I don't think so. I haven't heard from her since it all happened but I think she's on my side." Remembering the look on Mom's face when I was packing, the way she held me and cried. "I hope."

Irish stops mid-stride and turns to me. "Well, I think some shopping is in order and caffeine. Lots and lots of caffeine." She walks over, sits down again and smiles.

"Yeah, well, a cell phone first. I want to get Brock's back to him right after. Oh! And the bank! Then…." I look around the dingy walls and then back at her. "I think the hardware store for some paint." Irish's eyes light up and I know she'll be great in helping me. "Then to the store for some much needed small appliances and things for the kitchen and groceries. That should start me off."

She leans forward, her arms resting on her legs as she claps her hands and rubs them swiftly. "I love the way you think, girl. Let's do this!"

I grab my purse from the small table by the front door and we head out to her truck. We run to the bank first and I create another new account, transferring all my money over to it. I was smart enough when I turned eighteen to get an account and every time Dad gave me money I would transfer it from the account he created for me into it. Mom is on this account, just in case something happened to me, and even though she says she's behind us, I'm a little leery. I have more than enough money to help out for quite a while but I still need to get a job.

After getting my new cell phone, I texted Brock, and we headed to the construction site so I could give him his back. We pull in to the lot, and all the guys turn their heads when we get out of Irish's truck. She leans against her door as I walk to meet Brock. Nothing like getting leered and whistled at along with winks as I walk over. "Hey, baby." He smiles then gives me a quick kiss. More whistling ensues, and I think my face turns beet red with the heat of embarrassment I'm feeling, not to mention the bright sun. His bruises are magnified by the light of day but at least his swollen eye is open. Makes him look all kinds of tough yet I still feel bad that it happened because of me. "Don't mind them. They're harmless."
Yeah, right.

A light shines, hitting me right in my eyes. I turn my head towards the street. The sun glares off a black SUV. I squint, putting my hand over my eyes to shield them from the bright sun, and I almost could swear that's Jeffrey in the driver's seat. The car moves slowly by, the sun playing havoc with my sight and my head turns trying to follow it. "Uh, babe? You okay?" Brock's voice pulls me back to him, and I smile. No need in getting him angry when I'm not for sure that it was Jeffrey, but I have the strangest feeling.

"I'm good. Here's your phone back. I put my new number in your contacts." I hand him his phone and he tucks it in his front pocket looking at me with concern.

His face softens as he looks over at Irish's truck and then back at me. "And where are you ladies off to?" He takes my hand and suddenly everything around us moves out of focus, my eyes only seeing him.

"Oh, we are going shopping, you know, girl stuff." He smiles and moves closer until a loud whistle breaks our spell.

"YO, BROCK!"

He turns his head, and I look over his shoulder. Kane winks and cocks his head back at the building. *Party pooper.* Brock turns back around, rolling his eyes but chuckling. "Okay, I guess I gotta get back to work. You two have fun. I'll see you when I get home. Fuck that sounds so good." My smile couldn't be any bigger as he leans over and gives me a quick kiss. I turn just as the whistling and name calling starts up, our hands still locked and pulling away when we finally release them, and I walk to Irish's truck.

"Damn, there are some fine looking guys here," Irish mumbles as I walk around the front of her truck and then open the door, sliding onto the seat. After we both are buckled in, she starts it up and drives out of the lot.

"Uh, Irish? You just said there were good looking guys there. Feeling okay?" I laugh.

She pulls onto the street and turns her head to me. "What? I am a woman. Besides, there's never any harm in looking." She winks and then we're on our way.

We shopped for two hours, and I'm so excited about everything I got. Then we spent another three hours covering furniture and painting the walls in the living room and our bedroom and setting out the small appliances. By the time we hug goodbye, I am exhausted but happy. I unpack my things, did another two loads of laundry, and then took a much needed shower. I'm sitting on the couch with my laptop and looking at jobs online. I had to text Brock earlier to get the password for his internet. My head turns when I hear the lock click open on the front door, and I smile when the most gorgeous, filthy man walks inside. His head turns, his eyes immediately find mine. I watch the corner of his mouth turn up into a grin as he walks directly to me. I barely get my laptop set on the coffee table when he lifts me into his arms.

I immediately put my arm around his neck, giggling ensues, but it stops as I place my hand against his face, and our lips collide. He starts carrying me to be our room then into the bathroom. He begins to set me down, my body sliding down his front and feeling every single ridge of his muscular body. My breaths come out in pants, and I see he's equally affected when he presses his hardened cock against me. He leans down and starts kissing right below my ear, traveling down my neck. "I'm filthy. Need a shower," he whispers as his mouth moves back up my skin.

"You do smell a little raunchy," I whisper back as I tilt my head to the side so he can reach more of me.

He stops, smiling against my neck, then proceeds to kiss downward again. "I think I might be so dirty I'll need help cleaning."

My eyes flutter close and I moan as my head leans back, his mouth latching onto some skin. "I think that can be arranged," I whisper. His hand finds my breast, and I arch my back in response. His arm is holding me tightly around my back and in this position I feel as if I could fall, but I don't think I'd feel it if I did. Coolness sweeps across my neck when I feel his mouth release my skin, leaving wetness behind. I open my eyes and see he's staring at me, his eye swollen with dark purple all around it. Suddenly, I remember he was hurt and went to work today. I lean back up, his facial expression changing from desire to concern. My hands hold onto his shoulders, and I kiss his cheek, softly.

"What's wrong, Taren? Did I do something?" I watch his face change again into anger. "Did something happen today? What? Tell me?"

Never has anyone cared about me so deeply, loved me so fully. "No, it's not that. Everything's okay but…." I place my hand on the side of his face but his facial expression doesn't waver. "You're hurt because of me. I know last night we…. Maybe we shouldn't…."

His smile appears and relief spreads across his face. He leans into me, kissing my forehead then my mouth. "I'm good, Taren. Okay, I'm a little stiff and sore, and I'm not gonna lie and say that work didn't make me feel any better but a shower will." He kisses me again, smiling against my lips. "*You* will feel great. Best medicine ever." My heart beats faster with his words and the feeling of guilt fades, momentarily.

Brock

My ribs and face were throbbing by the time I got off work. I already got razzed all day from Kane about the beating I took and got the fifth degree about it. I explained what happened and he was fuming, stating we're to have a family meeting at Pops later tonight.

When I walked into the apartment, I couldn't believe the transformation, but I really didn't look at everything thoroughly because all I could think about was seeing my girl. She had on a loose tank top. Her feet were placed on the coffee table with her computer on her lap. I could see she was wearing black yoga pants that stopped mid-calf, showing her unblemished smooth skin. It doesn't take much for my body to want her and just looking at her, in my apartment, *our place*, makes it even harder to stay away. I couldn't take it anymore. I walked to her like I was the predator and she my prey but that's kinda how I felt. I barely gave her time to set her laptop down before I had her in my arms and taking her to the bathroom. I'm in bad need of a shower but don't want to be away from her, so I figured why not take one together. After feeling her luscious body slide against mine, my lips kissed their way down her neck then back up, stopping to suck on her skin. God she tastes so good. When she stilled I got concerned but when she told me she was worried about me, my heart just soared even more. God, I fucking love her.

I helped her undress then she did the same for me. Gotta say getting my shirt off hurt my ribs as I try to pull it over my head. I turn on the shower, adjusting until it wasn't too hot, then I pick up my naked girl and carry her in. She starts nibbling on my earlobe, driving me crazy. There was no more foreplay as I couldn't take it anymore so I drove my cock into her as her legs wrapped around my waist. I was careful not to slam her against the tiled wall, putting one of my hands behind her head. Our hips rocked as we made love in a frenzy. We kissed, our tongues rolling over each other's, and we barely came up for air. Her mouth leaves mine but her lips still parted, her forehead creases, and her moan echoes against the tiles, coming from deep within her. Sexiest sound in the world. It hits me hard, watching her orgasm completely rip through her, and I climax quickly after. "God, Taren!" I cry out then cover her mouth with mine. Her legs drop down in their weakness. My arm tightens around her as my hips buck a few more times, and I expel all that I have into her.

She opens her eyes, looking down into mine. The corner of her mouth lifts, a slight pink color on her cheeks. "I love you," she whispers. I kiss her again then ease my hold, letting her wet body down until her feet are stable on the ground.

"I love you, baby," I whisper back. She kisses me again then takes the soap in her hand and rubs it until there's a good lather. She places her hands on my shoulders, pushing so I'll turn around, and begins washing my back. Just her soft hands on my skin makes my cock start to harden again. I'll never have enough of her.

She finishes washing me, and I take my turn. I pay homage to every inch of her gorgeous body, taking special care of her breasts, then I turn off the water and dry my girl off. She puts on a silky tank top with a tight pair of jeans and after brushing out her hair, she kisses me and leaves the bedroom. I walk into my closet knowing I probably have no clean clothes, and my eyes widen when I see all of them hanging there. I can't believe she did all my laundry. I quickly put on a clean wifebeater and jeans then walk out into the living room stopping when I see her in the kitchen. My shoulder presses against the wall as I watch her move about, taking something out of the oven, poking her finger in it then bringing it up to her mouth and closing her eyes as she sucks on it. *Oh, to be that finger.* She puts on oven mitts that I didn't know I had, on her hands and picks up the pan. She turns, and her eyes widen. Her face softens and the smile I live for, the one that takes my breath away, appears.

"Oh, I made us some dinner." She walks over to the table which is already set and sets the pan down on a folded dish towel, again something I've never seen before. I walk over and as she sits in her chair, I lean down and kiss her luscious lips then take my seat across from her. "Looks like you were very busy shopping today and cleaning." She picks up my plate, a large spoon in her hand and looks at me, her eyebrows creasing.

"You don't like everything." It wasn't a question but a sorrowful statement. She starts spooning food onto my plate.

"No! No, I love everything." I look around and then back into her eyes that have now softened. "I don't think I've seen it all, yet. I was pretty preoccupied when I got home." I wiggle my brows, trying to lighten the mood that I somehow managed to dampen. "Taren, I hope you know I don't expect you to clean up after me. I'll try to do better and do my part. I've never really had someone live with me before. Thank you for doing all this."

Her mouth turns into a smile as she sets my plate in front of me, then picks up her own, scooping up more food for herself. "You're welcome. I've never lived away from home so this is all so new to me but I don't mind cleaning, cooking, doing my part. Babe, right now you work hard all day so the least I could do was get your laundry done for you. I didn't mind at all." She winks and then places her plate in front of her. My heart soars with her love, and even though she's here in less than great circumstances, I'm so glad she is.

I take a bite of food and close my eyes at the deliciousness. "Wow! You can cook too! Damn, this is good." She smiles, almost shyly. "So, after what happened to me, Kane wants to have a family meeting at Pops tonight." Her body stiffens, and she chews slowly. I set down my fork and reach across the small table, taking her hand in mine, and rubbing my thumb over her soft skin. "Baby, we have to talk about it. We need help. We can't do this on our own. Not anymore." She nods, slightly, and sighs.

"I know. I'm just…. Your dad doesn't like me and to be there, around him…. I know it has to happen at some point. He's your dad. But…."

"Don't worry about Pop. He won't be there tonight anyway." She relaxes. "He takes off a couple of nights a week and tonight some game is on that he wants to watch." She smiles, and I release her hand and take another bite of this amazing food. "So, are you gonna tell me what happened with your dad?"

She swallows, and I take a big gulp of my coke. "What I thought would happen. He disowned me and told me to leave." She shrugs her shoulders like it's nothing, but I know she's really hurt. She sets her fork down and looks at me, her eyes full of love. "It's gonna be okay. I figured this would happen eventually, even though I'd hoped by some miracle it would have gone differently. I knew at some point we'd be together and I would do anything to make that happen."

"God, I fucking love you," I tell her in all seriousness.

She smiles. "I love you too. So much."

We finish eating, talking about lighter things like everything she purchased today, her and Irish's decorating and her online search for a job. I told her again she didn't have to work, but she's adamant about it. I help her clean up the kitchen, taking a lot longer than it should with me kissing and fondling her every few minutes. What can I say? I can't keep my mouth or hands off her. We get in my truck and drive the short distance to the bar. I can tell she's nervous when we walk in, seeing how crowded it is. I take her hand, threading my fingers through hers, and kiss her lips.

"Yo, Bro!" Kane yells from a table at the back of the bar. We walk together hand in hand until we reach the table, and I point for Taren to slide into the booth first. "Taren." Kane nods and gives her a wink, relaxing her a little. I raise our hands and kiss hers. He looks at me and frowns. "Okay, so we need to figure out how to keep you both safe."

"Oh, no you don't!" Our heads turn and we see Irish walking towards us in a hurry, carrying a tray full of beers. She sets a beer in front of each of us, then one on the table next to Kane and sits down beside him, placing the tray on the floor standing it up against the booth seat. She takes a quick drink and then cups the bottle with her hands. "Okay, what'd I miss?"

Kane nudges her with his elbow as he lifts his beer, takes a drink then sets it on the table, looking straight at me. "You need to make sure someone is with you and Taren at all times if you're out and about. Even if you're here. The guys at work said they'd even help out. Just gotta let them know." I let out a sigh and roll my eyes. "Hey, this ain't over and I think we know what's at stake here." His eyebrows lift, his eyes staring a hole in mine. "We all know him and I don't think he'll stop at getting what he wants. Money tends to do that to some, especially him." He looks at Taren and smiles. "No offense."

I release her hand and slide my arm around her, pulling her closer. "No, I totally agree." She looks at me with a look of tenderness. "I hate that he came after Brock and I'd die if anything worse happened to him." I lean in and kiss her, hearing Irish sigh and Kane chuckle. She looks around the table. "I don't want anything to happen to anyone because of me."

"That's so sweet." Irish sighs again. I look over at her and she straightens her back. I pick up my beer and take a big drawl. "Well, I was here and I wish I would have known what the hell was going on outside or I'd have kicked his ass. If I'd only left a little earlier I…."

I set down my bottle. "Okay, enough of trying to blame what happened on yourselves. Irish, you couldn't have known. Hell, I didn't know and walked right into it." I look at Taren and smile. "And you. Stop blaming yourself. None of this is your fault. Those to blame are the ones trying to keep us apart and we ain't letting that happen." She smiles big and kisses me then we both look at Irish and Kane.

"It's true. Irish could have taken him," Kane states all serious and takes another drink.

We all burst out into laughter but he's right. She could have. She's one tough chick. Thank God, she's on our side.

Chapter Eight

Taren

I was so nervous, even though Brock said Pop wasn't gonna be there. When we walked in and seeing the place was packed, I felt a little better until I saw Kane and knots formed in my stomach. He's always stood up for us, been there when we needed him, but I'm just not sure how deep after what happened to Brock. He is Brock's big brother, and I know they're extremely close. Kane has a big heart but also is tough as nails. I had the idea that maybe after Brock being hurt, his feelings might have changed about me. After we sat down and listened to him, I relaxed and felt better. He showed me I still mattered to him. Brock's love for me means I'm still in his family, and that he'd do anything for me too. I felt overwhelmed with love and a closeness that is so foreign to me, making me wish I'd had this kind of family closeness while growing up. Then Irish showed up and we actually ended up having a good time, once all the heavy talking was done. Still, I hate how everyone feels that they need to protect us, even though I appreciate it and love them for it. It's just really sad it's come down to this. If only Brock and I could be a normal couple, do normal things without having to worry about someone coming after us or being angry and upset.

It's late, well after midnight, by the time we get home. I drove his truck home as he had a few too many beers, but he needed it, and I didn't mind. We made sweet love, and he fell asleep quickly after. He had to be exhausted, still being hurt, working all day, and then a night out. I lay here awake thinking about all that has transpired in the last two days. Feelings and emotions of love, betrayal, and loss, then my close knit friends. Everything is overwhelming me. My mind won't shut off thinking about being here, finally being with my love, living away from home for the first time, trying to find a job, and Jeffrey's horrific ways. I don't know how long I lay in the darkness, but I look at his alarm clock noticing it's three in the morning. I close my eyes and hope sleep finds me.

Waking up with your body being lavished is the best alarm in the world, especially when it's by the man you love with your entire heart, your whole self. I don't want to open my eyes as his strong hands push my camisole up slowly while his lips worship my stomach with kisses. His hard length presses against my thigh with need as his mouth makes its way up my ribs then captures one of my nipples that is already erect, taut, and waiting for him in anticipation. His hand slides into the waistband of my panties, finding me already soaked, aching for his touch. My hips buck, a moan leaving my mouth, as his hand slides up my folds then down. "Brock," I moan and begin writhing beneath him. His mouth leaves my breast and finds my mouth as his hands remove my panties. He thrusts into me hard, fast, and I moan again, muffled by his mouth.

"Fuck! You're so tight. So responsive to my touch. You're fucking wet for me so quickly," he whispers against my lips. His words make me squirm. So sexy.

I'll never get enough of him, never close enough. His smell invades my senses as we move together in the rhythm that is ours. The familiar tingles begin low in my core, traveling into my stomach. That small flame starts to ignite inside me, heating me up until I feel like I could explode. I grab his muscular arms, holding tight, feeling the strain of his strong muscles, every vein. "Ugh, Brock!" I scream as my release overtakes me and spots form in my vision. But I can see clearly enough as his face contorts, almost like he's in pain as he finds his own release. The look of relief shadows across his gorgeous face, the look of pure ecstasy. My body shivers, shaking with my own release as he calls out my name. He covers me with his body, his light sheen of sweat matching my own. I wrap my arms around him, lovingly, as his body still shudders slightly. His head rises, kissing me softly and with so much love.

"God, I love you so much it hurts," he whispers against my lips.

Suddenly, he leans up on his elbows on either side of me, his weight lifted making it easier to breathe. "I'm off today. Let's take a picnic to our special place." He smiles and my heart fills, stopping briefly as the look on his face makes me catch my breath. "We need to have a happy day, one with no cares, no worries. We need to lighten up and have some fun." He kisses me again and then leans back, his eyes lighting up. "Bring your bikini."

I smile, my heart beating fast with happiness but then I begin thinking. "Should we go by ourselves? You heard what Kane said last night. Maybe…."

His fingers sweep my hair away and he smiles, but his eyes tell me of his own concern. "No one knows about our secret place, Taren. But you're right. We do need to be careful. I'll just make sure I take the long way there and we'll drive around a bit. Just in case." His eyes search mine, hoping I'll agree.

I lean up and kiss him then lay back down with a smile. "Okay. Let's have a happy day." God knows we could use one of those or several.

We take our showers separately. He lets me go first since he says I take the longest. *Men.* By the time I get out and get dressed, put on some light makeup, brush my teeth and dry my long hair, he's fixed breakfast for us, and it's already on the table. "I think I'm getting better. I didn't burn the eggs." His smile is wide and the feeling of love and desire already fill my body and mind. Will it always be this way? Will my heart stop beating every time I see him or am near him, forever? I walk over and kiss him hard then sit down in my chair and dig in.

I clean up the kitchen while he takes his shower. He ends up being right as it only took him fifteen minutes to my half an hour to get ready but hell if I say anything. I manage to start packing a picnic lunch, making sandwiches, putting in assorted fruits and some cookies into his backpack, then filling the small insulated cooler with ice, bottled water, and a few sodas. I feel him behind me before his arms wrap around my waist, pulling me back into him as his mouth kisses the side of my neck. His hand sweeps my long ponytail over my other shoulder while he sucks my skin into his mouth. I giggle and push my bottom against him, feeling his hard cock press against me causing flutters to form deep inside. My head lulls back onto his shoulder as desire sweeps though me. "We'll never leave if you keep this up," I moan.

He continues kissing, his hands moving up to my breasts, and his fingers rub across my tightened nipples over my bra. "We have time, baby. We have all the time in the world," he speaks as he continues his way up the side of my face, nipping my earlobe and driving me insane.

We're late leaving for our special place, but I didn't mind in the least. Of course, we ended up taking another shower, this time together. That shower took a little longer than normal as we couldn't keep our hands off each other. So worth it. We laughed and held hands all the way to the tree filled area and parked his truck then he helped me across the creek, making sure I didn't fall. My knees and ankle are still sore from the other night. We bypassed the shack, pushing through the overgrowth of the field until we reached the pond. It almost feels like the ocean does with its small sandy beach but no waves, just stilled clear water. He lays out his old beat up and well-worn blanket as I remove my shirt and shorts, revealing my black bikini that he requested I wear. It's so skimpy that I'd be embarrassed but not with him. He's seen so much more of me than what this covers. I watch him remove his shirt, licking my lips as his defined abs and broad chest appear. I remember the feeling of my hand as it moved over the ridges and bumps of those muscles. Makes me wet just thinking about it.

He surprises me by walking over and picking me up. I laugh as he walks us out into the water, my skin not warm enough yet for the coldness, shocking me as he takes us underneath. I spring to the top, my hands pushing my wet hair away from my face and laugh. He's looking all kinds of sexy, water dripping from his hair, face, and smiling at me with such love in his eyes. I can't imagine not being with him, not feeling his arms around me, his touch. I love everything about him. Sure, he's hot, sexy and well built, but I've known him all my life. I see so much more than that. He's loving, caring, funny and smart. There's nothing I wouldn't do for him, nothing I wouldn't do to make sure we'll be together. Forever.

We make love in the water, my bikini forgotten after he throws it onto the beach, along with his swim trunks. The sun is getting warmer, helping with my shivers but the coolness of the water isn't the only thing causing them. We're kissing, my arms around his neck and my legs hugging his waist. "So, what else do you want to do today?" He asks between kisses.

"Mmmmm, I dunno," my response is breathless, coming out in heavy pants.

The sound of a cell phone vibrating from the beach makes us turn our heads and look. I reluctantly let go of him so he can go answer. My legs move as I wade in the water, but I'm curious as to who is calling so I swim back to the shore, get out and grab one of the towels on the blanket. He's standing there looking at his phone with his towel wrapped around his waist. "Who was it, babe?" He dries off with an extra towel then picks his phone back up, swipes it a few times, and then hands it to me.

Mom: Family meeting at your place. Tonight @ 6! I'll bring food.

"Another family meeting?" My heart beats rapidly as I look at him.

He shrugs. "Yeah, I dunno. But I know Ma and if she says family meeting, we meet."

I look back down at the message then hand it back to him. "Well, I guess our day just got cut short. She may be bringing food but we can contribute something." He laughs. We pick up our things and make the long walk back to his truck. Doesn't mean we don't stop along the way and have a little fun rolling around in the tall grass. What can I say? Now that we're finally together, we can't seem to keep our hands off each other, among other things.

Brock

My family is the best but how many family meetings can we have in twenty four hours? Okay, I know the fact that I let that asshole get the better of me is making everyone worried and acting a little crazy. I get that. I love their support, but we just need to get on with our lives and keep our eyes and ears open. We get home and take yet another shower, getting the muck of the pond off us. We don't make love, although it wasn't from the lack of me trying, but she's freaking out about everyone coming over in a couple of hours. So, I help make sure the place is spotless and have to hold in my laughter when there really isn't much of anything to clean due to her OCD about having everything sparkling already. Finally, I manage to corner her against a wall, whispering how we have plenty of time and what her body does to me. After conceding, I lift her into my arms and carry her to our bedroom, telling her on the short walk that we can remake the bed but also keep the door closed so no one will see it. There was no laughter, no giggles, only passion and desire when we get to our room. I'm proud to say, we barely shifted the covers as we showed our love to one another.

There's a knock on the front door as I leave our bedroom closing the door behind me. Taren's in the bathroom "fixing" her sexed up looking hair. Her words. I just run my fingers through mine, but it normally looks that way no matter what I do. I open the front door and step back as not only Ma and Mrs. Mills walk by but my eyes widen when I see Pop walk in behind them. I shut the door and follow them the few steps into the living room, no one sitting down as I walk past and turn to them. "Listen, if you're here as an intervention or to upset Taren, don't bother staying. You can just leave right…."

Ma steps forward and Pop raises his hands, palms up, as if in surrender. "It's not like that, Brock. Simmer down. We're just showing our support. Aren't we, Stan?" Her head turns to him, and he looks down then back up and into my eyes as he nods curtly. She walks to me and gives me a hug, whispering in my ear. "We all love you, son. Believe that. We love Taren too and we're just here showing you that." She leans back, and I see tears brimming in her eyes. I pull her back into a hug and squeeze. We all turn when we hear footsteps and see Taren standing at end of the room, her face pale and eyes wide. She looks at Pop, Ma, and then me. Her face questioning. I hear a sniff and watch as Taren's eyes move to her mom. I feel kinda bad when I see Mrs. Mills standing there with tears streaming down her face.

"Taren," she whispers, choking on her tears.

"Mom," Taren's voice cracks but then she straightens her slumped shoulders and raises her chin. "I'm not leaving. This is where I belong, where my heart is. I…."

Her mom's voice is so low that you can barely hear it over her crying. "I've left him, sweetheart. I can't even stand to look at him. I know it's something I should have done a long time ago. I'm so sorry for the hurtfulness he's put you through." She looks at Ma and Pop then at me. "On all of you. I'm so ashamed." Her hands cover her face, and Ma runs over, putting her arms around her, guiding her down onto a chair. I look back over at Taren and see her tears freely flowing down her face.

"Well, not that it's much privacy but Ma, Pop, how about we go into the kitchen and give Mrs. Mills and Taren a little time." Pop nods and walks over to the kitchen, clearly uncomfortable. Ma turns her head and smiles then walks there as well. I walk over to Taren and place a tender kiss on her forehead. "Take your time, baby." Her watery eyes move to mine then back to her mom. I walk to the kitchen and start making drinks for everyone while Ma puts food away that they'd brought. I walk over and sit down at the table with Ma and Pop. My eyes keep shifting over to Taren. I try not to listen. I really do. But it's hard when you're only several feet away.

"Mom. I believe you and I know you've had your reasons for staying with him. I'm sorry. I now know what it's like to be on your own for the first time but I can't imagine after all the time you've been with him that you've left. You know I'm here for you." She's squatting in front of her and they both suddenly grab each other and cry together. I can't even begin to fathom being in such a dysfunctional family. We all have our moments but living day to day for your whole life that way, in a place with no love, no regard or respect for the other, is unimaginable to me. It makes me have that much more respect for Taren, turning out the way she has. So loving, caring, respectful, and a beautiful heart. It also actually makes me feel so grateful to Ma and Pop. They've always been there for Kane and me. Supported us even when they didn't agree with our decisions. Loved us unconditionally. Suddenly, I'm feeling all emotional too.

We end up eating while Taren and her mom talk for a bit. The silence at the table is excruciatingly tense and awkward. I've always hated that there's been stress in our family ever since the accident and really even before that since our parents have always had a dislike for each other but Taren is my life, my entire existence and if Pop doesn't ever get that, be happy for us, then there will always be that strife between us. I love him but I need Taren to live, to breathe. Without her my life is meaningless.

Taren walks into the kitchen, hesitantly, looking at Pop then down at me. "Mom's freshening up. Can I talk to you for a minute, please?" I nod as I stand and we walk to our bedroom, shutting the door behind us.

"Everything okay?" I ask before she has a chance to open her sweet mouth.

"Yes and no. I mean…. We're ok but do you think…. Ugh, this is harder than I thought." She looks down, wringing her hands so I know she's nervous. She always does that.

I grab her hands, holding them tight. She looks up at me, worry in her eyes. "Baby. You can ask me anything." I move my hand to her face, tucking some of her long soft hair behind her, and leave my hand there hoping to reassure her. "I don't ever want you to feel like you can't talk to me."

A small smile lifts and she releases a breath. "I know we've only started our lives together but would you mind if she stay...."

"No problem," I interrupt, knowing what she's gonna ask.

"Really? You don't mind if she stays here for a couple of days in the spare room until I can help her find a place of her own?" She bounces, her smile widening.

I laugh. "No, I don't mind. I'll be at work most of the time anyway. She would be great company for you and I know you want to help her." I take a step closer and cover her mouth with mine. Her hand slides up my chest and around my neck, her fingers moving into my hair. She jumps slightly when the toilet flushes in the other bathroom. *Okay, that may be a problem. No making love for two days? I know she'll be too uncomfortable with her mom here.* A thought hits me. "Hey, you know what? There's an apartment for rent two buildings over from here. Would be close for you both and she might feel more comfortable being out on her own." Her brows raise, and her eyes light up.

She turns, grabbing my hand and pulling. "That's awesome! Come on! Let's go tell her."

I try to keep my laughter in as I let her lead me out into the living room where everyone has now gathered. Her mom got a plate of food and they're all sitting around talking. "Mom! Brock said there's an apartment just two buildings over for rent! Wouldn't it be cool to be so close?" Her mom looks at me and smiles then back at Taren.

"Oh, my! That would be lovely. Maybe we can go see it tomorrow?" Taren nods excitedly and everything is right with the world again. Well, almost.

"Uh, son?" My head snaps to Pop. "Can we go outside and talk?" My eyebrows raise, and Taren squeezes my hand. "Please?" I nod slowly, and he stands. Taren whips around, kissing me hard, telling me in her own way to be strong. He walks to the front door, opening it and waiting for me to join him. I kiss Taren once again and walk out into the hall of the building. I watch him close the door then walk to the front door, sitting down outside on the first paved step, so I follow and sit down beside him, his eyes looking at the ground below him. "Ya know. It's hard being a parent. Kids look up to ya and put you up on some kinda pedestal. But…." His eyes shift my way and then back down to the ground. "Ya know. We're only human too and can make mistakes just like anyone else." My brows lower at his words then he turns to me, looking straight into my eyes. "We've always been close and there's been such tenseness on us lately, ever since…. Well, you know. Always liked Taren. She's a good girl. Can't help where she comes from or who. Glad you're together now. You need me or my help, you ask. Ya hear?"

I smile in relief. We've always been close knit and the tension has really bothered me. Most important people in my life, my family and my girl. How could you ever decide between them? I clap my hand on his upper back, my smile can't be any bigger. "Thanks, Pop. I'm glad to hear you say that. How 'bout tomorrow night off so I can take my girl on a date?"

He lowers his head and laughs then looks back at me, smiling. "Don't push it, son."

And that's how my family rocks. Tight.

Chapter Nine

Taren

I watch the front door holding my breath. God, I hope his dad finally sees that I'm not the enemy and makes Brock's life easier. I know Brock's been really upset ever since his dad put more awkward and uneasiness on the situation. They've always been so close and up until the accident, Pop's always liked me, welcomed me into the family, so to speak. Then he changed, which made it so much harder on us. It's bad enough my dad has been horrible all my life, so I always kinda felt like Pop was kind of a dad to me too. Feeling unloved by both really weighed heavily on me, but I was more concerned about Brock.

The door opens, and I jump in my seat. My hands have been digging into the arm rest of the worn chair. From the corner of my eye, I see Mom and Mrs. Evans looking at the door too. Brock and Pop walk in, arm in arm, laughing. I release the breath I'd been holding in one big whoosh. I watch Brock walk into the kitchen and hear Pop clear his throat, my eyes snapping back to him. He opens his arms. "Come here, girl." I stand on shaky legs and walk over to him. He wraps his arms around me as I step into him, putting mine around his back. "I'm sorry we've been strained. Forgive me?" I only nod my head, pushing the fabric of his shirt up and down with my movements. "Good." I look up at him, feeling the wetness in my eyes. He rubs away a tear with his thumb, smiling down at me. He looks around the room and then over at Brock. "Now, where's that beer?"

We all sit around the living room, talking, laughing with Pop and Mrs. Evans telling childhood stories of us. Mom was fascinated by them, not knowing everything we did together growing up. How inseparable we were. Still are. She kept laughing with us and saying that she had no idea after a lot that was being said. I think she's finally realized we will never be apart.

His parents finally left around nine then Brock went out to Mom's car and got her things. I help her get settled in the spare room then we kiss and hug goodnight. I guess getting her that apartment in the morning, more shopping and decorating are at hand. I'm actually relieved that if she gets that place she'll be so close. I can tell she's a little apprehensive about being out on her own.

I go to our room and Brock is already in bed. Once I've gotten on my sleep attire, I climb under the covers and snuggle into him. We don't make love, him respecting how weird I feel with Mom not far away. He said he's good with just holding me, saying as long as I'm near he can get through a night or two.

"Mmmmm," I moan as Brock's lips travel down my body. I look over at the clock. Six in the morning. I stretch my arms up over my head, the sheet being pulled down my body, coolness sweeping over me. My nipples peak and it's not only from the cool air but from his mouth too as it covers one while his magical fingers play with the other. I shift my body around, feeling his morning wood pressing against me, trying to aim it where I need him the most.

"God, you feel so good," he moans as his mouth moves to my stomach, leaving warm kisses in its wake. He doesn't waste time and thrusts inside me, filling me completely. My legs spread wider then wrap around his slim waist, my feet pushing against his firm bottom. My fingers find his hair quickly, threading and tugging, spurring him on. We begin to get the rhythm that is ours when my head snaps to the door, hearing a noise outside. His mouth kisses my cheek. "Don't pay attention, baby." Not hearing anything else I latch onto his mouth with mine, our tongues beginning their dance. I feel the heat inside me starting to change from a low simmer rising to a boil, my stomach clenching. I can feel the pulsing of his cock as it hardens even more inside me and my muscles begin to tighten. My fingers leave his hair and grasp his strong shoulders as my fingernails dig into his skin.

"Ugh, Brock!" His mouth covers mine fast, muffling my scream, but he releases right after and our mouths pressed together helps to hide his loud moan as well. We both lay there, with sweat lightly covering our bodies, panting in our post-coital states as we hold onto each other.

My head shoots up over his shoulder when I hear another noise in the apartment. His lips kiss my neck up to my earlobe, and his warm breath makes me shiver as he whispers, "It's just your mom, baby." *My mom! Oh, my God! She probably just heard us having sex. Shit!* I push against his shoulders hard, and he laughs as he leans up. His cock pulls out, and I shiver for another reason. I jump out of bed, almost falling when the rug slides on the hardwood floor, my arms outstretched to balance me. "I'm sure she didn't hear us." I turn my head looking at him lying on his back on top of the covers. I can't help but scan his gorgeous body. He looks like a hot movie star. *I can't believe he's mine.*

Shaking my head, I lower my eyebrows. "Shhhh." He laughs again. He's still laughing when I go into the bathroom, shutting the door. I take a quick shower, put on some light makeup, and do all things needed then get dressed in a pair of jeans and a t-shirt, pulling my hair up into a high ponytail.

A delicious aroma hits me right in my stomach as I walk into the living room. I see Brock sitting down at the table in jeans and shirtless. There goes my dry panties. Mom is sitting down beside him and when I walk over to sit down, I see a plate full of food in front of me. "Mom. This is great!" I look up to see a huge smile on her face, happy to see it since everything was so rough on her last night. "I didn't know you knew how to cook." I take a bite, closing my eyes from the taste, and when I open them her smile is gone, replaced with a frown. "Oh, I'm sorry, Mom. Of course you know how to cook." I scrunch my face as I look at Brock, and he just shrugs. *I don't think I've ever seen my mom cook a day of my life.*

She sighs and my eyes snap back to her as I continue to eat. "Taren. Just because we had Mimi doesn't mean I didn't know how to cook. It's just…. Been awhile." *Mimi! I wonder if she stayed with Dad. Now I'm worried about her.*

"Uh, sorry. I just don't think I've ever seen you cook, much less eaten something you've cooked before. It's really great." Her smile is back. "Mom? Where is Mimi? Did she stay there?" I didn't want to say "with Dad". As far as I'm concerned I don't have a dad. He said he didn't have a daughter so that's fair, right? My heart drops. I wish things could have been different. I know he wasn't always this way. I remember when I was little, he was so loving. Then as soon as his business took off, I hardly saw him and when I did, he didn't have time for me anymore.

"Oh…." I focus back on her trying to shake off my thoughts and feelings. "She's going to be joining me. I wanted to find a place first. But she's not really going to work for me, more of a roommate. She and I have become so close over the years. She's always been more of a sister than an employee to me. She won't even need to find a job right away. She's been more than wise with the money she's earned." My smile is huge at this news.

"You know," Brock interrupts. "I could ask Pop if he could use another hand in the kitchen at the bar. We're always having to help out and it gets so crowded there they can't keep up with the orders of food as it is. It wouldn't pay much though."

Mom listens intently then smiles, patting his arm. "Oh, I bet she would love to. Money wouldn't need to be much with us living together and she loves to cook."

I lean towards him and kiss his cheek. "That would be amazing! She has some great recipes that she created that are easy and out of this world. I bet they would be a big hit at the bar." He smiles at me with such love in his eyes.

"I'll talk to Pop tonight." He looks at Mom. "When is she coming?"

Mom looks at him and then at me. "Well, we need to look at the apartment and if I get it, I will call her and she'll move in. She's just waiting on me." Her eyes sadden, and my heart melts. "You're Dad's going to be lost with no one there with him." She lowers her head, and my heart hurts for her. I look at Brock, who's watching her, and see the sadness on his face as well.

"Well." I smack the top of the table, making both of them look at me. "We have a lot to do today. Apartment looking, shopping." Mom smiles but I know her heart isn't in it. We end up finishing breakfast and I have a very hard time letting Brock leave for work, but I think he had just as hard of a time leaving too.

Mom and I cleaned up the kitchen and then walked over to the apartment. It's actually a lot nicer than ours. The landlord said this building is newer. She happily took it and signed everything. Now, time for shopping! It took us all day and into the evening to purchase everything. I've now learned that Mom's pretty persuasive.

She got the stores to deliver all the furniture tonight, and even though I told her Irish and I could decorate, she hired an interior designer to come in the morning. The landlord told her the appliances were only a couple of years old, but she ordered all new ones to be delivered with everything else. I'm starting to wonder if the brains in the family really came from her and not Dad. She called and talked to Mimi while we were out, and she was there when we got back, suitcases in hand, several boxes in the back of her car.

Me: @Moms. Need help
Brock: OMW

Now, if we can just get her settled then Brock and I will have our place to ourselves again. I think we're in need of a little shower time before we have to go to the bar tonight.

Brock

We were supposed to be at the bar a half an hour ago, but we got a little distracted. Okay, a lot distracted. Hey, we're young, energetic and totally in love. Who can blame us? By the time we get there the place is so packed there's a line out front. Strange. It's really crowded most of the time, people loving the down home and family feel, but this is beyond the normal crowd. Taren is just as confused as I. Taking her hand and keeping her close to me, we walk in and head to the counter. Kane's and my stools have a reserve sign on them, as usual, so I let Taren sit on mine as I stand beside her. Perk of having the stool at the end of the counter. I know at some point Kane will be here, he normally is.

Irish walks through the opening, carrying a large tray filled with drinks and food. "Hey, guys. You can take Kane's chair. He's out with some woman." I look at her in confusion. "Probably some cheap floosy. Normal." She rolls her eyes then walks behind me and out into the crowd. I look down at Taren, the same confusion on her face. No, it's not weird for him to be out with a woman, but it is very odd he would go out this early. Usually, he's here for several hours first then gets hit on or he hits on a woman. He's pretty much a no commitment kind of guy. Maybe he's adopted?

"You okay?" Taren asks in concern.

I run my fingers through my hair making it stick up all over. "Yeah. Just weird Kane's out so early. Seems strange." I put my arm around her and smile. "I'm sure it's no big deal." I know I'll be talking to him later.

We watch tons of food being brought out, the waitresses taking trays full out to the masses. I look up as Craig slides us both a beer and yells over the noise, "Hey, what's up with all the food?"

He leans his arms on the counter in front of us. We both have to move forward to hear. "Got a new cook! She's freakin' awesome!

Pop decided to give out free samples tonight, kind of a taste test. As you can see people are going crazy. We're getting all kinds of compliments." He smacks the bar and walks away smiling.

Taren and I both look at each other. "Mimi," we say in unison.

I look around and am amazed by all the people eating. Usually, most people come in to drink, play pool, or just hang out. We've always had pretty decent food for people to munch on but these people act like they're starving. "Uh, Pop? What gives? I know it's free and all but…."

Pop walks over and stands in between us, putting his hands on both of our shoulders. "Yeah, it may be free but the reviews are crazy great! Just think when it's not free tomorrow."

"But why free tonight?" I'm confused. Pop never gives anything away for free. Hell, he hates that Kane and I drink for free and we're his sons.

"Mimi talked me into it. Seems she has a good sense for business." We follow his eyes as he looks around. "People are eating it up. Pun intended. Tomorrow, they'll buy it like it's the last food on earth." He smacks our shoulders and grins. "You should try some. Craig! Bring over a plate for my son and his girl." *His girl.* "Well, I best get back there. I've been helping out. You both have a good night."

He walks off, and I turn to Taren and shrug. Craig sets down a plate of assorted food, and I don't wait to dig in. "Damn! This is amazing." My eyes shift to Taren. She's sitting there just watching me.

"Ha. I know how great her food is. Eat up." She smiles, leaning her chin in her hand watching me devour everything on the plate.

We sit there and have a few beers, laughing, listening to the music and seeing some people I know. Taren's smile is huge and as beautiful as she is. She overwhelms me with her gorgeousness as she meets everyone. Some she knows from a long time ago but hasn't seen them in a long time. A few hours fly by in no time and we're getting ready to go home. My girl has had a few too many, but it's been nice just to kick back and have some fun, relieve all the stress she's been under. "Come on, baby. Let's get you home to bed." She sways as I help her off the stool, so I tighten my grip around her waist. She giggles, and my heart beats faster.

"You don't have to ask, babe." More giggles ensue.

It takes me a few minutes to get her through the thick crowd. We're almost to the door when there's a firm hold on my arm. I turn my head to see alarm on Irish's face. She's out of breath, gripping my arm so tight it almost hurts. "Irish, what's wrong?"

As she tries to calm her breathing, I watch her swallow hard. "Kane. He…."

I turn and grab her arms, shaking her a little more than I mean to. "Irish! What the fuck?"

My eyes move to Pop walking up to us then look back at her. "He's in the hospital. They found his truck in a ditch. I don't...."

I grab Taren's hand, pushing through the last of the crowd then once outside, I run to my truck, not waiting to help Taren inside. "Brock! Wait!" Pop runs up behind us and gets in the back seat. My heart is beating so fast it's pounding against my chest. I feel like I can't breathe. I tear out of the parking lot, trying to be careful not to hit any of the parked cars. My eyes shift to Taren quickly then back to the road. She's got a firm grip on the door handle, her other hand holding on to the belt buckle around her waist. I make good time getting to the hospital, parking half crossed in a space by the emergency room, my tires squealing in protest as I come to a stop.

I run around the front, meeting Taren getting down from her seat. Pop is behind us as we run into the emergency doors and straight over to the front desk. "Kane Evans. Where is he?" My breathing coming out in heavy pants.

The nurse looks up at me, her eyes wide. "Uh, yeah. Just let me look." She looks down and starts clicking away on the keyboard in front of her. "Yes...." She looks up at me. "He's still here in emergency. Please take a seat and someone will let you know as soon as they can."

She jumps as I smack my hands down on the counter. "We're family. Now. Tell me where my brother is." I feel Pop's hand on my back, Taren's is around my arm. Both are trying to steady me.

"Sir. I'm sure you're...."

I'm about ready to go around the counter and look myself when someone speaks to my right, all of us turning our heads simultaneously. "Kane Evans' family?"

I pull away from Pop and Taren, jogging over with them right behind me. "We're Kane's family. How is he? When can we see him?"

The nurse's eyes scan mine then look at Pop and Taren then back at me. "He's stable. Has a broken right forearm, some pretty bad cuts and bruises. I'll take you to him but only family." She eyes Taren warily, and I put my arm around her.

"She is family," I state simply.

The nurse nods, turns, and we follow her through two wide doors. Everything's bright, smelling of cleaner. She stops at the last small room on the right and I peek in. He's lying in bed, eyes closed. His arm is casted from right below his elbow and covers down over his hand, only his fingers showing. "I'll let you have some time."

"Uh, will he be able to go home?" Pop asks quietly. I can tell he's really shook up.

"I'll tell the doctor you're here. He'll be by and will talk to you." She smiles then leaves and we all just stand there looking into the room. Pop moves first, walking into the room and right to Kane's side. He puts a hand on his shoulder and Kane's eyes flutter open.

"Pop," he croaks.

"Son. You look a little worse for wear. That woman must have been a wild one." Kane laughs then winces. "Sorry. Bad timing. We'll get you home, help you recoup. No need to go into what happened now but clearly I want to know."

"He's coming to our place," I state, matter of factly. I'd finally managed to get the nerve to walk into the room and stand at the foot of the bed. Pop looks over at me and nods. His eyes tired and looking older than he should.

We stayed in there, took a couple of hours with Kane nodding off and on, while we waited for the doctor and then for them to release him. Doc confirmed he has the broken arm, which we could clearly see, cuts and bruises, but he also has a bruised chest from his seatbelt when his truck went down in the ditch. He also said the seatbelt saved his life. They wheeled him out after I brought my truck up to the entrance. I helped him get inside while Taren and Pop got in the back. I dropped Pop off at home, and by the time we got to our apartment, Irish was sitting on the front steps waiting. Taren ran in to unlock our door, and Irish helped me get Kane inside. By the time we got Kane into the spare bedroom bed, I thought he'd want to go to sleep, but he stopped us before we could leave the room.

"It was a setup," he says. He struggles to sit up, Irish helping him quickly. He sits back against the headboard as she props a pillow up for him.

I sit down at the foot of the bed while Irish stands beside him and Taren behind me. "What do you mean? How do you know for sure?"

"SUV chased me then caused me to go over into the ditch. Kept hitting my truck with theirs. No plates. I saw the guys inside. Friends of Jeffrey Stratton." I hear a gasp behind me and turn my head. Taren's eyes are wide, brimming with tears, and her hands are covering her mouth. "Guess it was some kind of message. Never did make it to my night out with Colleen. Think she was in on it. Bitch."

"Colleen Maxwell?" Taren asks.

He nods, looking at Taren. "Yeah. Met her at the bar last night. Didn't know she knew him." He looks back at me. "The stakes just went up. We need a plan."

I nod, standing up, and walk over to Taren, putting my arm around her. She's shaking and looks so pale. "Maybe I should...."

I kiss the side of her head. "No. You shouldn't do anything. We're family. We stand together."

"Brock's right." We look at Kane. "We stand together. United front. Always have, always will." He looks at Irish and she nods then looks back at us. "He's not giving up. He must want the power and money of your families coming together really bad. From now on, no one is alone. You go somewhere, you take one of us with you." He looks at Irish. "That goes for all of us." She nods and I do too. "Now, let me get some shut eye. Got work to do tomorrow. Not having the use of one hand's gonna take a little creativity but no biggie. I got this."

Irish leans down and kisses his cheek, then we all walk out, closing his door. Taren walks into the kitchen, opens a cabinet and gets three glasses then pulls out the bottle of Jack from another cabinet, pouring us all a shot. She hands us our glasses then picks hers up, holding it out in front of us. We touch glasses, and I smile. *God, I love her!* "Here's to sticking together and to family." We all give our "Here, here," then clink glasses and drink.

I watch Irish go over and pour another one, downing it quickly. "You're not driving if you keep that up," I say as she pours yet another.

She tips her head back, slamming it down. "I'm sleeping on the couch. I want to be here in case he needs anything."

"I'll get you a pillow and a blanket." Taren smiles, setting down her glass, and walks out of the kitchen.

Irish has always been strong, been there for us whenever we needed her. Tonight's no different. I give her a kiss and then walk to our bedroom. By the time I've gone to the bathroom, removed my clothes and gotten into bed, Taren walks in and goes into the bathroom. I close my eyes and am about to fall asleep. The drinks I had at Pops and then what happened to Kane makes me feel exhausted. I feel the bed dip and open my eyes a crack watching Taren get settled up against me. I put my arm around her as she lays her head on my chest.

"It's all my fault. I keep causing your family so much trouble. I don't want anyone else to get hurt or worse." She looks up at me as I play with the long strands of her hair with my fingers.

"Baby, you *are* family. We protect our own. Besides, it's not your fault. Let's put blame where blame is due. Your dad and Jeffrey. What I want to know is, is your dad still pursuing this after everything that's happened or is Jeffrey acting out on his own now?" She bites the inside of her cheek. I reach over and push her bottom lip down, my way of telling her to stop. "I think Jeffrey is money hungry and wants this union to push your family's money together. He's an asshole and I don't think he'll give up." She nods but doesn't speak. I tighten my hold around her, and she closes her eyes, burying her head into my chest and laying one of her legs across mine. Suddenly, I can't sleep. I need to figure out what to do to protect my family. Especially my girl.

Chapter Ten

Taren

I awaken to a slight hangover, my head throbbing, but I know it's not just the alcohol I consumed last night. Stress has taken up residency in my head and heart. I feel beaten down with everything that's happening. I'm squeezing my pillow as I open my eyes. The brightness of the day shining through the blinds is not helping. I feel cold when I notice Brock isn't wrapped around me, so I get out of bed and go into the bathroom hoping a hot shower will help. Sadly, it didn't. I get dressed in a sluggish state and wonder how in the hell Brock is gonna work today. I walk out of our room and stop short in the hall. Brock and Kane are sitting at the kitchen table, eating breakfast and talking quietly. I move over behind the wall, feeling a little sneaky. Kane looks horrible. His face is bruised and cut, his casted arm in a sling.

"I know how her mind works. She's gonna think of something to get us all out of this and get hurt in the process," Brock's voice is serious.

Kane nods. "Yeah or worse. She's a little spitfire but I'm also concerned about Irish. She'll go after him, knowing her."

My eyes snap to the couch. It's empty with the blanket folded and pillow on top. I decide to quit spying and walk in there.

"Morning." I try to sound a little cheerful, but I'm sure I didn't succeed. I lean down and kiss Kane on the cheek then sit down in the chair between them and lean over to Brock, kissing his full lips. "Kane, you look horrible. I'm so sorry. How are you going to work?" I look at Brock. "And you. I feel like shit today so I can only imagine how you feel. How are you going to work? You can't feel any better than I do." He picks up his cup of coffee, and I look down to see I have a plate full of food and much needed coffee sitting in front of me. *Thank God!*

"Pop called off work today due to family illness. His words," Kane speaks as I take a drink of heaven. "I could have handled it," he whispers.

"Geez, bro. It's a day off. Chill." Brock laughs and then looks at me. "I'm glad he called it off. I feel like shit too. I see some napping in our future."

I giggle, but move my eyes to Kane. He's not laughing. I press my lips together and then pick up my fork. I set it back down, suddenly losing my appetite. I caused all this. Kane's hurt, they're both missing a day of work, and their dad has a day when nothing will get done for his business. I feel horrible and sick to my stomach. I feel Brock's hand cover mine on the table, and I look up at him. "Baby. It's not your fault. Quit beating yourself up."

"Brock's right," Kane's voice makes me look his way. "This is the doing of your dad's selfishness, his business." He leans his good arm on the table. "What I haven't figured out is if your dad knows what happened, orchestrated it, or if this is all Jeffrey's doing. Would be nice to find out."

"Kane! No! I told you. She stays out of it. I'll handle the asshole, find out what he knows and what he's up to. I don't want Taren anywhere near him." Brock growls, his eyebrows low and forehead creased in anger.

I shake my head. "Stop!" Their eyes both turn to me. "I'm a big girl. I can handle this. And it is my fault. If I had given in to what Daddy wanted you both wouldn't be hurt, none of this would have happened."

"But…."

I look at Brock and smile, not feeling it at all. "No. Brock, I can text him or talk to him on the phone. I won't meet him in person, unless one of you are with me. I'm smarter than that. I just think I should talk to him, find out what's going on. If he'll even tell me. Okay?" I cover our hands with my other one and squeeze. "Trust me?" My smile is genuine now as I look into his eyes.

His hand moves under my hair, grasping my neck and pulling me towards him. He kisses me then presses his forehead against mine. "With my life." I smile and kiss him again.

"Okay, you guys. Go to your room if you're gonna do that." Kane chuckles.

I chow down on my food, getting my appetite back but I do dread calling Jeffrey. Maybe I'll start with a text and hope that'll be good enough. Knowing him, it won't be.

Later that day, Kane and Brock are sitting in the living room, watching some football game and drinking beer. I kiss Brock and tell them I'm gonna take a nap, which doesn't sound like a bad idea. I did take some aspirin earlier and my head isn't as bad, but I am tired after everything that happened. Once I'm in our room and climb into bed, I decide to send the text to Jeffery before I lay down. Might as well get it over with.

Me: It's Taren. Need 2 talk

I start to lay down, thinking it will take him a while, when my phone vibrates.

Jeffrey: Ah, new number? Trying to hide?

My face heats as anger brews within me. What a jerk!

Me: No! Daddy shut off my phone
Jeffrey: Aww 2 bad
Me: Try and be just a little nice
Jeffrey: I wish u could see my eyes roll. What do u want Tare?

Tare. I wanna tear his rolling eyes right outta his head.

Me: Leave me, my friends and my family alone

Jeffrey: I don't know what ur talking about

Me: Save it. I know ur the one hurting everyone I love. Stop it

Jeffrey: Ha well even if I was which I'm not – what the hell would u do about it?

Me: I know it's you. Just stop. U have more than enough money. Why do u need my family's 2?

Jeffrey: Money is power. I want it all. But I grow tired of this "talk". I have no idea why u think it's me. Maybe u should find out who it really is. Until we meet again, Tare

Me: Jeffrey! I know it's u. Quit playing games!

I sit here staring at my phone. Nothing. He's not gonna reply. Asshole! Now, my head hurts again, and I'm too pissed to lay down. I get up and go into the bathroom, find the aspirin, and take two more. I hear the guys out in the living room yelling at the TV, so I lay back down. I'm worried about what Jeffrey will do. How can I protect the ones I love? I need a plan. A good plan. I just hope I can figure out some way to stop him. I close my eyes, trying to find sleep but all I see is Jeffrey's smug face and Brock and Kanes injuries.

"Baby," Brock's voice fills my head and I slowly open my eyes. "Hey." His gorgeous smile appears as my eyes focus. *I am the luckiest woman alive.* His thumb brushes back some of my long hair from my forehead, and he keeps rubbing into my hairline. *So soothing. So sweet.* "Irish is coming over so I thought maybe we could go to our special place. It's beautiful outside." I nod, lazily. He kisses my head and moves back. "Good. I'll get everything ready."

Yawning, I stretch and notice my headache is gone. Sitting up, I rub my eyes, get out of bed and take a quick shower. Once done with all my bathroom business, I put on my black, barely there bikini, throw on a t-shirt and my jean shorts, and step into my flip flops. I grab a duffle bag, put towels and lotion in it, and grab my sunglasses. Maybe we can have a fun day and leave all the horrible things for a bit. I'm a little worried about going out, but with Brock there I feel safe.

He makes me laugh all the way to where he parks his truck. I love how he always holds my hand as we cross the creek on the slippery rocks. Once we get to the beach area, he spreads out the blanket, and we lay there soaking up the sun for a while before we decide to take a dip. The water feels heavenly as we splash each other and laugh, and we swim around. I decide to get out after being in there for a bit, wanting to get some more sun and a little heat. When I step onto the beach, I look up and gasp. *Was that someone ducking behind a tree?*

"What's wrong, Taren?" Brocks asks, panting from running to me.

I point over to the thick area of trees. "I thought I saw someone. Over there."

"Stay here." He grasps my arm, and I nod. He bends down and hands me my phone. "Get ready to call 911 if needed." I nod, and he kisses me quickly. "I'll be right back."

"Please, be careful."

He turns his head as he walks, giving me his gorgeous smile. Suddenly, I'm cold and shivering as I watch him walk off. Soon, I can't see him anymore and my heart takes a leap into my throat. I walk over to our things and put my dry clothes on over my wet bathing suit. The thickness of the tall grass and brush beside the trees start moving, my hand moving up to my face as my heart feels like it's going to pound out of my chest. Brock appears and I slump in relief. I slip my feet into my flip flops and take off running towards him, throwing myself into his arms when I reach him. "Whoa! Baby! I'm fine." His arms wrap around me. His strong hands rub up and down my back as I try to slow my heart rate. Finally, I pull back and look into his eyes, concern showing.

"Did you see anything?" I whisper.

He looks down with a sad smile. "No, I didn't. Maybe it was something else you saw?" I shake my head. I know what I saw. I know it was a person. I just know it. I think. "Come on." He starts to walk back to the beach, his arm around me tight. "Maybe it wasn't such a good idea coming today. Let's get you home. I think we all need a relaxing night."

How he can be so calm, so self-assured, I'll never know. I wish I could be that way. Most of the time I think I am but all of this is too much. But he's always handled everything in our young lives with such calmness, confidence. It's one of the things I love about him. He keeps me grounded. We walk back to his truck all the while I look around and over my shoulder, still having a feeling that we're being watched. His arm tightens around me as I shiver.

Brock

We get home. Taren says hi to Kane and then runs into the bathroom to take a shower to get the pond water off her. I grab a couple of beers from the fridge and sit on the couch. Kane's sitting in the recliner with his legs up and watching a game. I look over my shoulder and see our bedroom door is shut, then I look at Kane. "So, someone was in the woods by where we were today." Kane's eyebrows raise. "Yeah, Taren thought she saw someone run behind a tree so I went looking. I didn't see anything but I did find this." I pull the button out of my pocket, leaning over and hand it to him.

"Interesting," he murmurs as he rolls it around with his fingers. "Any ideas?"

I let out a sigh. "Not really but I can guess."

He leans his arm on the chair, getting a little closer. "Look, Brock. I know you and Taren have had this "secret" place for a lot of years. I think maybe it's time you tell me where it is? Obviously, someone's found it."

He's right. I know he is. I just hate telling anyone without Taren knowing. It's always been ours. A place where we could go and hide. Be just the two of us where no one could interfere. No one could say I was lower than dirt and that I wasn't good enough for her or that she was too good for me. But if anything happened to her, I would blame myself. I look over my shoulder again, still finding our door closed. When I turn back to him I still hesitate but the look in his eyes tell me he knows this is hard for me. "Taren is going shopping with her mom and Mimi tomorrow. I'll take you then. It'll be easier than trying to explain. It's very well hidden. That's why I'm so surprised that someone found it." I take the button from his hand and stare at it. "He must have followed us." I look back up at him, my eyebrows creasing. "It's the only way he could have found it."

"Found what?" I hear her light footsteps across the hardwood floor and the gentle breeze as she walks behind the couch. She sits down next to me, refreshed and wide eyed.

I shove the button into my pocket and turn around. "Oh! Um, Kane found the ice pack I was looking for the other day. It was in the spare room the whole time." I bite my lip, my eyes shifting at Kane. His head is low, his body shaking slightly, and I can tell he's trying not to laugh. That was a stupid thing to come up with. She's gonna know I'm lying. I swore to her when we were very young I'd never lie to her, and I never have. My head is swimming. Should I tell her or should I protect her? It's not really lying, lying, if you do it to protect someone. Right?

"Oh." Her eyebrows raise into her forehead making it crease. She's even beautiful when she's frustrated or questioning. "I didn't know you were looking for it."

I look at Kane, who now has his hand covering his mouth. *Thanks for the support, bro.* I look back at Taren and smile. "I was trying to find it the other day when you hurt your knees. Guess I'll know where it is in case we need it again now." I reach over and take her hand, threading my fingers through, squeezing tightly. *Shit! I need to change the subject fast!* "So, you girls are gonna go shopping tomorrow?" Her eyes light up. *Nice save.*

"Yeah. Mom and Mimi decided they wanted some new bedding and some new pictures for their walls. I thought I might look at some things too." She smiles, and I'm relieved. I lean over and kiss her mouth. She tastes of mint and her.

"You go have fun, baby. Kane and I'll just hang around here."

"Okay. Well, at least it's Saturday and you'll have a couple more days of healing before getting back to work," she says to Kane. She moves towards me, kissing me hard, then stands. "I'll go get dinner going. You enjoy the game." *Shit, I love her! Now if I can just protect her and get this asshole out of our lives for good.*

We have a great dinner. Irish came over to eat with us and watch the rest of the game. Sometimes I wonder if she's really a guy in disguise but then the way she looks at Kane at times, I wonder if she has feelings for him more than just friendship. She never dates. I never hear about a guy interest or her even talking about going out on a date. Makes me wonder. *Nah!* It's Irish. She's like family. We have a great time laughing and reminiscing about when we were young, and how much fun we had. Kane embarrassing Taren with his own stories. We've always been together. She's always been a part of our lives, my life. I couldn't imagine us not being together. She completes me, fills me with love and desire, always.

After we cleaned the kitchen and sat around with Kane and Irish, Taren starts yawning, and soon kisses me and Kane goodnight. I tell her I'll be there in a bit, wanting to finish the movie we'd started watching. I watch her walk to the bedroom, her cute tight bottom swaying in those damn yoga pants that fit like they're painted on. Damn, my cock has hardened past the point of painful. When I get into our bedroom, I see her passed out, the covers riding low on her waist. Her long dark hair is fanned out across her pillow, her hands underneath her face. A vision. I should go take a very cold shower to relieve my ache, but I'm too tired. After removing my clothes, I slide under the covers and up against her warm body, my arm moving over her waist. She stirs as I snuggle up close but doesn't wake. I take a big sniff of her hair and lay my head close to hers. *Someone should really bottle her unique smell. People would buy the shit outta it.* Sleep doesn't come easy, lying next to her, but finally I manage to drift off.

Warmth

Wet

Her lips encase me fully, her tongue sweeping over the tip. Sucking, stroking. Moaning. My cock hits the back of her throat. She doesn't even gag.

My eyes flutter open. My heart races as her teeth slide up the tender skin of my hard cock. I look down, watching the sexiest thing I've ever seen. My eyes almost close as I watch her mouth pull up to the tip then back down, taking it to the back of her throat. I expected her to gag, but she doesn't. *Shit! I thought I was dreaming this.* My head tilts back, my fingers finding her hair as her hand grasps my balls, rolling, tugging, then fondling. "Ugh, Taren!" I scream. She starts sucking harder, her hand squeezing my balls as they tighten, and my release begins to stream into her mouth. I look back down as my body shudders with my climax. She smiles as she releases me, her mouth leaving my now softened cock with a "pop". I lean up, taking her by her arms, bringing that hot mouth to my lips as she slides up my body. I can taste myself. It's weird but then I can taste her uniqueness too so it isn't as bad as I thought it would be.

"You're amazing," I tell her as I start kissing all over her face. She giggles.

I push her over, leaning up on my hands so I don't crush her with my weight. We stare into each other's eyes, searching for something. For what I'm not sure. I lean back on my legs, resting into between hers, and lift her thin top, pulling it up and watching her soft unblemished skin appear. *Shit, she's fucking beautiful.* Leaning down, I begin kissing up her luscious body, taking one of her pert nipples into my mouth while I play with her other breast, fondling, and rubbing my thumb across the nipple. She starts squirming a little beneath me when I suck harder. I think turnaround is only fair play, so I make my way back down, kissing and licking as I go. I take the waistband of her lacy panties in my hands, looking into her desired filled eyes as I pull them down. I have to back up to get them off then drop them on the floor. I place my hands on her inner thighs, pushing them open further, licking my lips when I look at the bareness before me. "God, you're so fucking beautiful." Her hips move, her legs trembling. I don't make her wait. My tongue dives into her sweetness as my thumb circles over her swollen clit. She's already dripping wet. I rub faster as I suck in her wetness, her hips bucking against my mouth.

"Ugh, Brock," she moans. Her head thrashes back and forth as her thighs clamp around my head. I pull back, her legs stilling until I move up, and thrust into her wetness. I glide easily in her slickness. It's not long that her legs begin to shake, and her body shivers with her release. I can feel my balls tighten, my climax reaching its peak, then my own body shudders, and I pour everything

I have into her. I collapse on her, trying to move off a little so she can breathe. Our bodies covered in a light sweat, our heavy panting the only sounds in the room. "Wow," she whispers breathlessly. I turn my head, looking into her half-mast eyes. The corners of her mouth turned up in a smile, satisfaction showing on her gorgeous face. "That was amazing."

I kiss her shoulder, smiling with my own sated feeling. "You're amazing." Her smile seems frozen on her face until she pushes against me.

"I need to go to the bathroom." She giggles. I laugh at her cuteness as she runs to the bathroom. "I'm gonna take my shower. Mom and Mimi should be here in…." She looks at the alarm clock. "About half an hour." Her hand rests against the door frame. Her body relaxed against it. "Of course if you wanna join me I could always have them come later," she says breathless. She's more than beautiful, standing there naked, looking at me with those lust filled eyes. I watch her breasts rise and fall from her heavy breathing. *Damn! How can I resist that?*

I rise, walking to her quickly, my body already heating up. "Text them you'll be late." She giggles and I put my arm around her, pulling her into the bathroom. She was about a half an hour late to get ready to go. I couldn't help it with an invitation like that.

Shortly after they left, Kane and I headed to our secret place. I start to feel weird as Kane and I approach the area where I turn off. We worked hard, getting the shack built, setting it up just how we wanted it. Now I understand why she was creeped out thinking someone had found our own private little pond area and so close to our shack. I wonder if that asshole found the shack too or since we didn't go there that time, he just followed us straight to the little beach? "I gotta ask you to keep this between you and me, Kane." I look over as I drive down the dirt road, Kane looking around out the windows. He turns to me, concern definitely on his face. "This has always been ours, somewhere we could go and have alone time without anyone intruding." I look at the road nearing where I turn off. "I mean. It was so hard, rough, trying to be somewhere all our lives that her parents wouldn't find us. We don't want to give that up, ya know?" I look at him and notice he's listening intently, watching me. He nods, and I feel a bit better but not much. He may be my brother, and I trust him with my life but I'm still having a hard time about anyone knowing about it.

I pull off the road and through the heavy trees, parking where I always do. We get out and Kane shoots me a look when he sees the creek we have to cross. "I'll help you. You're injured." He gives me a smirk and starts across the slippery rocks. He almost falls twice, but I didn't try to help him. He'd beat the shit outta me. Tough dude. He follows me through the tall brush until we reach the shack. I open the door, letting in the light, and walk to the window, raising it to get some fresh air in the small room. "Wow! You both really put some work into this. Nice," Kane says as he walks around the area. "Well hidden too. You all really put some thought into this. Gotta hand it to ya." He smacks my shoulder. "Now, show me this pond and where you saw someone." I nod, leading him out and then through the overgrown grass again. We reach the small beach area, and I watch as he looks around. "Dang. Got your own little paradise here. Nice."

I turn around and point to the heavy tree area. "They were over there. I looked around pretty thoroughly and that's where I found the button. I'm pretty fucking sure it's Jeffrey's though. He's the only one, outside her dad, that's out to get their families together. All for money. Selfish bastards."

He nods, and I follow him over to the trees. We walk around for what seems like hours. "Think you got the only piece of evidence. I think it's time to get Dean involved." My heart races thinking about letting the police know. However, Dean's a good friend so maybe he'll be discreet. We've known him for a long time.

"Okay. Maybe you're right. I can't let anything happen to Taren or our friends and family. I just hate having this public, ya know?"

He places a hand on my shoulder. "No. He'll keep it under wraps. If it's announced, he knows Jeffrey will hide. Not gonna help to pin him with this. Gonna be tough enough as it is. His family is pretty influential in town. Come on. Let's get back and take a ride to the police station." I nod, silently wishing this was all over. I will do anything to protect my girl. Anything.

Chapter Eleven

Taren

"Oh, my God, Mom! Are you trying to kill me?" We're sitting in a coffee shop in the mall. She smiles then winks at Mimi. "Death by shopping." I take a drink of my mocha and sigh in relief of having a few minutes to sit down. My feet are killing me. I wanna bring up about Jeffrey's attempts to still get our families together but suddenly feel ill thinking about it.

"What's got you thinking so hard, sweetie? I hope you know by now that I'm on your side and am always here for you." Mom's voice shakes me from my thoughts. I look up and see her beautiful smile. I really wish she would have come to her senses about Dad a long time ago, but I'm thankful she's here with me now.

I look down putting my hands around my cup, feeling the warmth. "Um, well." I look up at Mom and Mimi, finally landing on Mom's eyes. "Mom. Jeffrey's still trying to get us together. He's already hurt Brock and Kane. He's money hungry and I'm afraid he'll stop at nothing to get our families joined."

She gasps, laying her hand over her heart. "I wondered how Kane and Brock got those injuries. Oh my!"

My eyes snap over to Mimi as she speaks. "Boy's been nothing but trouble. Never liked him and I certainly never wanted you to be suited up with him."

Their reactions tell me they don't care much for him either. "Never did like his parents. Stuffy and always thought they were better than anyone. I told Tom at the beginning that you shouldn't be subjected to all that but he was bound and determined to get our families joined," Mom says angrily. She sighs, a frown appearing on her face, sadness in her eyes. "I should have left him so many years ago. Back in our day, you didn't leave your husband, let alone divorce them. But times changed. I guess those of us already stuck in our old ways didn't. I'm sorry, sweetheart. I wish I would have gotten out from under this thumb so many years ago, taking you and Sebastian with me."

I reach across the table, placing my hand on hers and squeeze. "Mom. Stop. I turned out okay, I think." Her frown turns into a sad smile. "It's gonna be fine. We'll figure out what to do." I sit back, taking a drink of my coffee.

"How are you going to stop him, Taren? Have you gotten the police involved? What's it going to take, *you* getting hurt?" Mom's eyes search mine with worry and concern.

I sigh. "I dunno what to do. I don't want anyone else getting hurt because of me." Tears fill my eyes and I close them tight. I'm tired of crying, tired of feeling weak. I open them and sit up straighter. "I think maybe the police would be a good idea. If anything happened to Brock I'd...."

Mom and Mimi both smile. "There's my strong girl. Now, let's finish up. I think we've shopped enough today. You have some business to do." *Thank God. No more shopping!*

They drop me off at my apartment. I stop at the mailbox on the way in and push my key into the lock, opening the door. I'm looking down, sorting through the mail, when the best smell fills my nose. I look up and notice the lights are off. Candles light the small table which is already set. A beautiful bouquet of fresh flowers is setting in a vase in the middle. The mail goes flying out of my hands and onto the floor as I bring them up to my mouth. The room looks so romantic and smells heavenly. A mixture of spaghetti and flowers. I hear a noise and turn my head. Music begins playing softly from his iPod dock in the living room. I feel anxious, like I don't know what could come next but can't wait to find out.

My eyes flit to the hall doorway. He's standing there in black jeans and a black button down shirt. The top two buttons are undone showing the soft skin of his broad and muscular chest. Self-consciously, I lick my lips. *Damn, he's so fine.* His short brown hair is sticking up all over the place, just how I love it. His eyes sear into mine. *He's so freaking sexy.* Slowly, he walks over to me, his slim waist swaying with his movements. When he reaches me, his hand moves under my long hair, cupping the back of my neck, pulling me closer until our mouths touch. *One of my most favorite things he does.* His tongue doesn't need to ask for permission to enter as I part my lips immediately. My heart beats frantically, my chest hitting against his. My arms move around his waist, but he grabs one then tears his mouth from mine and leads me around the couch, the mail on the floor forgotten. I look down, seeing our old ratty blanket laid out on the floor. He helps me down then walks over to the gas fireplace, turning it on low.

"I thought we were eating at the table?" I question but not really caring what the answer is. Right now, I'm not even in the mood to eat food. He gives me his sexy grin then leaves me. I follow him with my eyes, watching him pick up the place settings, except for the plates, bringing them over and setting them on the coffee table. He walks back and gets the flowers, setting them there as well. He returns to the kitchen, filling our plates with spaghetti and garlic bread then adds them to the setting. I can't help but let out a small laugh. "Why didn't you just set this all up here in the first place? I've missed you."

He kneels down beside me, his sexy grin still adorning his gorgeous face. "Changed my mind." He takes my hand, bringing it up to his mouth and kissing the top. His eyes widen. "Oh! I forgot something." He leaps up and runs to the kitchen, returning with two wine glasses and a bottle of wine, sitting down again and pouring some in each glass. "Now. That's better." He hands me a glass, clinking his with mine, and I take a sip.

"Mmmm," I moan as the taste sweeps over my tongue and down my throat. Tangy. A little fruity. "That's really good." Suddenly, he seems different. That sexy grin turns down a bit. I smile, trying to lighten things up. "Are you trying to butter me up?" My smile fades when his eyes snap to mine. Telltale sign that something's most definitely up. I set my glass down, putting my hands in my lap. They start fidgeting immediately. "What? Did something else happen? Did someone get hurt?"

He reaches up, pushing my lower lip down with his fingers until I release the inside of my cheek I was gnawing on. "No. No one's been hurt. I guess that's why I did what I did today, to make sure that doesn't happen."

My eyebrows raise. "What did you do?" I whisper.

He stares straight into my eyes, his never wavering. "Kane and I went to see Dean Weston today." I breathe a sigh of relief. He takes my hand, rubbing his thumb over my skin. "Sorry. I didn't mean to worry you. I just wasn't sure how'd you react, I guess."

"Anymore, I just want everyone to be safe. So, what did Dean say?"

He looks down, watching his thumb move across my hand. "Well, he said there's no real evidence, yet." He looks back up into my eyes, his long dark lashes fanning out above them. *Every girl would be jealous with envy for those.* "He said he would keep an eye on him. Problem is they don't have anyone to stick with him and watch him all the time. He said to call or text him if anything happens and of course to dial 911 if it's an emergency and he can't be reached." I press my lips together, my brows lower with frustration. I had a feeling if we went to the police, that's what would happened. "Hey," he whispers as his hand cups my face. I look up into his softened eyes, full of love and caring. "It's gonna be okay. If you're out you need to make sure to have your phone. There's GPS tracking in there. I set yours up on my phone and mine on yours. I'll show you after we eat. Okay? Kane has both of ours too." I nod, not knowing if I can eat. But my stomach has other plans and growls. He laughs, my mood changing quickly. "Come on. Apparently someone needs food." I relent, knowing I need to eat something. I think most of my food intake today was coffee. After eating the first bite, I close my eyes with the delicious taste. I had no idea he could cook this good.

We don't clean up after we're done. Instead, we undress each other, wanting to take advantage of the romantic ambience. We make love on our old blanket, the smell of the beach still embedded. We lie in each other's arms until I look up and see he's fast asleep. I carefully get up and walk to our bedroom, grab a blanket from the foot of the bed then return to my position, and cover us up. I bury my head into his chest and close my eyes. *Best night ever!*

The next morning I fix a nice breakfast. It's the least I could do after all he did last night. Even though it's Saturday, he and Kane are going over to the construction site because missing the last couple of days has put them behind. I have no idea how Kane's gonna manage with only one hand but he's pretty resourceful. I busy myself with cleaning up our mess, taking my shower and then I find by noon I'm bored stiff. I power on my laptop, hoping to find a job, when a knock sounds on the door. My heart races. *Shit, Taren. You're being silly. Why would he come over here and in broad daylight?* I stand, setting my laptop on the coffee table and walk to the door, stopping short. *Because he knows Brock's at work?* I answer myself.

"Taren!" I jump at another knock and Irish's voice.

Sheesh, Taren. Get a grip, I mumble to myself and laugh at my behavior.

I open the door and Irish walks past me. I close it and turn around watching her sit down in the recliner, pushing up the foot rest and plopping her feet there. "Took you long enough." Her eyes look at me and she frowns. "You look really pale. Are you okay?" I walk over and sit on the couch, letting out a big breath. I jump again when my phone vibrates in my pocket. After pulling it out I see a text from Kane.

Kane: If Irish is there tell her to answer her damn phone! Thx

I answer him that I will, finding it odd, then turn to her. "Um, Kane wants you to answer your damn phone." I tilt my head and look at her questioningly.

She scrunches up her face. "He can bite me." She grabs the TV remote from the end table and turns it on.

"What the hell, Irish? Why don't you want to talk to him?" She ignores me at first then shuts off the TV slamming the remote down on the table. I bend over, leaning my arms on my legs. "What's up, Bestie?"

"He just makes me crazy. A different woman every night. He gets hurt because he thought he was meeting a woman. Don't you see? He'd do anything for a woman as long as he can get some. Ugh! This! This is why I don't date! Men are the scum of the earth!" She leans her head back, hitting her fists against the arms of the chair. Suddenly, it all makes sense. Now, I know why she doesn't ever date. *Oh, my God!*

"Holy shit! You like him!" I yell. My eyes are wide, and I'm screeching inside.

She turns her head as her eyebrows lower. "Uh, yeah. I like him. We've known each other all our lives. You know this, Taren," she says sarcastically.

I straighten up and smile. "No. I mean, you like him, like him." Her mouth opens then closes, continuing like she's a fish trying to get air. I lean back, crossing my legs, and laugh. "Wow! You do! You really like him!" I slump back on the couch. "So, that's why you haven't dated anyone. You don't want to take the chance that maybe he'd have feelings for you in that way and you're hoping he'll calm his wild ways and you'll be there waiting."

Her feet press against the foot rest, slamming it back into place as she sits up. Her eyes are staring daggers at me, and I laugh harder. "I do not! You wench! Why would you even think that?" She leans back again and stares at the TV. "Most ridiculous thing I've ever heard leave your mouth and I've heard plenty of things leave there." Her eyes shift to mine then back to the TV. I just stare at her with my smile plastered on my face. She raises her arms then slaps her hands down on her jean covered legs. "OKAY! Okay, are you happy?" *I knew it!* "So I like him, like him. Who wouldn't? Have you seen him with his shirt off?" I start giggling. "And he's just so nice, caring, strong, and have you seen him with his shirt off? Okay, so he has some wild women ways right now but that's not gonna last forever. Right?" Her eyes widen as she turns towards me, and then she seems to deflate. "Is it?"

I burst out, laughing even harder. I never thought I'd see the day. Irish really likes Kane. Wow! Okay, I gotta admit. Kane is rugged, muscular in all the right places, works hard and works out even harder but damn, he's such a womanizer. I finally settle myself down, my breathing out of control with laughing so hard and my sides hurt. I get serious and tilt my head, looking into her eyes. "Why don't you just tell him?"

She jumps up, my eyes following her as she paces the floor, her arms flailing around wildly as she rants. "Are you fucking kidding? He doesn't like me that way and probably never will. It will ruin our friendship because he'll think I'm a lovesick twit! Kane's too much a man and even more a big womanizer. He's young and out to live life his way!" She stops and looks at me and gets serious. "I'm not sure he'll ever change but I am sure he would never think of me more than a sister." She walks over and slams herself down into the chair, sighing loudly while her head bounces off the head rest.

I never thought I'd see the day, but I don't know what to tell her, how to console her. She's right. Kane's out to have sex with all the women who come up to him or that he can find. I've never understood why he's that way. Doesn't he ever want to find "the woman" and settle down or is that what he's trying to do, in his own way? "Irish." Her eyes shift to me. "Maybe it's supposed to be this way. Maybe Kane's not the right one for you. Have you thought of that? You've spent so much time hoping for something that's maybe never gonna happen, wasting precious time, when there's someone out there that's right for you."

She turns in the chair, her legs curling up around her. "How do you shut off feelings you've had since you were young. Look at you and Brock. Could you just stop feeling what you're feeling for him and look for someone else?" *Damn. She's got a point.*

"No one said it would be easy. But honey, without looking at all, how would you ever know?" I try to sound reasonable, but I know what she means. If I couldn't have Brock, I'd be forever alone. There's no one that could ever take his place in my heart.

She closes her eyes briefly and sighs again, looking down at her fingers, picking on some invisible thing on the arm rest. "I know you're right." She looks up at me, sadness written on her face. "I guess I've always known but it's so hard. I look at other guys and it's just not the same, ya know? Besides, most of the guys I see, women just put out and they just go with it. I'm not sure there are any guys worth it. I want a guy who'll work for a relationship, same as I would."

I rise and walk over, squatting down beside her. "I know, bestie. But all you do is work and it's normally in Pops Bar. You're not gonna find the right guy there." I reach up and tuck a long piece of her hair that came loose from her ponytail behind her ear and smile. "You're a beautiful woman. You have a killer body and a kind heart. Not to mention you can kick the ass of any man." A laugh bursts from her mouth. I grab her arm. "Come on. Let's go workout or something, your favorite thing. Sounds like you need to release some pent up energy…." She stands, and I try to hide my laugh. "Or something."

Brock

Works been tough. With Kane only having one hand, he's done what he can but the other guys and me end up working more, making up for him. I don't mind. I'd do whatever's needed when it comes to him. I keep thinking about how weird Irish has been acting around him, wondering what's up with her. Secretly, I think she has a thing for him, but then I shake my head and just think, nah, couldn't be. I mean, we've all been together since we were young. She's almost been like "one of the guys". She can play ball better than some men, works out every day, and has muscles that most women don't. Oh, she's beautiful, no doubt about that, but a rough exterior too. I must be crazy. I know Kane doesn't think of her *that* way. At least I don't think he does.

It's close to the end of the day when a big truck pulls into the lot. Most don't notice it but Kane and I immediately lift our heads and then look at each other. I guess we're both on alert. He's got his hand on his phone, probably ready to call 911 or Dean, just in case. The truck's loud motor shuts off and a huge guy steps out of it. He's got red hair, cut short. The same red color scruff on his face. His eyes are hazel green but the thing that I notice the most is how massive his shoulders are and how broad his chest is. Definitely works out and keeps in shape that's for sure. I watch carefully as Kane walks over to meet him then I slowly walk closer so I can hear them, making sure this isn't a set up or a plant.

"Caylan Dorn," he says as he shakes Kane's hand. "Lookin' for work, if you got any."

He seems nice enough, has a huge smile on his face. But I know looks can be deceiving.

"Kane Evans." He turns his head to me, and I cross my arms over my chest, trying to look tough. "My brother, Brock." He turns back to Caylan. "As you can see…." He lifts his casted arm. "I'm working with one hand for a while. You got experience in construction?"

"Yes, sir. Been working construction for about two years now," he answers quickly.

"Oh? Where?" Kane asks just a fast.

"Just moved here from Kentucky. That's why I'm needing a job," Caylan responds without hesitation. "I have papers of recommendation." He hands the papers to Kane.

Kane studies him and the papers, and I'm wondering if he's as suspicious as I am. "We could use the help, especially from one that has experience." He reaches out his hand and Caylan takes it, shaking as Kane smiles. "Welcome aboard." He turns to me and nods. "Brock. Show Caylan what we got going on." I nod back, my apprehension soaring. I guess he could be legit, but I just have a strange feeling about him.

Surprisingly, we end up working well together. He does know what he's doing and is a strong guy. He can definitely lift way more than I can. Around noon, we sit down on the scaffolding and I open my sack lunch Taren made me this morning. I watch him from the corner of my eye, opening a small bag, brings out an apple and bites into it. "Uh. I got two sandwiches. Want one?" I offer.

He shakes his head and smiles. "No. But thank you. Got fruit and a couple of granola bars." He takes another bite, looking out at the scenery in front of us.

I chuckle. "I'd die with only eating that stuff, man." He looks at me and laughs.

"Gotta watch my weight. I have a photo shoot coming up in a month."

My brows raise. "What? Are you a model?" I start snickering as his face grows serious.

"Actually, yes."

My eyes widen. "Really? Wow! Kinda like a celebrity, huh?" Now he laughs, really hard.

"Nah. I just do photo shoots for some photographers for business and some authors buy them for book covers. Kinda weird, really. Never thought I'd be doing that kind of thing." He takes another bite and looks like he's thinking. "Strange really. I'd done my first shoot a few months ago, just for business." He turns and looks at me. "I'm a fitness trainer. So was doing it to get some pictures to advertise with. This one photographer is pretty well known on social media and had shared some of the pictures around so some authors asked about selling them for covers. He asked me and I figured, why not?"

"Wow. That's pretty cool. Seems you got quite a bit going for ya. Nice to have all that in your life, huh?" I ask and take a big bite of my sandwich. Hell, I don't gotta watch my weight.

His brows lower. "Yes and no. I mean…. It's cool and all but moving here is kinda harder than I thought. I found an apartment yesterday that's pretty nice and now this job but I need to find a gym, see if I can get a job as a personal trainer there. But there's so many that I wouldn't work at. Gotta be the right one."

I'm starting to feel more at ease with him. He really is a nice guy. "Well, you can ask Kane about a gym. He works out daily. Maybe the one he uses can use a personal trainer. It's pretty nice."

He smiles big. "Thanks. Appreciate it."

I take another huge bite, chew, and swallow. "Eh, it's nothing. Whatever I can do to help a celebrity." We both start laughing, and he play punches my arm. Holy shit, that kinda smarted.

I'm impressed that by the end of the day he did more work than Kane and I combined. Mind you, Kane is one handed right now but Caylan did way more than one and a half men. We walk together to our trucks and invite him to come hang at the bar later. He declined saying he needed to get settled but thanked us and said another time. He did take Kane's offer to follow him to the gym, so I get in my truck and drive home. I need a shower and spend time with my girl. Since Mimi's working at the bar now, Pop said I don't need to come in every night unless it's to have fun or if he needs help. Fine by me.

I walk in the door and my eyes immediately zone to Taren sleeping on the couch. I lean back against the door and just stare.

She's a vision. Memories wash over me of the first time I saw her. I think we were about six or seven. Even though we lived on different sides of the "tracks", we went to the same school. I guess it was what they call a district thing. We weren't in the same class though. I'd been playing ball with a couple of guys at recess and felt her before I saw her. I stopped with my foot on the ball, moving it back and forth, and the guys were yelling at me. I looked across the small field and there she was. It was clear that even in first grade you could see the segregation between girls and boys. She was standing with a few other girls, but I really couldn't tell you how many. I only had eyes for her. I felt the guys hitting my arm, yelling at me to kick the ball, but I was mesmerized by her. She noticed me right away, her eyes looking at me from beneath those long lashes. A light pink graced her sweet face as the corner of her mouth lifted. I dared not approach her or speak to her. I was too nervous, yet I wanted to so badly. I stared at her and watched her every move any chance I got. A week had gone by and   I'd finally decided to sit down on the ground against the brick of the school and let the warm breeze blow against my heated skin. She walked over and sat down right beside me. I didn't know what to say, what to do. I'd been dreaming about her ever since the first moment I'd seen her and now it was like my dream came true.

"Hi," she said quietly.

I looked at her and smiled, my heart beating so fast I thought it would choke me, making me unable to speak. "Hi," I managed to get out.

It was on that day moving forward we became inseparable. Here I was supposed to be the guy, the strong one, but it took her coming to me that broke the ice. Thank God she was strong as well. Of course we started getting razzed from other kids immediately. Her friends at even such a young age were appalled that she would even speak to me. My friends just whooped and hollered that I was moving up in the world to have such a fine wealthy girl even look at me. It's sad that in this world there are so many invisible lines drawn everywhere, but we stepped over this one and have been together ever since.

I push off the door and walk over to the couch, toeing my shoes off, and even though I need a shower desperately, I step over her sleeping form and gently push her forward with my body as I cuddle behind her. She doesn't stir but let's out a sigh as I put my arm around her waist. I lay my head against hers and close my eyes.

It was a great nap, one that made me think I may never be able to get to sleep later tonight. I awoke to her kissing my face, down my neck, and then she lifted my shirt and started peppering kisses on my stomach. I couldn't take it for long and startled her a bit when I jumped over the back of the couch. She soon started giggling when I reached down and lifted her in my arms, marching us right to the bathroom. We took a long shower, the water turning cool as we made love then washed each other. Then we had the most relaxing night we've had in a long time. We made dinner out of popcorn, chips, pop and other snacks as we watched a marathon of movies. It was the best time and the first time since she moved in that nothing was in our way of just enjoying each other, no worries of anyone hurting us or stopping us. I wish it could always be this way.

Chapter Twelve

Taren

When I woke up from my nap, one that I hadn't intended on sleeping quite so long, the warmth of his body incased mine. I turned in his arms and watched him sleep. Flashes of memories invaded my mind. My mouth turns into a smile when I remember the first time we kissed. I study his face as I remember being on the side of the school, sitting against the hard brick of the building, talking like we had so many times. Suddenly, he turned to me, not giving me a warning, and cupped the sides of my face, his lips pressing against mine. It was a sweet kiss, romantic yet definitely not long enough. I remember the feeling of electricity flowing from my face down my body, thinking that odd yet wonderful at the same time.

When Mimi picked me up after school, I was so excited to tell her about it and was crushed when she told me I shouldn't speak a word of it to Mom or Dad. She told me I needed to be discreet and I had to look up that word when I got home because I had no idea what it meant. I was confused when I found the meaning. I didn't understand why I couldn't be happy about it. I wanted to shout it to the world that I liked him, that this boy had already captured my heart. However, I soon learned why. Being so young and so filled with happiness, I told my parents and the small war between them and Brock's family began. If only I'd listened to Mimi and kept it to myself. However, because of Brock, I met Irish. She was the one person I could talk to, show my excitement about him to and we became best friends.

After a long shower and much needed time together watching movies in each other's arms, we finally turned off the TV and lights and went to bed. But after such a long nap, neither of us were tired. We had no problem finding something to do until we became sleepy again. Then a while later, he held me in his arms as I feel asleep.

The next morning I stretched my arms above my head, feeling happy. I reach over to find his side of the bed cool and open my eyes feeling the warmth of the sun from the window above the bed. I move my hand and hit paper, bringing it up in front of me.

I wanted you to sleep in, for once. I'll see you after work.

Love you with all my heart and soul.

Brock

My mouth instantly forms into a huge smile. I decide to forgo a shower and get on my yellow bikini, wanting to take advantage of the sun. I walk out onto our small deck, put a towel on the wooden floor and lay down, closing my eyes to the brightness. After a while I nearly fall asleep and turn over to get some sun on my back. It ends up being a lazy morning but after all the shopping, I deserve it. Once I've taken a shower, scrunching up my hair as I blow it dry, then putting on one of my silky tank tops and jeans shorts, I decide I'm not in the mood for anything we have to eat. My stomach growls and the thought of Mimi's cooking hits me hard. Without thinking it through, I decide the twenty five minute walk to Pops will do me good so I lock up the apartment and head out of the building and down the tree lined dirt road.

I get only about fifteen minutes into my walk when the sky opens up and starts pelting me with rain. It's not even a sprinkle, but a full out downpour. "Great," I mumble jogging off the road and into the trees for cover. I'm drenched and all I can think about is how horrible my hair probably looks. I lean against the trunk of a tree hoping the rain will stop soon. My stomach growls louder than the thunder and I sigh. The sky darkens to black. Should I take the chance and run home? I'm closer to the bar now. I start to move when a hand clasps around my neck. My eyes squeeze shut with the force, my airway cut off.

"No need to run, Tare," his voice sends shivers down my spine. I open my eyes slowly and look up, staring into dark green eyes. My lips part and I'm ready to scream, not sure if I can even take a breath, when his other hand covers them. "Aw, what's wrong, my love? Aren't you glad to see me?" His mouth turns up into an evil smirk. His hand is replaced over my mouth with his. I start to struggle, but his hand tightens around my throat. Sick feelings stir throughout me as his hand squeezes my breast through my bra. It doesn't stay there for long. I kick out, trying to hit his legs when his hand moves down and cups me in between my legs. His leg moves in between us, spreading my legs further as bile rises at the base of my throat underneath his hand that's covering it. I slide in the wet grass, trying to gain my footing. "You will be mine," he growls. My heart beats out of control in fear. One of my hands is around his arm, trying to push his hand away from my neck while the other is against his chest. My hand moves under his shirt in a panic, the force popping off the top button and my fingernails dig into his skin. Suddenly, a horn honks, his hand leaving my throat quickly, and as I drop to the ground, my nails sear across his chest as my body slides roughly down the bark of the tree.

"Bitch!" He screams.

My eyes are closed tight. I hear his running footsteps growing faint. I feel the tears running down my face intermingling with the heavy rain. My hand moves around my throat as my airway opens, and I struggle to take deep breaths. Finally, I open my eyes, searching around for him, but he's nowhere. The rain is coming down in buckets. I turn, pushing my hand against the tree and finally manage to stand on shaky legs. I'm numb as I walk back to the road, berating myself for leaving it in the first place. It feels longer than the ten minutes to the bar. The parking lot isn't full, thank God. I push open the front door, heads turning around and so many eyes are staring. I must look as scared as I feel when Pop jogs over to me, putting his arm around me, and silently leading me down a short hallway and into a room. He helps me sit down in a folding chair, my eyes darting to the door when Irish runs in.

"What the fuck, Taren?" Her eyes dart to Pop, but he doesn't correct her language, his face only showing concern. She squats down in front of me and places a hand on my upper back. I wince, and her eyes widen. "You're hurt."

"Call Brock, Irish," Pops says. She nods slowly and rises, pulling her phone from the front pocket of her jeans. He sits down in the chair next to me and covers my wringing hands with his. "Taren," he whispers. My eyes snap to his worried and caring face. He looks at Irish as she squats back down in front of me.

"He's on his way." Her hand comes up, pushing back some of my drenched hair and suddenly my entire body begins to shake.

"I'm gonna go get the first aid kit. You okay, Irish," he asks, his voice filled with worry.

"I'm good," she responds removing her hand and leaning up on her knees. I bend over as she pulls up my drenched tank top so that she can look at my back. I hiss when her fingers touch part of my skin that feels scraped. "Not too bad but I'm sure that stings." She stands and we both look at the doorway to see Mimi standing there. She walks in quickly, sitting down in the seat where Pop was and immediately puts her arms around me, not caring that I'm dripping wet.

Sobs rack my already shaking body, but suddenly I feel so violated, so scared. She holds me tight whispering words in my ear. I barely get my crying down to a sniffle when I feel myself being pulled into strong arms. His smell invades me as I rub my face into his chest. "What the fuck happened?" He growls angrily.

"We're not sure. She came into the bar, drenched and scared to death. I saw that her neck was beet red and she was shaking so badly I thought she might collapse but Pop got to her and brought her in here," Irish speaks quickly and I hear him growl again, feeling the vibration against my face.

"I'm gonna kill that motherfucker," he sneers. I pull back, my tear filled eyes clouding him.

"No," I whisper, my voice hoarse. "That's what he wants. Anger. Don't you see he just wanted to get a rise out of you? Yes, he wants me but I think he wants to get you all out of the way first. Just…." my voice cracks. "Just hold me. Please, hold me." He pulls me back into his chest, his face rubbing against my head, soothingly.

"It's okay, baby." He moves back a bit, his eyes looking at my neck. "Where all are you hurt?" I know he's trying not to show his anger, but I know he's boiling mad. I arch my back when his hand starts to rub. "Ow." I lean back and look into his worried eyes.

"Here. I brought the first aid kit," Irish breathes out in a rush.

"I should take you to the hospital," he says matter of fact. He begins to stand but I grab his t-shirt, fisting the cloth.

I shake my head. "No. Please don't make me go." A tear falls from my eye.

Irish looks at him. "I can take care of it. How many times have I tended to your wounds?" She gives him a smirk. My eyes move back to him and watch him nod at her, then he holds my hand as she begins to clean up the scrapes on my back. I hiss a few times and he wipes away a couple of tears from my face. "It's not too bad," she says as she continues. "You're gonna have some bruising but the scrapes are minor." She leans back and smiles then starts to put away things into the small box. "You might want to put some ice on your throat and uh, wear a scarf for a few days." I roll my eyes. *Wear a scarf in this heat? That won't be obvious.* I almost let out a laugh but I'm too upset.

Brock bends down behind me looking at my back. I can't tell by his facial expression when he sits up and moves around to where I can see him, how bad it is. "Let me take you home, baby." He stands, helping me up.

"I actually came here to get something to eat. Now I'm not so sure I'm hungry."

His brows lower. "Irish. Go get two specials from Mimi." I look at him and smile. "To go."

Brock

When she told me what happened, I was ready to take off and find that motherfucker. It's one thing to hurt me, another to hurt Kane, but to hurt Taren made me want to kill him. Then I almost wanted to shake some sense into her, except I knew it wasn't the time to talk to her. She was so shaken up. I know I've asked her not to go anywhere alone, so did Kane, though she should have just been able to walk to the bar. Such a simple thing yet something she can't do right now. While waiting for Irish to get our food, I sent off a text to Dean asking him to meet us at our place.

It takes a little bit to get our food, and then I help her into my truck. She's quiet on the short drive home. When I pull my truck in front of the building, she sees Dean standing on the front porch immediately. There's really no reaction except for the widening of her eyes. I put it in park and turn to her, taking her hand. "He needs to know, Taren. He'll probably want a statement." She turns to me and nods. Again, no reaction really. Maybe she's in shock or maybe she's just done with it. I'm a little worried of which it is. We both get out of the truck, and I take her hand in mine, my other hand carrying the sack with our food. I nod at Dean and open the front door of the building, Taren following behind me to our door. After getting inside she walks straight for the bedroom, and I take our food into the kitchen.

"Sorry about what happened, Brock. Think she's willing to talk? Maybe give a statement?" Dean asks. I can see the concern on his face.

I turn to set the bags on the counter and turn back around, placing my hands on it behind me. "I think so. I mean, she's pretty shaken up though." Both our heads turn when she walks into the kitchen. She's changed into one of my t-shirts. It's so long on her. It hits her mid-thigh over her yoga pants. She smiles and reaches behind me, so I move over a bit. I watch her take out plates and then begins taking the food from the sack in silence. I shift my eyes to Dean, who's watching her intently. She fills our plates and turns around, looking at him.

"Would you like a plate of food? There's more than enough." She smiles, waiting for him to answer.

His eyes shift to mine then back at her. "That's very kind, Taren. Actually, a cup of coffee would hit the spot, if you don't mind." He smiles at her, and she nods then walks over to get the coffee pot set up.

I grab the plates and take them to the table. "Why don't we sit?" He nods and pulls the nearest chair out and sits down. It's quiet except for the sounds of the coffee perking and her getting silverware from the drawer. She bring forks and knives over and sets them by the plates then fills coffee cups and brings them over and sits down between us.

"I hate interrupting your dinner," Dean begins.

She looks at me and then back at him. "It's okay. I'm not that hungry anyway.

He sits up and clears his throat, taking out a small notebook from his jacket pocket. "I hope you don't mind, Taren. Can you tell me what happened?"

She sets her fork down on her plate. "I decided to walk to the bar. It was so beautiful out, at the time. I was so stupid. Stupid and should have known better than to be out by myself. I don't know what I was thinking. I was just hungry for some of Mimi's cooking. Then the rain started and came down so hard that I ducked into the trees for shelter. I wasn't there long before he grabbed me by the throat. He…." She looks at me and then sits up straight, looking back at him. "He touched my breast and then…. You know, down there, over my shorts. My back was scratched from the bark of the tree trunk when he released me, hearing a car nearby, and I dropped to the ground." Her eyes shift to mine then back to his quickly. She clears her throat again. "It was Jeffrey Stratton."

He's looking down, writing on his pad. I look at Taren, watching him. I'm so fucking proud of her but hearing what happened in full makes me want to leave and go find him. Show him what it's like to have someone surprise him then beat him to an inch of his life. Dean clears his throat again and looks at us both. "Thank you. That's a really great description. Uh. I have to ask you." He looks at her again, leaning his arm on the table. "Taren, do you want to press charges?"

She doesn't hesitate. "Yes."

He smiles. "Good. I'll have this typed up and you can come by in the morning to sign it. I'll get some men out now looking for him. I'll call around the other counties and get more men to help, if I have to." He stands and takes a quick sip of the coffee that had sat there forgotten. I stand and follow him the short distance to the door. Once I open it, I reach out my hand and he shakes it. "I'll text you in the morning when it's ready." He looks over at Taren and smiles. "Thanks, Taren. You all try to have a good rest of the evening."

I shut the door behind him and twist the lock then take my seat again and pick up my fork. I take a bite and then push the food around. When I look over at her, she's just sitting there watching me. I set my fork down and give her a smile, holding out my hand. "Come here," I whisper. She doesn't delay in taking my hand, standing and then sitting down on my lap as I push my chair back. My arms wrap around her as she lays her head down on my shoulder. "I couldn't be more proud of you," I tell her as I run my fingers through her long hair.

Her beautiful eyes look up at me from beneath her long lashes. "I shouldn't have walked there. It was just such a nice day. I feel so stupid. I'm just done. I'm tired of looking over our shoulders. It's like we went from the disapproval of my family to this maniac who won't take no for an answer, who won't leave us alone." She looks down and rubs her finger across my chest. "I just want to be a normal couple and be able to do normal couple things without worrying about people trying to keep us apart." My hold tightens around her, my fingers releasing her soft hair. She sighs. "I know we'll always have some obstacles. I mean that's how life is. I'm not stupid about that. We've fought so long and so hard to be together and now he's trying to break us up or worse get people out of the way that I love." Her eyes move back up to mine. "I'm just tired."

I run my hand over her head, down her long hair, soothingly, knowing she loves when I do it. I keep doing it until her eyes blink a little. "I know, baby. Life has had a way to try to come between us. We're stronger. We're meant to be together and I won't let anything tear us apart. Together, we can get through anything. I think we've proven that time and time again." I reach up and flick her cute nose with my finger and smile. However, I don't think my smile reached my heart. I'm just as tired of it as she is, but right now I'm more concerned with her safety. "Are you hungry?" She shakes her head slowly. "Then how about you go get in bed and I'll clean up the mess." She leans up and kisses me then slides off my lap. "I'll be there in just a bit. Promise." She smiles sadly, and I watch her walk away.

I pick up the plates, rinse them off and put all the dirty dishes into the dishwasher. I lean back against the counter and take out my phone, find the name and push call. It only rings once.

"Talk to me."

Kane's voice is alert, like he was waiting on my call. "She gave a statement, signing it in the morning. Dean has men out looking for him. I wanna kill the motherfucker," I growl.

"We need a plan. Meet me tomorrow night at Pops. I'll get the guys together. Fill Irish in and ask her to keep Taren busy. Irish won't answer my calls or texts for some reason. Is Taren okay?" His voice is steady, sure.

"Yeah. Just worried and tired of all this shit, just like me."

"I'm sure. Okay. See you tomorrow at work." He hangs up and I quickly find Irish's number.

"Is she okay? Do you need me to come over?" Her voice is fairly quiet and hard to hear over the racket at Pops.

"She's okay, for now. We have a meeting at Pops tomorrow night. Can you come over and stay with Taren?" I'm waiting for the yelling I know that I s about to ensue.

"WHAT? I should be at the meeting. Seriously, Brock? What the fuck?" Her voice is loud in my ear, so much I have to pull the phone away until she's done.

"Are you done yelling at me?" Silence, except the background noise. "Good. I need someone I can trust and do you really think if something happened her Mom or Mimi would be able to defend themselves or her?" I can hear her sigh. She knows I'm right. "So just plan on coming over, okay?" I hear her sigh again. She's always been one that would be in the middle of any fight and can hold her own fairly well. We've never really had to look out for her. In fact, she's walloped us a few times.

"Okay. I guess you're right. This time." I hear a bunch of voices. "Hold on to your boxers. I'll be right there!" My smile overtakes me. Good ole Irish.

"Good. Now, what in the hell is with you and Kane? He says you won't talk to him and you've ignored his texts. You all have a lovers quarrel?" I snicker to myself. Sometimes I crack myself up.

"None of your fucking business."

And then the noise stops and I pull my phone away from my ear and see she's hung up on me. What the hell? I don't know what's going on between them, but I'm sure I'll find out. They've always fought like siblings, but this is taking it to a whole other level. I set my phone down on the counter and turn off the lights on my way to the bedroom, pulling off my shirt as I get to the door. When I open it, I see she's already in bed, lights off, and fast asleep. Good. She has to be exhausted emotionally and physically. I remove my shoes and jeans quickly then climb into bed. She moves over in her sleep, cuddling up to me. Her arm moves over my waist as her head lays against my chest. I put my arm around her. She sighs but doesn't open her eyes, her breathing still light and even. God, what I wouldn't do to keep her safe, to take all the madness out of her life. I close my eyes and dream about her and finding that asshole and beating the shit outta him.

I'm up earlier than normal the next morning. I guess I'm antsy to get her to the station before I have to leave for work. I texted Kane and reminded him I'd be a little late. He was cool with it, of course. Everything anymore seems to make me anxious. I guess I'm feeling like she is. I just want this to be over. Dean's team of guys are good, but it feels like that asshole may be a little slicker. I guess money can buy a lot of things, maybe even getting away with murder? It's always been about money with him, with so many people. My life has been so much better. Granted it's been hard at times but the love I've had, the closeness, and the support makes it a ton better. Maybe that's the problem. No love in his life. Now, I kinda feel sorry for him. Just a little.

We don't wait for breakfast. She tells me she's not hungry anyway. I take her to the station and as Dean promised, the statement was ready for her to sign. She reads it quickly, and I watch her sign it. He tells me he's had men out all night looking but nothing yet. I figured it wouldn't be that easy. I take her home and kiss her goodbye, not wanting to go to work, not wanting to leave her alone. As I'm closing the front door, I wait until I hear the lock click then I about knock Irish over as I walk out the front door of the building. I grab her arms to steady us both, almost pushing her off the steps.

"Oh, sorry." I move my hands from her arms when she looks at me with a sneer. "What the hell, Irish. What's got your panties in a bunch anymore?"

"Nothing, okay?" She tries to move past me but I grab her arms again. She shakes herself free. *Strong woman.*

"Seriously. I get that this whole thing is a mess but you've been acting strange for a while now. What's going on?" She looks around like everything around us is more interesting. "And what's up with you and Kane? Did he do something?" Her eyes quickly snap to mine. "What did he do, Irish? I'll kick his ass."

"No! Um…. He didn't do anything. I just…." She looks down at an invisible spot on the ground. *Women! She's acting so weird. Wait! What the hell?*

I put my hand under her chin and lift her head then stare into her eyes. Her eyes lower. She can't look at me. "Irish. Do you have a thing for Kane?" It all seems to fall into place. She never dates, never seems even mildly attracted to anyone but hangs on his every word, watching every movement. No way! We've been friends forever. Could she? Nah! Maybe? No Way! She's always been like one of the guys. Maybe that's where we've all been blind. She isn't a guy. Not by any means. She's beautiful, strong, willful, and has a killer body. I guess I've just never thought of in that way. "Oh, my God. You fucking like him. I mean, not just like him but, like him." I smile, thinking I've just unlocked the secret to the world. Like I just found the meaning of life. "Shit. Does he know?" She tugs out of my grip roughly and pushes me, starting to open the door to the building. I turn and laugh. "Aw, come on, Irish. I won't say nothin'." She turns her head and growls then walks inside. Well, that went well. Now, do I say anything to Kane, let him know what's been crawlin' up her ass, or do I keep my promise and not say anything? This is gonna be a tough one.

Chapter Thirteen

Taren

"Your boyfriend is so.... infuriating!" is my greeting when Irish comes storming in the front door once I've unlocked it. She stomps her feet straight over to the coffee pot and pours herself a cup. She leans back against the counter and closes her eyes as she takes a drink.

"No coffee yet this morning?" I smile when her eyes open, stabbing mine with her stare. I slowly sit down at the table as she takes another sip. "Okay, bestie. What's up so early in the morning? Or what's not up might be the better question." I tilt my head and raise an eyebrow. She gives me another mean look and stomps over to the table, practically throwing herself onto the chair. "Aww. It can't be that bad." Her eyes snap to mine and a frown graces her beautiful face. "Can it?"

She slams her back against the chair and sighs, loudly. "I'm just over it." She looks at me, her face so sad. "Face it. Kane's never gonna want me in *that* way. We're like siblings and he's out with a different woman every night, like musical women. Even if he did like me, like me, I wouldn't want to go out with him anyway, just because of that. I mean, sheesh." She starts twirling a bunch of strands of hair, hanging from her ponytail. "Right?" *She's asking me?*

"Well, I dunno if I'm the right...."

"I mean. He's like the whore of men. The king of man whores. Who needs that, right? Why have something so used when there are plenty of men in the sea. The ocean. Right?"

"Uh, yes. Well...."

She leans up and pats my arm then takes a big drink of coffee. "Thanks. I knew you'd help, bestie." She gives me a huge smile.

My mouth turns into a little smile, and I nod, slightly. "Sure. Don't mention it."

There was no more talk of whores or men or salt water places. We sat around all day. Me, feeling like the sexiest babysitter was flipping through the TV channels and after many attempts and to my relief she finally settles on a good romantic comedy. Her, finally realizing that she and Kane wouldn't work. I started feeling sad for her. All these years she'd been holding out for him when she should have been dating, doing what normal teenage girls did by playing the field, having fun going out with different guys and seeing if there's a chance with someone else out there. She looks at me as I bite my fingernail. "What's wrong, babe?"

I look up and sigh. "I really need to go to the grocery store but I'm leery to go anywhere now. He's out there somewhere, waiting."

She gives me her devious smile. "I got your back. Come on, girl." She stands, and I run and collect my purse and then follow her out the door. Yeah, I feel pretty safe with her. She's a pretty tough chick, and I'm fortunate she's my best friend.

We end up going to the mall instead and by the end of the day, I start getting nervous. "I swear someone's following us," I whisper to her as we round a corner in the mall. She shifts her eyes, and I roll mine. Kind of like telling someone not to look, but they do anyway. "What the hell? Don't look!"

"How am I supposed to catch them if I don't look," she whispers back.

I lace my arm through hers and get closer. "Don't be stupid, Irish. You'll get yourself killed."

From the corner of my eye, I see a guy quickly move behind a pillar and stiffen. "Where? What did you see?"

I lean in again. "To the right, behind that pillar."

She starts picking up her pace, my sacks hitting against my thigh as I try to keep up. My heart is racing. My feet are cramping as we head outside the mall door and around the corner of the building. She pushes me back against the stone, her arm across my waist. I wince from the impact, the scrapes on my back hitting the rough surface. I hold my breath because my panting is so loud. I watch her peek around the corner, so many footsteps from others walking in and out of the mall, but then I hear some that are running this way. Her head lays back against the building, and I feel like I'm gonna puke. Suddenly, she jumps out, and my heart lodges in my throat. She grabs this guy and throws him down on the ground, his body hitting rocks, grass, and the shrubs lining the walk. She's on top of him, sitting on his waist, her hands belting him right, then left. She continues beating the shit outta him until he grabs her upper arms and swiftly turns her over, pinning them down above her head, straddling her lap. I run over and jump on his huge back, my sacks flying everywhere. Wrapping my arms around his neck, I start screaming.

"Get off her! Dammit! Get the hell off her!" My thighs are pressed into his side, squeezing as he tries to push me off.

"Will ya'll just give me a minute…. To explain," he croaks as I literally choke him. Before I can scream again, I'm on the ground next to Irish, his hand grasping both of my wrists and the other hand still pinning hers down above her. Everyone is breathing heavy, and I notice we've drawn quite a crowd. I also notice no one is running over here to help us either. He looks back and forth at us, panting a little himself, but not much, not seeming winded. "Give me a second to explain." Irish squirms beneath him and he looks her in the eyes and growls. *I swear he growled.* "Give me a damn minute." She finally stops, nodding slightly. "Good. Now. I was hired to protect you." My face scrunches, and Irish's eyes widen. "Can I let you two up now and talk rationally?" Irish and I look at each other, and I just shrug. She turns her head back at him and nods. He slowly releases our wrists, and I struggle to stand, my body aching from all the running and being thrown down on the ground. I step back and turn, noticing he's still sitting on her, and they're just staring at each other.

"You can get up now," Irish sneers.

His mouth turns into a slight grin. "Not unless you promise you're not gonna attack me again." Her eyes move away then back at him and nods. He rises, his feet still on either side of her legs, and holds his hand down to her. She pushes her hands against the ground and slides back then stands, wiping the grass of the back of her jeans. He steps back and shakes his head, a grin on his face. "Stubborn," he mumbles. I actually have to cover my mouth with my hand to try to not laugh out loud. He's right, of course.

She crosses her arms over her waist, lifting her breasts, and scowls. "So. Talk."

Now that I get a chance to really look at him, without all the throwing around of bodies and being pinned to the ground, he's really quite a good looking guy. Red hair, hazel green eyes, and matching red scruff on his face but it's how huge his arms and shoulders are underneath his t-shirt that really catches my eye. He could be a bouncer at a bar. Seems like Brock mentioned a new guy at his work that is red haired. You don't see that many around or at least I haven't noticed them. Huh. I look over at Irish and can tell she's really casing him out too. Hmmm.

"Okay, well…." His big arms cross over his chest, and I swear her eyes widen. "I just moved here and took a part time job at the police station. I've worked helping out in law enforcement prior so they asked me to keep an eye on you, ladies." His eyes scan over to me and then back at her.

"So, they just hire anyone? Seems weird to me. You'd think they'd want to trust the individual that they'd hire to…." She does air quotes with her fingers. "Keep an eye on people."

His head lowers, and I watch him cover his mouth with the side of his hand, but I can see his small grin. He clears his throat and straightens up, looking right at her. "I have an outstanding record with the police station I worked for before. The sergeant gave your police station, a one Dean Weston, my file. So, you see…." He crosses his beefy arms again. "I come highly recommended." Her lip turns up, and I think she's holding back a snarl. "Anything else?"

She shifts, uncomfortably, then straightens her demeanor. "Well. Someone should have told us." She walks around him and starts picking up sacks. I jump and start helping her. We get all our belongings, and then I follow her to her truck. Footsteps sound behind us and she stops, abruptly, causing me to plow right into her. She turns her head and looks over her shoulder, and I take a step back. "Do you mind not following so closely?" she sneers at him. I turn my head and smile, slightly, when he bows, his hand moving out in a gentlemanly fashion. I have to clamp my mouth closed so my laugh doesn't explode. I turn back just as she huffs and starts stomping off and turn my head again and shrug my shoulders at him. He just gives me a wink, and I have to stifle my giggle.

It's loud on the way home. Not the radio that's playing but the sound of her voice shrilling about what happened. "The nerve of Dean not telling us about this and the bigger nerve of this mammoth guy pinning me down." She huffs loudly, and I can see the white of her knuckles as she grips the steering wheel hard. I startle when she starts again. "I mean, who does he think he is? Acting like he's all that and what an asshole, huh?" She looks over at me, and I stay quiet but nod slowly. "And what's with the bodybuilder body and trying to be all suave and everything? Does he think he's a model or something, some fitness pro?" I shrug when she looks at me again. "Did you see the size of his shoulders and arms?" I nod eagerly now, this much I agree with.

It went on like that until she parks at my apartment, but the loudness of the truck door slamming tells me she's still fired up. I grab the sacks from the back and run to catch up to her, grabbing the door and watch as she flies into the building. I turn just before I walk in and see a huge truck parked down the dirt road, hidden in the trees, the sun hitting the chrome on the front bumper. Hmm, doesn't seem that concealed to me if I can see it. I let the door shut behind me and see my front door is wide open. When I walk in and close the door, I immediately set all the sacks down on the small kitchen table and look around, not seeing Irish anywhere.

Slam

Slam

Ah, she's in the bathroom. I let a giggle slip out as I start taking items out of the sacks, placing them on the table. I hold up a new lacy camisole and visions of Brock flitter in my mind.

"Dammit! Where's your fucking aspirin?" She walks into the kitchen, her fingers pressing against her temples. "Killer headache." I lay down the camisole on the table and walk over to the small cabinet, open it and grab the bottle of aspirin then take a glass from the next cabinet and fill it with water. I turn and see her sitting down at the table and place them in front of her. Her eyes look into mine, and she tries to smile. I say "try" because it really is a halfhearted attempt. "Thanks."

I sit down in the chair beside her and place my hand on the camisole, feeling the softness under my fingertips. "What's the big deal, Irish? I mean. If Dean thinks he's a good man to help keep us safe, why are you so upset?" I watch her head jerk back after she pops the pills in her mouth and takes a drink, then swallows. She looks back at me and scrunches her face.

"He just rubs me the wrong way. Thinking he's all that and what the hell with the scene at the mall? I mean…. He could have handled that so much differently. Making a spectacle out of himself was not a good impression. Not like no one noticed us being pinned down on the ground right out in the open." My brows lift, and my mouth turns into a huge smile.

"Oh, my God!" I shout.

She sits up straight. "What?"

My face softens. "You like him."

Her arms cross over her middle as her brows lower. "I do not! What the hell, Taren." My smile broadens. She gets up and grabs her glass, takes it over and places it in the sink then opens the fridge and grabs a beer. She turns around and leans back against the counter, twists off the lid and take a big swig. "I'm swearing off all men. Especially one big, burly redhead." My hand covers my mouth but not before my laugh escapes. Her eyes snap to me, and she scowls. Hmm. Maybe this is just what she needs to move on from Kane and who knows. Maybe there's a redhead, big burly man in her future.

Brock

Another long day of lifting, hammering, and screwing, and not the kind of screwing I'm longing for. I'm sweaty, dirty, and tired by the time I get on my motorcycle to go home. After mid-morning, this new guy, Caylan, tells Kane he has to leave and I watch Kane just nod. What the hell was that? Sheesh, if I ask to take off early, he throws a fit. Something's up. I can feel it. Now if I can just find out what it is.

The breeze invades me, cooling me off a bit as I drive home. *Home.* It really is a home now. It smells like her when I walk in. All perfume and Taren. But the darkness of the apartment changes my feelings of excitement to worry in a heartbeat. We'd worked a little later than usual, with having one man gone. I try to keep that anger at bay as I set my tool belt down inside the door. I look around and focus on all the candles around the living room, our old worn blanket laying out on the floor. Suddenly, the worry changes rapidly into longing and the ache in my filthy jeans escalates.

I hear a noise and look at the doorway, leading into the hall, and see Taren standing there. Her arm lifted up high as her hand molds around the frame, her hip jetted out and her other hand grasping it. She wearing a t-shirt, cut off right underneath her ample breasts. My hands ache to hold them, feel their weight in my hands and squeeze them as my mouth captures one of her perk nipples that are pressing against the fabric. It doesn't go unnoticed that she's not wearing a bra. My cock presses instantly against my jeans, wanting to be released as my face lights up, my mouth turning into a smile. I look into her eyes, darkened with desire, and everything around me fades, the only thing that's in focus is my girl.

"It's about time you got home," she whispers, her chest lifting and falling with her heavy breathing.

I walk quickly straight to her and start to put my arms around her but step back, her brows lower immediately, her face turns into sadness. "I'm filthy, Taren."

Her face softens and that desire fills her eyes again. "I wanna be filthy, Brock." She breathes slowly. *Fuck me.* She takes my hand, hers so small compared to mine. As her fingers thread through mine, I follow her into our bedroom.

She turns abruptly, releasing my hand, and pulls up on the hem of my dirty shirt. "So dirty," she whispers as her eyes burn into mine.

My heart accelerates as I allow her to bring my shirt up to my neck then I reach back and pull it over my head. Her eyes instantly move to my chest. My hardened cock straining against my jeans. She's killing me here but I let her continue her lead, curious. Her eyes move back to mine, the blue darkened even more. She reaches out and I feel my belt being undone, then the button on my jeans opened and my breath hitches. Our eyes keep glued to each other's as she pulls down the zipper, and I feel my length spring out. Her eyes move down and widen. Yes, I'm commando. Who needs boxers making you sweat even worse on a hot day?

Her small hand grasps my cock, and I hiss from the feel of her touch. I tear my eyes from hers and look down, seeing how her small hand doesn't fully wrap around my hardened length. I can feel it pulsating as she tightens her grip then strokes it hard all the way down then back up again. "Taren," I growl, my voice coming out in a broken whisper. The smile on her face is sexy as hell, her hand leaving my cock cold as she pushes my jeans down the rest of the way. She only gets them halfway down my thighs when I place my hands over hers and help her remove them. I step out, pushing them aside with my foot as she leans up on her tiptoes and her luscious mouth presses hard against mine. My arms immediately move around her, my hand moving up underneath her shirt, feeling the soft skin of her back. My fingers reach up into her long hair, and my tongue dives into her sweet mouth. Her moan fills me, and my cock pushes against her.

I can't take it anymore and pull her into me as I walk backwards into the bathroom, bringing her with me. Our mouths don't disconnect as I make quick work of removing her clothes. We break away long enough for me to get her shirt off her head then connect again quickly, frantically. I walk us over to the shower. My hand reaches for the knobs and turns them on as our kissing becomes more heated than the water spraying against my arm. I fumble, turning the knobs every which way, my eyes opening long enough to see what I'm doing. As the water adjusts to where it won't scorch us, I bend and lift her into my arms. I step into the shower, losing my balance as my mouth presses harder against hers. Her back hits the tile and sounds of her gasp echoes in the small area from the impact. I tear my mouth from hers looking at her in concern, but I know she's okay when she captures mine again in a hurried frenzy.

"God, Taren," I moan as I push inside her. Her legs are wrapped around my waist clenching me as her hips buck, making me go even deeper. "I love you," I whisper into her ear then capture her mouth again. Our rhythm begins, and I'm amazed how she keeps up as hard and fast as I'm thrusting into her. It's like a dam was broken, and I can't seem to get close enough, to get deep enough inside her, feel her. It doesn't take long when I feel her muscles squeeze my growing cock. She screams out my name, and I follow closely behind her. I stand here, wet from the water spraying on us but yet feeling sweaty from our activity. We both are breathing heavily, our chests hitting each other's in our sated states. She slides down my body, and we make quick work of washing each other.

Once clean, I lift her again, and she giggles as I walk out of the room, grabbing a couple of towels from the linen closet on our way past, then laying her beautiful body down on a towel on our bed, and hover over her. My mouth seizes one of her perk nipples, and I begin lavishing, sucking, and nipping as she wiggles beneath me. My cock already engorged again spurs me on. My hand moves across her smooth skin, down her flat stomach and onto the place I ache to touch. I cup her and her hips buck, pressing it harder against my hand. My thumb begins to circle her clit, pressing every so often, and she releases a guttural moan. I kiss across her peak and valley until I reach the other nipple. "Brock." Another moan escapes, throaty yet soft. I push a finger inside her. Her walls slick and already soaking wet with need. I love how she's so insatiable, so ready for me. Always. The feeling it gives me how my touch alone makes her this way, the way she looks at me, full of longing and want, how she wants me as much as I want her. "Plea…. Please," she moans. Those blue eyes darkened and fill with desire for me.

God, she makes my heart stop, my breathing hitch when I look into them.

I push another finger inside, her heat and wetness making them glide in and out. Her hips buck hard, her body pushing against my hand. My cock is straining, throbbing to be where my fingers are. Not able to wait anymore, I hear her whimper as I pull my fingers out but quickly replace them with my aching cock. I moan loudly as I slide into her, bending down and kissing her hard. This time I make love to her slowly, passionately, full of all the love I feel for her. As our bodies become one, emotions overtake me. Memories of our past together flood my mind. Placing my hands on the sides of her face, I watch her come undone. The most beautiful sight I've ever seen. My head tilts back as my release overwhelms me, my eyes closing with the pleasure. When I look back down as my body shudders, the look on her face is reverent. She reaches up, her hand soft against my stubble, her thumb rubbing over my jaw. Such love in her eyes as her finger rubs underneath my eye, and I feel wetness fall from it. I'm taken aback as I feel the tear leave me, not realizing I'd been crying.

"Baby," she whispers as I lean down and nuzzle my face into the damp skin of her neck. Her arms move around me and tighten their hold. I've never been more comfortable, more loved than I am in this moment. I never want to leave her embrace, feeling her heartbeat against my chest. But her stomach growls and that's my cue.

*　*　*　*

"So what's with this new guy?" She brings the chopsticks in her fingers full of food to my mouth. I snatch it, of course, and smile as I chew.

I fill my chopsticks and bring them up to her full lips. She smiles and I watch them wrap around the sticks. *Lucky sticks.* "What new guy?" My brows lower as I sit back up. "Wait! How'd you know about the new guy?"

She chews and swallows then picks up her glass of wine and takes a drink. "He showed up at the mall today, started following Irish and me around. Didn't know who he was until Irish tackled him well then he kinda tackled both of us." She starts biting her fingernail as anger wells inside me. Why in the fuck would he be following them and who the hell does he think he is tackling my girl? Just the thought of him touching her makes me want to hunt him down and tell him how much he should never, ever, lay a hand on my love. My face must show her just how angry I'm becoming 'cos she starts looking worried. "Hey," she whispers as she places her hand on my face. "Nothing happened. Come to find out, Dean hired him to follow us, protect us."

My face now scrunches in confusion. "But Kane hired him as a construction worker. What the hell is going on?" She startles as I jump up, half jogging to get my cell phone from the bedroom, where it dropped on the floor along with my jeans earlier. I pick it up and find the number as she comes sliding in on the wood floor only in her socks and one of my t-shirts. I don't give him a chance to speak as I hear the call go through. "Over here. NOW! And bring that…. THAT, Caylan guy with you!" I hang up and look at her. "You might want to get some clothes on." Her eyes widen, like a deer in the headlights look, and she takes off scrambling to get her clothes on. I'd laugh, but I want to hold onto my anger. I'll need it when Kane and that asshole gets here.

I barely get my shirt over my head when banging sounds on the front door. I glare at Taren when she starts to walk, stopping her in her place. I walk heavily to the door, open it and stand aside as Kane and Caylan walk in. I slam the door, a little more forcefully than intended, and when I turn around, Kane's right up in my face, his finger poking me in my chest. "What the fuck, little brother. I don't appreciate being called up, yelled at, and then hung up on. What the hell's gotten into you?" His face is beet red, and his finger starts pushing harder.

My anger swells. I move my arm under his and push his away from me then get up into his face. "Why in the hell didn't you tell me this guy…." My arm stretches out, pointing my finger at

Caylan. "Was following my girl? Why am I the fucking last to know? And he scared the shit outta her at the mall!"

He starts to push up against me with his bulky chest until Taren slides between us and places a hand on both of our chests. Her hair sweeps out around her as her head turns back and forth at us. "Stop it! Both of you!" We both take a step back, our anger still consuming us. "Pick your battles, guys. He's not the bad guy," she says pointing at Caylan. "Yes, it would have been nice to know he would be around but shit, it's not the end of the world. I, for one, am glad to have someone who's trained to protect me. No offense." She looks at Kane then at me. Her face softens as well as her voice. "I love you guys and always feel safe when you're around but you can't always be around." Both Kane and I look at each other. "You guys are brothers. Stop acting like you hate each other." She looks back at Caylan. "And you should have been honest with us." Then she looks at me. "He was only doing what he thought would help protect me." The tension in the room dies a little.

All heads turn when Irish walks in the door. I have no idea how long she'd been standing there. "Yeah. You should have told us. I almost kicked his ass."

Caylan's head lowers, his hand covering his chuckles as Taren bursts out laughing. "Not the way I heard it," I say laughing myself. Kane just looks confused not knowing the whole story yet. I walk around Taren and put my arm around his shoulder. "C'mon, big brother. I'll tell ya all about it." I lead him into the kitchen as

Irish hands out beers from our fridge. I notice Caylan doesn't take one. Strange dude.

Chapter Fourteen

Taren

The evening changed from anger and tension to one of laughter and lots of talking in a heartbeat. Thank goodness. However, I can understand Brock's concern. I have to admit, I was a little shaken up at the mall until Caylan told us he was there to protect us. Guess his plan of being hidden didn't work too well with Irish there. As usual, she was badass. Even she would have to admit, which she won't, that Caylan is a little bit too large for her to take. I had to keep my snicker to myself when she left tonight, mumbling how she needed to increase her workout routine. I noticed Caylan overheard her though and had to snap his mouth shut. He's a quick learner, I'll give him that. I also noticed how much Irish kept sneaking looks at him, the entire evening. I would have called her out on it but there are too many around. Although, she caught my questioning eyes more than once. I wish she could find someone, or someone would find her. I still wonder about her being alone all these years, never hearing of even one date, and why she would wait for Kane knowing how he's always been.

Brock and I have a lazy evening the rest of the night, snuggling on the couch and watching a movie. It's like he couldn't quit holding me, kissing the side of my head, my face, and keeping my hand in his. I think after everything today he's even more concerned. I know I am especially after texting Jeffrey over a dozen times and hearing nothing back from him. I have a bad feeling.

The next morning I awaken to more snuggling with my love and hate when he finally tells me he needs to take a shower and leave for work. I decided that yesterday was just too much, so I'm staying inside today, not even chancing going out on our deck to sun bathe. I hate that I feel trapped in my own home. About mid-morning, Irish called and said she'd be over soon, telling me I needed company. Secretly, I think she wants to girl talk. At least I hope she does. I'm dying to know if my suspicions are right.

"So, I worked out hard last night and guess who's a new personal trainer at the gym?" she says while getting out the tub of left over spaghetti from the fridge. My brow raises in question. She plops a big spoonful on a plate and zaps it in the microwave then turns around, crossing her arms over her chest, which only pushed her girls up. Hard not to notice when she's wearing one of those workout half tops, her flat stomach and belly piercing being displayed. Seriously, I don't know how she eats like she does and still has that great figure. "Caylan." *Go figure.*

"Oh, really? Hmmm," I say watching her grab the plate, a fork, and start shoveling the food in her mouth. Shoveling. Not daintily. Not one fork full at a time. Shoveling. "Hungry?"

Her eyes move up to mine. "No. Not really." She continues to shovel and I sit back in my chair, picking up my cup and taking a heavenly drink of my coffee. "Anyway," she says, coming up for air. "So, I walk into the gym last night, get changed and then after working out for about forty-five minutes, sweat covering me, my hair pulled back and damp with that same sweat, and I'm dying by that point. I mean, I looked like shit. Well, I don't hear him from having my iPod buds in my ears, and I look up and see him standing in front of the treadmill, looking all…. His big arms crossing over that massive…. Yeah, well." *Huh?*

"What the hell, Irish. Can you slow down and speak English, please?" I have to stifle my laugh. I've never seen her so flustered before. It's actually kinda cute, like a normal woman would do. But Irish is anything but "normal". She's the toughest woman I know, hard core, brutally honest, but a hard worker. She's feminine yet strong and not just muscles but strong willed too. That's why I love her.

"Well, he just gets on my last nerve. That's all." She shrugs and dishes out more spaghetti from the tub onto her now empty plate and puts it in the microwave, slamming the door. *Okay, that's not what I got outta that garblish chatter, at all. Garblish. That's a word, right?*

"Irish. I don't think he gets on your nerves. I think he gets on your…."

Her head whips around, kinda like that girl in that movie *The Exorcist*, or maybe it was like that girl in *Carrie*? Anyway, really fast and kinda spooky. "What? Wait! You think I'm interested in him?" A loud laugh bursts from her mouth. "That I like him?" Another one and I purse my lips. I'm busting inside, wanting to walk over and shake her, tell her to loosen up and take a chance.

I take some deep breaths, trying to calm my inner self and place my hands in my lap, sitting up straight and posed. "Irish. There's nothing wrong with "liking" a guy. I mean…. How will you ever know if there's a connection or if he likes you too if you don't take a chance? Who knows? Maybe he'll end up being "Mr. Right" and you blow it by blowing him off. Well…. Uh…. You know what I mean." Suddenly, my face heats and thoughts of how big his, you know, is compared to his arms. Oh, my! I have everything I want in a man. Why would I be thinking like that about another one? Because I'm a girl. We all think like that, right?

She laughs. Not a burst of laughter. Not a snicker or giggle. But a full out, put your arms around your waist, bend over, your hair falling down over your head, kind of laugh. Okay, it wasn't that funny. When she finally calms herself and stands back up, pushing her hair behind her, she gets the plate out of the microwave and starts shoveling food in her pie hole again. "Are you nesting or something?" Her brow raises. "Never mind. Point is, if you don't allow yourself to actually form a relationship, get to know someone, you'll forever be single." Now her other brow raises. "Is that what you want? Seriously?"

She sighs, heavily, and sets the plate of uneaten food, which isn't much, in the sink. She grabs a cup and fills it with coffee then walks over and sits down across from me. "I dunno, Taren. I'm just really guy shy. I wasted so many years thinking that I wanted Kane, all the while knowing of his man whore ways and that he may never change, and now I'm not sure I want to try again." She takes a drink and so I do too then she sets down her cup and sighs again. Her eyes look up and meet mine. She really is beautiful. "He's okay looking and all." *Really? I saw her looking at him and know she feels way more than that.* "I guess I'm afraid of being hurt. I don't want to put all the effort into someone, again, and then find out they don't feel that way about me or that they're really the scum of the earth. Besides. You can't just change your feelings, the ones you've had most of your life, to someone else. Doesn't work that way. At least not for me."

"Dramatic much?" I smile and see the corner of her mouth lift. I can tell she's trying not to smile. I can understand what she's saying. Of course, if something happened to Brock and me, I'd die a lonely life. There's no one that could ever come close to him, there's no way I'd have even half the feelings that I have for him with someone else. No way.

She startles me when she sits up straight and squares her shoulders back. "Besides. I'm trying to keep on my game with trying to protect you right now. Can't let my guard down." *Wow, so that's gonna be her excuse? She's gonna use me to get outta trying again.* "And. I applied for this tech job at *Millerbeck Technology*. I have an interview next week." *Wait! What?*

"Oh, my God! Irish, that's amazing! Wait! When did you decide to leave Pops Bar and go into technology? You've worked at the bar since you were old enough to work there." Suddenly, I feel things shifting, changing, and I'm not sure I like it. What happened to the old times, the fun times? Okay, some of that already changed with this whole *running for my life-Jeffrey thing*, but still.

Now her smile is huge and genuine. "I know, right? I just decided that I'm tired of just working all the time at the bar, constantly being hit on by all the guys. You know me. That's not my thing." *She's right. It never has been. Can't blame all the guys for trying though. She's a knockout. She can also knock out a guy who messes with her.* "Anyway. It sounds like a great job. I can put my degree to use, finally. I'll still work at the bar on weekends. I can't ever leave that place completely. It's part of me, of who I am."

I reach across and cover her hand with mine. "That's great, Irish. I'm proud of you. How about I text Brock and we can all go to the bar tonight for a few drinks. Kind of an early celebration?" She nods, excitedly.

The rest of the day we watched soap operas and laughed at them. When we were younger, we used to do this and loved seeing the hunky guys and laughing at the poor stories and lines that they made those actors say. It was a great time, and I was glad to take things down a notch after all the pent up frustration earlier. Then by late afternoon, Brock came home – the changing of the guard I like to call it now – and Irish left to go home and get cleaned up for tonight. Brock and I cleaned up too. Slowly. In the shower. Together.

With no more things happening with Jeffrey, and no more hearing of anything new about finding him, we left for the bar to hang out with our friends. It was crowed for a Thursday night but with the weekend approaching, it was less crowded then it will be. We sit in our normal booth. Beers spread out amongst us, pitchers half empty in the middle, and it was one of the best times I've had in a long time. Until….

"Oh, my freaking, God! Look who just walked in and is headed our way," she whispers loudly in my ear. We're all a little tipsy now and I guess have lost our sense of hearing. I start to turn my head to see when she grabs my chin and pulls me back to her. "Don't look!" I scrunch up my face and pout. *How am I supposed to know who it is if I can't look?*

"Hey! Caylan!" Kane shouts across the table from us. *Oh!*

My eyes shift to my left, and they fall on a mammoth body standing there. They scan up and find a large man with a tight t-shirt, showing the flatness of his stomach, his sculpted abs, and broad chest until they reach his face. His hazel green eyes are staring right at…. I shift my eyes to my right, following his gaze to Irish, who's looking over at Kane. Well. This is awkward.

"Come have a sit and a beer," Kane says, sliding over in the booth, which makes everyone move over. Being brothers, Kane and Brock leave a bigger gap so Irish and I are squished together at the end. Caylan smiles and I swear he has the whitest teeth I've ever seen. He's now sitting directly across from Irish and me, who is squirming up against me in nervousness.

Caylan covers the glass in front of him as Kane tries to pour him a beer. "Thanks but no. Gotta keep my wits about me." Kane shrugs and fills his own glass then tops off everyone else's too.

"Can't even hang with people and have a beer," Irish leans into me and whispers, not that she has to lean much.

"Actually, I can." His voice rings over the chatter and clatter. We both snap our eyes to him. He's smiling with a raised brow. "I just choose to stay alert. Someone needs to." I grab her hand, which is fisted, when she sits up, ready to pounce. "But you all need a night off. I don't blame you." He suddenly becomes serious, and I feel her hand unclench underneath mine. No one else notices him staring into her eyes or how she stares back. Everyone else is talking, drinking, and laughing. But I notice.

I look up as Mimi walks over, carrying a large tray of food, and I can't help but smile. I haven't seen her or Mom in a couple of days and of course her food is to die for. So to speak.

"Do you eat?" My head swings back around and I look at Irish. Oh, she's so toying with him. One of them is gonna get hurt. I'm just not sure which one.

He laughs and sits up, grabbing one of the small plates Mimi sets on the table, and raises an eyebrow at Irish. "Oh, I eat. I just watch my calories." He winks at her and she sits back in a huff, making me bounce forward from the force. These two may be the death of me before anyone else gets to me.

Brock

We had a great time tonight being with our friends. Plenty of laughs, great food, and beer. I think something weird is going on with Caylan and Irish. They jabbed at each other all night. Then again, she's been acting weird for a long time. At least she and Kane are talking again. Never did know what was going on there for sure. Kane didn't either. Weird.

I take my girl home, getting excited for the upcoming weekend. We plan to go to our special place and hang out Friday night and come back Sunday morning. Kane thinks it's a bad idea, saying he's the only one that knows about the shack, besides us and then reminds me about the so called person that was out in the woods by the pond. I know, he's right. I know we'll have to be careful, so I'm am a little nervous. She is too, but we agreed on one thing. We can't stop living because of asshole, we just need to stick close together and be aware. That night we laid in bed on our sides, playing with each other's fingers while we made our plans. Once she's fallen asleep, cuddled up as close as she can to me, I think about what a lucky guy I am. My dream has finally come true. The love of my life, that I've had since I was young, is living with me, sharing my home, my bed, and will someday become my wife. I wonder what our kids will look like. Will they have her blue eyes or brown like mine? Maybe they'll have a combination, a unique color all to their own. I keep thinking of all the possibilities as I drift off to sleep.

The next day is more of the same. Construction all day but the building is almost done on the outside then we can start working inside without the heat of the sun beating down on us all day. After work, I run home, take a quick shower, only because Taren didn't get in with me, and we take off for our place. We stopped by the grocery store on the way out of town, loaded up my truck with bags of food, more matches, drinks, ice, candles, flowers, oil for the lamps, batteries for the radio, and a couple of new flashlights. The news said there's a chance of rain tomorrow late afternoon. You never know around here if it could turn out to be another bad storm. Since we only packed one bag together, we should be able to take everything in one trip to the shack. I hope. When I get to the place where I always park my truck, I jump in the back and try to fit all the food into the big cooler I brought. Most of it fits except for a few things, so we only have two sacks to carry. Being the sensible woman she is, Taren decides to carry the bag and sacks so I can haul the full cooler. Smart woman. She grabs the cooler handle as we walk across the slippery rocks, so she doesn't fall, and then we make it to the shack, taking much longer than normal.

She walks in before me, opening the window and lighting the lamps. I set the cooler on the floor by the small make shift fridge, fill it with ice, and fit as much stuff in there as possible. I leave out a couple of steaks and the veggies we're gonna make tonight on the small grill outside. I pour the rest of the ice into the cooler and arrange the bottled waters, soft drinks, and beers in there then when I stand I watch her put clean sheets on the cot. The aroma fills the air with freshness, the flowers and burning candles she's lit around the small room, makes it feel homey. We've spent so much time here in our young lives, and she's always given it that woman's touch. I look around the room, feeling all kinds of pride that we actually had built this together. It's not much but it's always been ours, something we've shared, laughter, sadness, love, and the first time we made love. *Special.*

The night has been great. Dinner was delicious. She brought things to make a small salad, and we ate until we were so full we could bust. We laid on the cot and watched a movie, eating strawberries with whipped cream. Needless to say, we didn't finish watching the movie as we started having a whipped cream fight.

Luckily, she'd brought another pair of clean sheets. There's nothing like laying in our shack, on this old cot, with Taren in my arms after making love. I listen to her light breathing and the nighttime sounds surrounding us. I'm keen to hearing any noise that isn't a normal sound for outside but the rustling of leaves due to the wind is making it hard to decipher. I may not get any sleep tonight.

"Mmmmm," I moan. I must be dreaming of her mouth on me, but it feels so real that I'm about to jump outta my skin or on her. One eye opens a slit, just in time to see her head move down, her lips covering my more than eager cock. "Ugh, Taren!" Another moan moves up through my chest, my throat, and out of my mouth when her teeth lightly scrape my tender skin then she sucks, hard. My eyes open wide as she takes me until I feel the back of her throat. My fingers tighten in her hair, not even realizing they were on her head. When my balls begin to tense, I raise up enough to grab ahold of her arms and pull her up to me. She straddles my hips quickly, the look of surprise on her face as I set her down right over my cock that's dying to be inside her.

"Brock," she moans as her eyes close, taking me all in. She begins to move as she leans down and presses her mouth against mine. My hand finds its way under her thick hair and around the back of her neck, the other holds onto her hip as we find our rhythm.

My lips move to her jaw over her silky skin. "God, what you do to me," I whisper.

She starts moving fast. My thrusts meeting every move. I feel her clamp around me, and my hips buck even more. "BROCK!" she yells, her eyes closed and her brows lower. The look on her face is pure gratification. Love. I shout out her name as I release into her. She lays on me, her head on my chest as we pant together in a total state of satisfaction.

"Best way to wake up in the morning," I tell her as I rub her back. She giggles. Her head rises and she looks at me, her chin resting on my chest. Her smile is beautiful, happy. I smile back, not being able to help it. Her happiness contagious. "What do you want to do today, beautiful?"

Her brows lower, like she's thinking about it then they lift. "A storm might be coming later. Why don't we eat breakfast, make love again, pack a picnic lunch, and make love again, then go play in the water at the pond, make love, then lay out on the beach, and make love."

My heart speeds up, and my smile widens. "I love the way you think." I wink, and she giggles again. I'll never tire of that sound, of her. "How about you make breakfast and I'll get the water boiling for a bath. We can take it together. You know, save on water." I waggle my brows and she giggles again. I grab her sides and roll her over, tickling her. She starts squirming and laughing, but her movements cause my cock to pull out of her. I feel that loss but am having too much fun making her laugh to care too much. Not like I won't be right back in there in a little bit anyway.

We play around a little more. I finally concede when she couldn't catch her breath from laughing so hard. Finally, I swat her cute, tight bottom and she gets up and starts making breakfast. I get the water boiling and then we eat. It takes us three trips out back to fill the tub, boiling more water, and another three trips after, before the tub is full enough. Okay, so maybe this wasn't the best setup but when you're young and building something of your own, this seemed like a good idea at the time. Someday, I'd like to buy this piece of land and actually build a house. But I'd leave our shack. Some of our best memories are here.

As she had said, we made love again, then we washed each other. It didn't take long for the water to grow cool so we had to hurry to get clean. Worth it. I helped her pack up a picnic lunch, the sun still shining overhead, but I heard from the radio it's gonna turn stormy later, just like Taren thought. We head out hand in hand to the small beach area. She spreads out our beat up blanket and then runs into the water. I set the basket down and watch her for a minute.

She ducks under the water then bobs back up, pushing back her long hair from her face. Her eyes open and those blue wonders stare at me, filled with desire. My heart flutters as I wonder how she can be horny after this morning but hey, I'm a man. I'm always horny. I smile as I pull off my jeans and practically skip as I walk towards her. She shrieks when I jump in beside her. I grab her slim waist and pull her to me, her legs immediately wrapping around me. Since I have plans to do a lot later, and being afraid she won't be

225 | P a g e

able to walk later or do anything else if we continue to make love like rabbits, we just kiss like horny teenagers and do other teenager *things* then end up splashing each other and swim around.

After about an hour, I watch her walk out of the water and lay down on her side on the beach. She looks over at me, one leg over the other. One hand rests on her thigh while the other on the sand. Her long dark wet hair lays over her shoulder, the long layers almost touching her arm. She looks like a model. Beautiful. Sexy. My heart rate speeds up, and my cock pushes against my swim trunks. I start to wade through the water, my eyes boring into hers. Eh, she doesn't need to be able to walk. I'll carry her wherever she needs to go.

Chapter Fifteen

Taren

Laying on the beach, I watch him walk to me with hunger in his eyes. Sexy. His hips sway, and I lick my lips. I'm already feeling a bit sore but who the hell cares. I can't get enough of him. He made love to me slowly, passionately on our blanket. I'm not even sure the last time the blanket was washed because it smells of us. After we both climaxed, he held me in his strong arms, covering us with our towels.

It's been the most perfect day until the clouds hide the sun and darken the sky. We both knew a storm was going to end up coming, but I thought it wouldn't be until tonight. We hurry and pick up everything and head back to our shack, eating our forgotten picnic lunch at the table. I cut up some fruit with the large butcher knife, setting it on the counter. I lean my hand beside it and a loose board springs up. "I'll fix that tomorrow before we leave," Brock says, smiling at me. After we eat and then clean up, we put in a movie and lay on the futon, our hands clasped together, his arm hanging over my shoulder. The rain begins to beat on the window and the roof as we start watching the second movie, lulling me.

Pretty quickly my eyes start to grow heavy, and I finally let them shut, so comfortable in his arms.

BANG!

"Ugh! Omph!"

I sit up with a startle. My eyes heavy and trying to adjust to the darkness. I hear struggles and sounds of fighting and grope my way over to the table, feeling around for the matches. The sounds of a storm is raging outside, and I fumble around trying to find them. "Omph." *Damnit! Where are those matches?* My hand finally hits them, pushing them over, but I grab onto them shakily as I remove one from the box and try to strike it against the outside of the small box. The sounds of a fight echo through the small confines as the match finally catches, lighting up the area in front of me. I open the small door to the lamp, placing the flame against the wick. Soon the area brightens, and I turn up the flame. I pick up the lamp and turn, a gasp leaving me loudly. I almost drop the lamp.

Jeffrey has Brock pinned against the wall. I can only see Brock's bruised face and only hope Jeffrey's is the same. Quickly, I set the lamp down on the table, and run over to them. Grabbing Jeffrey's upper arms and digging my feet into the floor, I start pulling and trying to get him off Brock. I'm knocked off balance and onto the floor with a *"thud"* when his arm pushes back, his hand smacking across my face with the movement. The wind is knocked out of me, briefly, my face heated and stinging, but I get right back up. I know my strength, or lack thereof, is no match for his, so I grab one of his arms with both hands and start tugging as hard as I can. "Let him go, Jeffrey!" I yell.

"Fuck you, Tare!" His mouth turns into a snarl. I keep pulling and look at Brock. His eyes are half closed, his face turning a light blue as Jeffrey's hand presses against his throat. "This ends now. Tonight. You'll come home with me and we'll marry tomorrow. I'm done playing this fucking game."

My heart starts beating even faster than it was at his words. He wants to end this. Tonight. Deep in my heart, I know what that means, what he intends to do. The hold on his arm tightens as I lean back, trying desperately to get him off Brock. Fear envelopes me. My stomach ties up in knots and queasiness overtakes it as I struggle with him. Suddenly, arms wrap around my waist, lifting me into the air and I land on the floor hard. My head hits against the cabinet with a force and spots fill my eyes along with tears. I cover the spot on my head with my hand and hear the sounds of scuffling, looking up and blink rapidly so I can see, trying to clear the haziness.

You know that part in a thriller movie, when your eyes open wide, you feel like your heart is gonna pound outta your chest as you watch everything happen in slow motion? This feels just like that as I watch the horror unfold before me.

When the spots finally leave my eyes, and I brush away the tears, I see Dad pulling Jeffrey off of Brock. I push against the cabinet, trying to gain footing enough to stand. My legs feel weak, and the pain in my head makes me sluggish. I watch Jeffrey turn around, the look of surprise on his face. My dad is strong but Jeffrey is younger, stronger. His arm pulls back then his fist hits Dad square on his jaw. Dad lets out a sound, and I watch him topple over and onto the ground. Memories flash in my head. Times as a child, sitting on his lap as he read to me. All the times I felt his love, before he changed, before Sebastian died. Maybe this is his way of telling me he still loves me. That he was wrong. Fighting for me.

I feel like I can't move, my hands covering my mouth when Jeffrey raises his arm, his hand aiming a gun down at Dad. I begin to move when shots are fired. I jump, my lower back hitting the cabinet as I grab the counter with my hands to steady me. I watch blood making a huge puddle on the floor around him, a small river of red coming from his body. A sob breaks free but stops quickly when I turn and see Brock struggling with Jeffrey for the gun. They move towards me, and I start backing away. I keep edging my way until I'm next to the door.

"Dammit, asshole! Drop the fucking gun!" Brock yells right before Jeffrey put his arms around his head, putting him in a headlock. He slams Brock against the cabinet, and I watch as the butcher knife I was using earlier slides around with the impact until the blade is facing out into the room. I begin to stagger over to see if

I can get around them and grab it when Jeffrey grabs blindly behind him and the loose board pops up and he grabs it. He reaches down around Brock's head and hits his forearm hard with it. Brock cries out as Jeffrey releases him and jams his fist into his stomach. I scream as Jeffrey steps back, then pitches forward and does it again. Brock bends over, his arm trying to protect himself. Jeffrey steps back again and I watch as Brock barrels into him, pushing him back against the table. Jeffrey reaches out with his free hand and grabs Brock's t-shirt, fisting the fabric pulling him with him. He hits him hard with the butt of the gun against his head. Brock's eyes close halfway, blood running down the side of his face, and bile reaches the bottom of my throat.

I see an opportunity to get the knife again but when I start in that direction, the door opens beside me, and I'm pushed down, hitting my injured head on the hard floor. My vision is clouded, along with the dim light making it hard to distinguish what's happening as I try to regain my senses. The slow motion from before speeds up and then so many things sweep through my mind as I watch. Kane grabs Jeffrey, who still has a tight hold on Brock's t-shirt, turning him around. Jeffrey's hold on Brock causes him to follow until Kane places his hands on Jeffrey's chest and with a loud groan, pushing him hard. He grabs Brock around his waist with both arms, pulling him back against him as Jeffrey soars in the air, stopping abruptly when he hits the cabinet. His eyes widen. His mouth opens, and turns his head. His body turns, and I gasp as I see the butcher knife protruding from slightly above his lower back. His head turns towards Kane, who was pushed against the table still holding onto Brock. Jeffrey raises his gun, and I push up from the floor trying to stand. My head is hammering as I stagger. "NOOOOOOOOOOOOOOO!" I scream, my body jolts and my eyes close when shots are fired, and I watch in fear as Kane and Brock fall to the floor.

My body is shaking hard when I open my eyes. Jeffrey is in a heap on the floor, blood pooling around him. His body is still, his eyes open and lifeless as they stare ahead. I turn to my left, sounds of sirens blaring outside, coming closer. Is there a fire? The room begins to get lighter yet hazy. The odor of something burning fills my nose. I look over at the futon, the lamp laying on its side in the middle of flames that are growing by the minute. They say in an emergency your adrenaline kicks in that you become stronger than you ever imagine. That may be true but not when you're injured. I manage to push against the wall with my hand, struggling until I stand.

Coughing ensues as I limp over to Brock then rest my knee on the floor. His eyes are closed. Blood still drips down his beautiful face. I reach down and put my hand on his face, tears flowing down mine. Some are from the smoke filled room but most are in fear. I scan down his firm jaw, his neck, until I see his blood drenched shirt. "No," I whisper. I hear a groan behind him, and my eyes snap to Kane, who's laying beneath him. He's trying to sit up, Brock's weight heavy on his legs. Quickly, I look back at Brock and try to shake him, the warmth from the fire getting hotter, closer. "Brock! Baby, wake up! We have to get out of here!" No movement except for what my shaking causes.

"Taren! You need to leave. Now!" Kane's voice sounds from my left but I can't move. I can't leave him. I won't. I shake Brock harder, desperate in my attempts to wake him. The sirens outside are loud now, the roar of the fire even louder. "Dammit, Taren! Get out now! I'll get him!" I look over at Dad, my heart breaking. "I'm sorry, Taren, but, he's gone. We have to go!" Suddenly, I feel arms around my waist, and as I'm lifted, I begin beating on them.

"NO! NO! I won't leave him!" I scream, the smoke and my tears making Brock hazy as I'm pulled out the front door. "PUT ME DOWN! BROCK!" My legs try to kick back, kick the person taking me away from my love, but they're so weak so I keep hitting his arms. Rain beats down on us, soaking us instantly. My fists keep sliding off their wet skin.

Kane speaks into my ear, my body shaking, shivering. "Taren. I'll go get him. I can't do that and take care of you. Stay here." I nod, my head wobbling with the effort. In trying to get Brock to wake up, I hadn't noticed that Kane had managed to get himself out from under him. He sets me down on the ground, and I fall to my knees. Even through the darkness and the onslaught of rain, I can see the smoke bellowing from the door. I watch him run inside, and I bend over, purging everything within me.

"Miss. Are you okay?" I startle when I feel a hand on my shoulder but don't look up as my stomach continues to heave. "Taren?" A familiar voice rings in my ears but I can't stop to figure out where I know it from. "Dean! Stay with her! Get the paramedics here now!" My arms wrap around my waist. Dry heaving begins, but I can't seem to stop the cramping in my stomach. I start coughing again, my lungs needing air desperately. "I'll get them, Taren. Don't worry." I finally manage to lift my head slightly and see Caylan running into the shack. Our shack. Our love. Brock. Is he still alive? Did Jeffrey really end this? Did he finally get what he wanted and end Brock's life? What did he gain? He's dead, lying in the shack that Brock and I built together, in our love for each other.

I jump when someone tries to place an oxygen mask over my mouth, and my eyes snap up into the eyes of a paramedic. "Let me just put this around your head. I need to tend to your wound too. Okay? Let me just help you move back from the fire." I shake my head wildly, the movement makes me close my eyes with the pain and a groan escapes me. I feel strong arms around my waist and am lifted. When I open my eyes, I see Caylan walking out the door with his arm around Kane, half dragging him. They both fall to the ground. Kane isn't moving. His eyes closed, and Caylan is leaning on one arm beside him, breathing heavy.

My heart feels like it could strangle me. I start to struggle, pulling forward. "BROCK!" I scream, but it's muffled by the mask. My feet slide on the wet ground as I'm pulled away. Another paramedic appears and blocks my line of hazy vision as he picks up my legs and I'm placed on a thin mattress. I try to sit up but strong hands push me back down. "NO! BROCK!" I try screaming again. Suddenly I still when the other paramedic moves to the side and I see Caylan running back into the shack. His body is bent as he half limps through the door, his movements slow. Flames roar above the roof and out the sides. I startle when I hear a loud crash, imagining the glass in the window blowing out. Brock's face enters my mind. Bruises all around one side, the same side that was hurt before. The blood that was flowing so readily, not only on his face but his shirt. Stomach cramps return and I turn to my side and bend over, my hand ripping the mask from my mouth just in time to start dry heaving again.

I turn my head back, my hand grips the side of the gurney as I stare at the doorway. "Here. Let me…." I wince as I feel the paramedic tending to my head. Pain sears through me, clouding my already hazy vision. "Looks like you'll need some stitches." Stitches. I hit my head on the cabinet and the floor. Confusion sets in but then I sit up, my hands pushing against the mattress. He keeps fooling with my head as I see Caylan walk out, Brock's lifeless body over his shoulder. Caylan gets only a few feet when he collapses and Brock falls onto the ground. Moving my legs over the side, I begin to get up but am pushed back down. "Hey, you can't get up. I'm not done yet and you're losing a lot of blood."

BR…. BROCK!" I yell and start to struggle in the man's hold. Several men run over to Caylan and Brock. Two men are carrying Kane to another gurney a few feet away from me. "I need to…."

More men show up, carrying Jeffrey and Dad's bodies out of the shack, laying them down on the saturated ground.

BOOM

The earth seems to shake, and everyone ducks. The kerosene. I feel the gurney I'm on moving away from the shack. When we stop, hands grip my arms as I try to get up again. "Please." I cry, my body racking with sobs. Men pick up Caylan and Brock and lay them down closer to me. As they lay Brock down, his head turns my way. My head tilts to the side as I study his battered face. His eyes are still closed, but it's hard to decipher much in the rain and darkness. I still when I look at his chest, trying to determine if he's breathing. Men in police uniforms and paramedics run around everywhere. Talking, yelling of needing oxygen, and various sounds are all around. I feel a prick and look down just as a needle pulls away from my skin. My head snaps back to Brock, the pain in my body making my vision more unclear. A paramedic kneels down over him blocking my view.

Then my eyes are obstructed by a body and I look up. Dean is standing beside me, his eyes full of tears, and his face solemn.

"Taren. I'm so sorry." I don't want to believe my eyes or what he says. I try to look around him but can't. He places his hand on my arm, and my eyes snap to it as it tightens, squeezes. I can't live without Brock. There's no life for me here, no hope. For most of our young lives, we've been together, shared almost every moment, good and bad. Our families tried to keep us apart, but we always stayed together. Our love held us, comforted us, and was the only thing that saw us through all the bad times, knowing in the end we'd be together. He's all I've ever known. All I've ever wanted. All I've ever needed.

"Brock," I whisper. "Please, don't leave me." A sob escapes and I start feeling woozy. I look up at the man trying to bandage my head and anger swells. "What did you give me? I need…." my voice sounds strange, my body becoming light. "No. I…." I need to make sure he's okay. Doesn't he understand my whole life is laying on the ground dying? My world is crumbling around me as confusion sets in. I turn my head and see the man beside Brock look up at another man shaking his head. "No." My chin quivers. Another sob bursts free. They begin to stand and walk away. "No." my voice comes out a little louder. The rain begins to hit me harder and the gurney I'm on starts to move. "NO!" I look over at Dean. His face changed to alarm. Lightning strikes, shedding a little light in its flash. A glimmer makes my eyes look at his hand. He's holding the butchers knife, a cloth wrapped around the handle. In the blink of an eye, I reach over and grab the handle, pulling it free from his hold. I sit up halfway, grasping the handle with both hands, turning the blade around and plunge it into my stomach, my mouth opening in silence as my face scrunches in pain.

"TAREN! NO! WHAT HAVE YOU DONE?"

Screaming and yelling is all around me. My body falls against the mattress. I look up to the sky, the raining causing me to blink rapidly as it hits my eyes. Pain floods through me and my body begins to shake uncontrollably. Brock's face appears over me, and my mouth turns into a smile. I feel hands all over me, the small bed shaking, moving. I feel numb, but I keep my eyes on Brock. His face isn't bruised, his eyes not swollen. There's no blood, only his breathtakingly beautiful face. He smiles, and I feel him. *"Come with me, my love,"* he whispers. *"It's over now. We can finally be together. Forever."* My eyes become heavy but I strain to keep them open, to keep them on him. *"It's okay, Taren. I've got you."* I feel his warm hand cup my face, and I let my eyes close with his touch.

Brock

I swallow. My throat feels like sandpaper. I struggle to open my eyes, but I'm sluggish, feeling like I've been drugged. Flashes and scenes play in my mind. The shack. Fire. Jeffrey. Was Taren's dad there or did I dream that? What's real and what have I imagined? Maybe when I finally open my eyes the whole thing will have been a bad dream. Taren's in my arms, her breathing light in her sleep. I remember that I finished watching the movie, too comfortable to take her to bed.

Opening my eyes, I saw the blue showing on the TV screen, telling me I'd fallen asleep. Then I'm pulled up off the couch, fists hitting me repeatedly. Everything after that is so scrambled, so confusing. I open my eyes a slit. A hospital room. Small with no window. Is it day or night? I look around. Tubes filtering from my hand, my arm. Tilting my head back I see machines. Beeping sounds waft into the tiny area from behind me, counting my heart beats, continually taking my blood pressure. I've seen them before. In movies as well as others I've visited in the hospital. Question is why do I have them? But the bigger question is: where is Taren? My hand lifts and reaches over, my finger pressing on the button that looks like a woman's face. I'm hoping this is the nurse's button because I want answers. Now. Quickly, I hear footsteps, the door already ajar. It moves open further and a nurse walks in, immediately coming to my side and picking up my hand. Her fingers are pressed against my wrist as she looks at her watch.

"Taren. Where is she?" my voice doesn't sound like me. My throat is so dry and scratchy. She looks down at me, her brows lower. "Taren Mills. Where is she?" I ask again and then swallow hard. Damn, that hurts. Her silence causes my heart to race and a machine starts becoming louder. "Taren! Where the fuck is she?" I yell, pain searing through me. My eyes close tight as I wince.

"Please, stay calm, Mr. Evans. I'll go find out." I open my eyes and see her push a needle in the top of a tube. "You must stay calm. You haven't been out of surgery long and you'll cause yourself more damage."

She turns and starts to walk away but I grab her arm, squeezing tightly. Well, as tight as I can. I feel so weak. "Where's Taren," I say through gritted teeth.

Her other hand lays on mine that's gripping her arm. "Sir. I promise I'll find out." Her eyes are full of concern, and I slowly release her. She jogs out of the room, and I lay back. The pain intensifies, but I have to find her. Flashes of memories keep sweeping through my mind. I remember Jeffrey choking me, knocking her away, and she hit her head against the cabinet. The sounds of her screaming. I kept trying to fight him, get him off me, so I could get to her but his surprise attack left me weak and injured. Still I tried, hard. Then I remember seeing his face as the knife went into his back, his look of surprise and confusion. But when his gun went off and hit me in the chest, I flew back into Kane, knocking us both down. My hand moves over the bandage covering my chest. I don't know anything that happened after that, and now I'm left wondering how Taren is. Was she hurt more after that? Is she okay now? All these thoughts make me even more anxious to see her, hold her in my arms. I need to know that she's okay.

I look up when a doctor walks into the room. His face is full of concern and something else I can't decipher. He walks to the end of the bed and just looks at me. I open my mouth to speak, to ask him about Taren, when he starts talking. "Mr. Evans. Good to see you awake. The injuries you sustained made me fear losing you. More than once." My eyebrow raises. "I had a difficult time removing the bullet from your chest. It was very close to your heart. Another inch and you wouldn't be with us now. Your heart stopped twice and you had to be revived. Your facial and head lacerations will heal but you could be left with some light scarring."

"Uh, Doc. I'm sorry but I don't really care about me. Taren Mills. Is she okay?" I interrupt, anxious as ever to find out about my love.

He clears his throat. "You're not a relative. Are you?" His brows lift and mine lower.

"She's my girlfr…. She's my life. Tell me or I'll go find her myself." I throw the covers off, pain shooting through me as I try to sit up. I lay back and close my eyes, the machine behind me sounding with loud beeping, echoing in the small room.

I feel his hand on my leg. "Please, lay still, Mr. Evans. I don't want to you undo everything I've done and have to take you into surgery again." I open my eyes, squinting through the pain. "Her mother is with her. I'll go talk with her and make sure you're allowed information about her then I'll return. I won't take long. Okay?" I nod. It's the only movement I can do at the moment.

"Good. I'll be right back." I watch him leave the room and wince. Dammit. I need to find out. I need her. I need to know she's okay. Then my thoughts move to Kane. I wonder where he is, if he's okay as well. I place my hand over my heart, closing my eyes as the pain starts to die down again. A sound makes my eyes snap back open. Caylan walks into the room and straight to the bed. He lays a hand on my arm.

"You okay? You had me worried." His eyes are full of concern.

"I'll be fine," my voice sounds rough and raspy. He turns and does something that I can't see then turns back with a big cup with a straw. I take it from him and drink some cool water. The liquid feels so good on my throat. I push the straw out and hand the cup back to him and watch him set it on a table, rolling it over me, so I can reach it. "Taren. No one will tell me where she is, if she's okay." I reach out and grab his arm. "Do you know?" His eyes widen. "Tell me." He opens his mouth then we both look at the doorway when the doctor walks back in. I release Caylan's arm, anxious to hear what he has to say.

"Mr. Evans. I've been given permission to speak to you about Taren, however...." Mrs. Mills walks in right behind him. "Mrs. Mills would like to speak with you about her instead." I can't take my eyes off her as I watch her walk to a chair, pulling it up beside me. She takes my hand in hers, my heart causing the machine to go off again as I look at her tear streaked face, wetness still brimming in her eyes. "I'll just leave you all alone." I hear him walk out but still can take my eyes off hers. She's dead. I know it. I can feel it.

"I'll leave you all too. I'll be right outside," Caylan speaks.

"No! You need to stay, dear. After everything you've done, you have the right to be here and are more than welcome." *The right? What does she mean?*

"Thank you," he replies. From the corner of my eye, I see him sit in another chair close by.

She squeezes my hand and I swallow hard, thankful of the water I'd drank. "Brock, dear. I'm going to tell you about Taren but I need you to remain calm. Can you do that for me? For her?" I nod and swallow again, nervous for what I'm about to hear. It must be bad if she's telling me to stay calm. I don't know if I can take it. My feelings are all over the place, but I have to know. I need to know. "Honey. Taren is okay. Well, as good as expected." *I'm relieved, but that scares the shit outta me at the same time.* "Let me step back. She was hurt pretty bad, not as bad as you of course, in the beginning. She has a bad concussion and some bruising and scrapes, a cut on her head, but…." Tears flow readily down her face now and my heart stops.

"Brock. She thought you were dead. When she was laying on a gurney, ready to be brought to the hospital, she thought you had died so she…." I watch her swallow and look away. She brings her other hand up and wipes away some tears, keeping her other hand in mine, then looks up at me again. "She took the knife that killed Jeffrey from Dean's hand. He was standing by her side. Brock, she stabbed herself in her stomach, wanting to end her life." *What? Why would she do that?* My eyes fill with tears. Knowing she would take her own life to be with me in spirit makes me want to shake her hard then hold her in my arms so tightly. I can't believe she did that. *Romeo and Juliet. How many times had we watched that over the years thinking our lives sounded so much like that story?* Mrs. Mills squeezes my hand again, bringing me back to the present.

"She had to have surgery." Her voice now sounds rough with emotion. "She's better now but still not awake yet." She leans closer, her grip on my hand tightening. "Honey. She's pregnant." The heart machine goes ballistic, and my breathing escalates. She places her other hand on my arm. "I need you to take a deep breath, Brock. I need you to relax." *A baby? But she stabbed her stomach. How can...* "The baby is fine, dear. Calm down for me." I swallow hard, multiple times. *A baby. We're gonna have a baby.*

"Is everything okay in here?" The nurse shows up, concerned. "If you can't remain calm, Mr. Evans, I'll need to sedate you and your visitors will need to leave." I open my mouth to speak but nothing comes out. Mrs. Mills turns to her and smiles.

"He's fine. I'm sorry. I'll make sure he stays calm." The nurse looks at her wearily then finally nods and leaves the room again. Mrs. Mills turns back to me, her smile faltering slightly. She pats my arm and then lays her hand on her lap, keeping the other tight around mine. "She really is okay, honey, but doesn't know about the baby yet." I take a deep breath, expelling the air quickly. "Brock. She'll need you when she awakens. Do what you're told by the nurse and doctor. I'll talk to him about getting you to her room. Okay?" I nod and swallow again.

"When do you think…. When do you think she'll wake up? I want to be there. I have to be there." Thoughts of her waking up without me there makes me cringe. She thought I'd die, tried to take her own life not realizing she was carrying a life inside her. A part of me. A part of her. I feel the wetness of my tears on my cheeks.

"The doctor told me it will be today. He's had her sedated. Brock. I'll talk to him as soon as I leave here, okay? You need to be there with her." I nod again, unsure if I can speak. She removes her hand from mine and pats my arm. "I'm gonna go back to her. I don't want to stay away long. Mimi and Irish are with her now. I'll send one of them as soon as I talk to the doctor. Okay?" I nod again, swallowing hard. She stands leans over and kisses my cheek. "You just stay calm and heal. She'll need you more than ever now." I look up at her and then watch her leave the room. A clearing of a throat reminds me that Caylan is still in the room. I turn my head and look at him. He's sitting in a chair, a few feet from where Mrs. Mills sat. His head is down, his hands in his lap clasped together.

"Um. Can you move closer? Some things we need to talk about," I ask him quietly. He looks up, nods, and moves to the abandoned chair beside me. "Thanks. I mean…. What did Mrs. Mills mean about you having a right to stay? What don't I know?" He looks down, suddenly shy or maybe embarrassed? Definitely don't know him well enough to know his expressions. "Fill me in?"

He looks back up at me and takes a deep breath. "I just did what most people would do. I got you and Kane out of the shack. That's all." He shrugs like it's no big deal. Like he didn't just save two people's lives.

"That's all." I smirk, and his mouth turns up into a small smile. "I'd say that's quite a bit." He shrugs again, but his smile widens. "Thank you, man. I mean it. If not for you, Kane and I might not be here today." I reach out my right hand. My movements hindered by the pain and my left forearm in a cast weighing me down.

"You'd have done the same for me. No thanks needed." He smiles.

We release hands and I just look at him. He seems uncomfortable, but I still have so many questions. I'm still confused about some things, but I know Taren would be the only one to answer a few of them. "Did you see…." I almost can't get the words out and feel like I'm choking on them. "Did you see Taren stab herself?" *I can't believe she'd do that. I know our love is strong but to want to end your life because she thought I was dead scares the shit outta me.*

He nods slowly, his smile gone. "Yes. I wasn't too far from her. She thought you were dead. I saw her grab the knife that Dean was holding. She didn't even hesitate. I envy you." My brows raise. *Envy me?* "You two have a love like none other I've ever seen. She was willing to die because she thought you had. Kinda reminds me of that story *Romeo and Juliet.* You know the one where the families try to keep them apart but their love was so strong and in the end they both end up taken their lives because they think the other is dead?"

"Does sound vaguely familiar." I smirk but then sadden. "Good thing it didn't turn out that way in the end for us." He nods and sits back in the chair, relaxing a bit. I feel a little more relieved and raise one brow at him, giving him a half smile. "So you read that shit?" A burst of a laugh leaves him, and he smiles.

"Yeah, well. I like to read. You know that book has a movie out too." I laugh, my hand moving to my chest. Okay, it hurts to laugh. We end up talking for a long time, getting to know each other better. I like him. He's a good guy, and I'm so thankful to him for saving Kane and me. After an hour, the doctor walks in, the nurse behind him pushing a wheelchair in tow. He tells me that I can go be with Taren, that they'll be bringing her out of sedation and after talking to her mom, they feel I should be with her to help with her recovery. If I have my way – I'll never leave her again.

Soon after he leaves, Ma and Pop walk in. She runs over to my bed, throwing her arms around me. "My baby boy!" She cries into my neck. My arms move around her, the tubes making it difficult. Pop walks over to the other side of the bed, laying his hand on my shoulder. Tears brim in my eyes as well as his. "We were so worried."

I look up at Pop, my tears threatening to fall. "Son," is all he can manage.

We stay like that for a long time. My tears keep threatening to fall but I hold them back. Until I see Taren.

Chapter Sixteen

Taren

I lick my dry lips. A voice reaches me. The sound of his beautiful voice fills me. I don't want to open my eyes, fearing it could be a dream. A beautiful dream.

"And when I found out you tried to leave this world, not knowing I was alive, I almost lost it." *The dream is so real I can almost feel his hand squeeze mine.* "I found out…. I found out you're pregnant." *Now this dream has gotten strange. I can hear him choking on his words, and I feel the warmth of his hand on my forehead, his thumb brushing against my skin. I always loved when he did that. So soothing. Loving. Pregnant?* "I know that had you'd known you wouldn't have tried to take your life. You would have been strong for our baby." *Wait! What? I need this dream to stop. I need him.* "Come back to me, baby. I need you. I need to hold you in my arms so badly."

My hand moves, slightly. I try to squeeze his hand but feel like I can't move. I'm tired. So tired. "Taren! Come on, baby. Come back. Please." I try again, actually feeling his skin, his warmth, but I'm afraid I didn't do it hard enough. "That's it. That's my girl." Maybe I did. I try again, a little harder. "Thank fuck." I hear his heavy breathing. He has to be exhausted and hurt. I thought he died. Now I feel his finger wipe away a tear from my face I know I'm shedding. "Don't cry, sweetheart. I'm here. I've got you. I'll always be here." His hand leaves mine, and I don't feel his warmth on my face any longer. *Wait! Don't go!* I hear movements, shuffling of a chair, and then the mattress dips and I'm in his arms. His strong arms. His warmth. I sigh. Out loud. I think. "There now." My mouth turns up a little at the feel of his lips against my cheek. "I'll never leave you again. Never." I bask in his warmth and then I return to darkness, comforted.

*　　*　　*　　*

"And then she smiled. It wasn't much but it was there."

"Oh, Brock! That's fantastic news. I'm sorry I missed it but I'm so glad you were here."

Brock. Mom. Their voices seem so far away. "I'll never leave her again." This time his voice sounds close. Then I feel his lips press against my face.

"Mmmm."

The bed jerks. "Baby? Taren? Are you awake?" I try to open my eyes or even one eye, but I'm still so tired. He kisses me again.

"Mmmmm."

He laughs. What a beautiful sound. "It's okay, baby. You sleep. As long as you come back to me." Once again his lips press against me but this time they're on my lips. I moan again and he lays his face against mine. He feels so good. I wish I wasn't so tired. I want to kiss him back. So badly. "Sleep, love. I'll be right here."

*   *   *   *

"It's very normal. Her vitals and reflexes are good and you heard her make a noise. Between the sedation and the severeness of the concussion it may take her a lot longer to fully come around. Don't worry. She's doing very well and the baby's heartbeat is strong."

An unfamiliar voice rings in my ear and I feel someone poking and prodding me.

"Thank you, Doc. I'm just anxious for her to wake up."

"I can understand that, Brock."

Brock.

I feel my heart start to speed up and a warm body beside me immediately. "Baby? Open those beautiful blue eyes for me." My eyes roll around underneath their lids but I'm still too tired to open them. "That's it, my love. Try for me." *For him. I'd do anything for him. Anything.* I take a deep breath and crack open one eye, just a slit. "Ah. Hi, my love." He's hazy, clouded, but I can see his gorgeous smile.

"Brock," I whisper/croak. My voice sounds strange. Probably from lack of use.

As I open my other eye a slit, I see him leaning on the bed, his face so close to mine. He leans in and starts to kiss me but stops. "You're about to close your eyes. I know it's easy to do when we kiss but please don't close them. I need to see them." My mouth turns up into a smile. He reaches up and cups my face then his lips press against mine. Warm. It's short. Sweet. He lays his forehead on mine. "Hi."

My smile grows. "Hi," my voice is quiet yet rough.

He moves back but only a breath away. "So many things I want to tell you. But right now, all I want to do is look at your eyes. I'm so thankful you came back to me. I love you, so much."

My chin quivers. My eyes open a little more. "I thought you were…. Dead," I croak. "I didn't want to go on without you. I'm so selfish."

His hand cups my quivering chin, softly. "No. You're not. I would have felt the same way, if I thought you had died. You didn't know." He leans in and kisses my lips quickly then moves back to where he was.

"A baby?" I whisper.

His smile grows huge. His eyes light up and sparkle. "Our baby. Made from our love." He moves again and rubs his scruffy face against mine. I don't remember ever seeing him with scruff before. I kinda like it.

I swallow hard and my eyes open even more. "Hold me?"

He doesn't hesitate and climbs onto the bed. He helps me up, slightly, then puts his arm around me. I try to move, turn on my side in my favorite position but I feel too weak. Like he reads my mind, he helps me turn. I wince with a little discomfort but I'd take any kind of pain to be in his arms. I sigh as I bring my arm around his waist, laying my hand on his flat stomach. "Better?" he asks as he rubs my shoulder. I nod and snuggle into his chest, loving the feeling of his fingers on my skin.

"Talk to me." I yawn, still a whisper. Suddenly, my heart beats harder, and I raise my head. "Daaad." I let out a quiet sob, and my eyes fill with tears. "Mom."

His hold tightens and I lay my head back down, too tired to keep it up for long. "I'm so sorry, Taren." He kisses the top of my head. "Your mom is doing okay. She'll be back in a while. She's been here since we were brought in." I nod and sniffle as a tear rolls down my cheek. "I think she still really loved him, ya know? I know she believes he was there to save you. He did love you." I nod into his chest unable to speak. We lay here in silence. Thoughts of my dad overwhelming me. Little did he know he would have been a grandfather. So much time past. If he hadn't turned into the man he was, we would have had a happier life. Brock and I would have been together. Dad would have welcomed his grandchild into the world with us. I let out another big yawn mixed with another sob and nestle into him. "Sleep, sweetheart. You've been through a lot and need rest now. Sleep." My eyes grow heavy and even thought I don't want to, I let sleep take me again.

I open my eyes to a bright room and turn my head to the window. Sun bellows in through the blinds and I take a deep breath, grateful to be alive. The bed is cold next to me, and no one is in the room. I startle when the door opens and a doctor walks in. "Well, good morning, Miss Mills. I'm Dr. Gammon. How are you feeling?"

I smile and push my hands against the mattress, moving myself up a bit. "I feel tired and weak but I'm good. Thank you."

"Good. Well, you have visitors, even though in ICU we normally only allow one in at a time but I'm making an exception. I'm thinking I can remove the catheter now. I think we should get you out of bed today. But not too much. Don't want you to overdo." I nod and he pulls back the covers. I wince a little as he removes it but I feel relief when it's gone. He sets it down and checks my vitals, telling me everything is good.

"When can I go home?" I give him a smile, hoping he'll tell me that I can go soon.

"Hmmm. I think we'll see maybe tomorrow. I want you to get some more rest and check the baby again before you leave. Sound good? You'll need to continue to rest at home." He gives me a smile and I nod. "Very well. I'll just take this and go and tell your visitors you're ready to see them." I like him. He seems very nice. I watch him leave and suddenly I'm feeling yucky, dirty. My teeth feel coated and I reach up and try to thread my fingers through my snarled hair without much luck.

"My baby!" Mom runs over and throws her arms around me. "Let me look at you," she says as she moves back, her hands on my face. "You look so much better today." I love her smile.

"Bestie!" I look around Mom and see Irish walking in carrying sacks. I look back at Mom and frown.

"I wish I could brush my teeth and take a shower." Mom's head turns and then looks back at me.

"I'll be right back." She leans in and kisses me then leaves the room.

Irish sets everything down on a very small table then walks over to me. "God. It's so good to see you awake," she whispers as she gives me a hug.

"Where's Brock?" It's not like I could miss him in this tiny room.

"Oh, they took him for some tests and to check him out. He said he was gonna take a shower then come straight back. He told me to tell you not to worry." A small laugh bursts from me but inside I'm feeling all warm and loved. She walks back over to the table and begins taking things out. The smell of food makes my stomach growl. Mom walks back in with a nurse behind her.

"Brought some help." She smiles. The nurse gives me a smile too and pulls back the covers. They both help me up, and I'm glad they're holding onto my arms tightly as my legs feel so weak and wobbly. The bathroom is tiny but as soon as they help me get the gown off, they walk me into the even smaller shower and help me sit down on a plastic stool in there. I'm grateful to be able to sit. "I brought you a pair of your jammies and some clean panties," Mom says as she turns the shower knobs. The water is cold at first but then turns to warm and it feels so good. She leaves me and the nurse then returns with a small bag, placing it in the sink, since there's no counter. I smile when I watch her bring my shampoo and conditioner and can't wait to be clean again. I know it'll make me feel better. The nurse steps out and Mom washes my hair. I close my eyes at her loving touch. Once my hair and body are clean, the nurse returns and help me out, dry off, and get my jammies on. I feel so much better already. Then after relieving myself, I sit on the toilet seat, and Mom gets my toothbrush, paste, and a small container and I almost moan as I brush my teeth.

Feeling more like myself, they help me back into bed and Mom pulls the covers over me. I smile and thank the nurse s she leaves. Irish brings over a plate of food, setting it on the table. She moves the table over me and the aroma hits me hard. "That doctor said you should only eat soft and light food today so I brought you a heap of scrambled eggs and some Jello." Her smile makes her beam. She leaves me and I dig in. God, I hadn't realized just how hungry I am. I get halfway through the eggs and start on the Jello when I feel his kiss on my temple. I look up and see the most beautiful thing in the world. My love.

"Glad to see you eating." He smiles, and my heart skips a beat. He's gorgeous and all mine. I notice his wheelchair and suddenly want him beside me. He always knows what I think, what I want. He stands, his arms shaking but manages to turn and sit on the mattress. I use my hands to push off the bed and move over, giving him some room. He pulls his legs up under the covers then stretches them out underneath the table. Feeling a bit clearer, I notice his left arm is in a cast.

"Here. Doc says you can have a little more substance." Irish smiles and sets his plate down beside mine. I pout when I see the eggs, biscuit and gravy, bacon, and sausage. He picks up the plastic utensils and cuts off a small piece of the sausage link and hold the fork up to my lips. I smile and snatch it into my mouth.

"I don't think one or two small pieces will hurt ya." He smiles, showing his straight white teeth, and I melt.

Breakfast is full of love, chatter, and laughing. Kane walks in with a limp and cane and heads directly for me. He bends down and kisses my forehead then sits next to my leg on the bed. "How are you, kiddo?"

I swallow my food and smile. "Much better." My face changes into concern. "Are you okay?" Now I feel bad. Since I awakened I've only thought about myself, the baby, and Brock. I did think about Dad and Mom too but never did I think about Kane or even Caylan. "I'm good. Just hurt my leg a bit." He looks at Brock and something passes between them. My brows lower as flashes from that night enter my mind. Kane on the ground, Brock on top of him. Smoke. Fire. Kane being helped out of the shack by Caylan.

"You're looking much better," Kane's voice breaks me free from the nightmare, and I smile. "You really had me worried." He places his hand on mine, and I start feeling my tears coming.

"Thank you, Kane. Thank you for everything. Really." He winks and pats my hand. I look around the room as Kane stands and walks over to the small table. Everyone I love is here, everyone that means something to me except two people. "Where's Mimi?"

Mom looks over. "Oh, sweetie. She's working. She was here on and off the whole time and she said that if you get to go home tomorrow, she'll see you at your apartment and whip you up all your favorites." I smile and nod, thankful again for my family.

After a while I start to get tired. Doesn't seem like I have to do much to get that way but I guess I have some healing to do and so does Brock. Once everyone leaves, Brock turns the TV on low and finds a movie. *Romeo & Juliet*. How fitting. I always felt like we've been living that in the modern day world. I'm lying in his arms, feeling full, loved and warm. I move my head up from his chest and see his eyes starting to close. "Brock?" They flutter back open and look down at me. "Where's Caylan? I really want to thank him."

His arm tightens around me. "He'll be around. Probably tomorrow. Maybe over at the apartment." He sighs. "I know what you mean though. I thanked him already, but it doesn't seem enough." His face snuggles into my head as I cuddle into him. "We should do something…." He yawns. "For him." I nod, not being able to keep my eyes open a second longer.

Brock

We're lying here, the love of my life in my arms, and the tears I've been holding back begin to leave my eyes. I've tried to be strong for her but now that I know she's okay, I can't stop them anymore from falling. I listen to her light breathing and thank God again that she's here with me. Angry thoughts of what she did to herself enter my head but then I wonder what I would have done if the tables had been turned? In my heart, I know if she had known she was carrying our baby, she would have never tried to take her own life. I also know that had I died, that she wanted to follow me, stay with me. I get it. Would I have done the same? Unless I was in that situation, I'm not sure. I know one thing, though. I wouldn't have wanted to live without her. There could have never been anyone else in my life. Oh, I'm not stupid. I know everyone dies at some point. But we're young and have been in love our entire lives. It's too soon, too much. The hospital counselor paid her a visit, and once she told our story they understood. At least enough that they didn't feel she was crazy. Well, we both may be a little crazy. Crazy in love.

Her body begins to shake in my arms, her eyes twitching underneath their lids. I strengthen my hold around her and finally she stops. She must be having a bad dream, or maybe she's reliving that night. I know I have several times now. After I woke up, all I could think about was Taren. Was she okay? How badly was she hurt? Then after she finally woke up, which scared the shit outta me wondering when she would, the nightmare's hit. I replayed that night over and over again. The same fear I had that night of protecting her, feeling helpless in my struggles, came back in full force. I woke up in a sweat each time.

She stirs again, and I look down at her. She's a vision. So beautiful, so sweet and loving. I sigh and hold her even closer. I'll never be able to get her close enough. I want to hold her in my arms forever, never letting go.

I laid awake most of the night as she kept having bad dreams. I couldn't protect her as much as I wanted to that night but I'll be damned if I ever let anything bad happen to her again. She's gonna need me more than ever now. A baby on the way and what happened to her dad is gonna hit her even harder once she's more lucid. I know her too well, even better than she knows herself. By the time the sun rises, I think I might have dozed off and on for a couple of hours. I watch her stretch, her mouth opening with a yawn. So beautiful.

"Morning," she whispers as she leans up and kisses me. We've been past the "morning breath" quite a few years ago. I've been telling her for years that hers tastes sweet but she just laughs at me.

"Morning, my love," I whisper back and kiss her back, harder.

"I need a shower and to brush my teeth in the worst way. Help me?" she asks. Damn, if only she was healed and had her energy back.

"Of course I will." I sit up and help her off the bed, walking with my arm around her waist to steady her. After we both relieve ourselves, she brushes her teeth while I get the shower ready. Under better circumstance, helping her remove her jammies would have been sensual. Her body is a bit battered and bruised and then there's the bandage that covers part of her stomach, reminding me that she had surgery. I look down at her tummy and imagine a small baby cocooned inside. She looks up at me as I place my hand there, lovingly. I lean down and kiss her forehead, then bend until I place a kiss on her tummy. Her hand covers mine and smiles. No words are spoken. None are needed. We stand there for a few minutes just relishing in the fact that we'll be parents. Our own child to love.

I help her into the shower, wash her hair, and help wash her body so we don't get her bandage wet. It's a tricky task but one I do gratefully and am certain it will be this way until she gets her stitches out. Her mom had told me that the knife wound was close to the baby and that a mere inch to the right would have torn into the sac, probably killing our child. Taren had also lost a fair amount of blood and had to have a transfusion. To think that I could have lost both of them makes me crazy. After I dried her off and helped her into a pair of sweatpants, wanting something loose around her waist, and a t-shirt, I help her back into bed just in time for the doctor to walk in. I stepped back so he could check her and am relieved when he announced that she can go home as soon as he gets the discharge papers ready. He recommended she still eat light for a couple of days but the way her eyes widen, I have to hold in my laugh. I know she's starving. He also said she should stay in bed, laying down, for at least a week. She nodded to that, probably still exhausted. Can't blame her. I have no problem lying in bed with her. You know. To keep her comfortable.

I grab my phone from my front pocket and call Ma to tell her that we're coming home and asking her to call everyone. She told me Pop and Kane would be by to pick us up and that our apartment is ready for us to come home. I'm not sure what she means by that. I mean, how can an apartment be ready? I just shrug and nod, like she can see me, then end the call. Two hours later and a lot of pacing on my part, we're finally in Pop's truck heading home. To say I'm anxious for us to get there would be a huge understatement. Even though the hospital staff was beyond great, the mattresses on the beds were so thin it felt like you were laying on a board, the pillows were not fluffy or soft, but thank God I didn't have to eat any of their food. Thanks to my family and friends. Suddenly, emotions overtake me. Family. Friends. They were all there for us. Holding my hand as I await the news about Taren. Being there for us at the shack when our lives were in danger. Bringing us "real" food during our hospital stay. We couldn't be more blessed. I look over when I feel Taren squeeze my hand, the one that won't let hers go for anything. She looks at me with worry but I give her a smile, letting her know I'm okay.

I've never seen a better sight then our apartment building coming into view. She turns her head to me, her gorgeous smile big, and she squeezes my hand. I feel the same and cannot wait to get her home. Still moving a little slow myself, Kane helps me get Taren to our apartment door and as I pull my keys out to unlock it, it flies open. "Surprise!" I hear Taren gasp. We stand in shock in the doorway. Balloons and streamers are all over the living room. A big "Welcome Home" sign is hanging on the wall over the recliner. Both of our family and friends are inside waiting for us to enter.

"Sheesh! Go in already." Kane's voice penetrates my ears as he practically pushes me inside. I put my arm around Taren's waist and help her walk until we're finally standing in the living room.

"Took you all long enough to get here. I had to make sure the food on the stove and in the oven didn't burn," Irish's voice rings out beside us. The look on her face is anything but annoyed. She's smiling and quickly walks to us, putting her arms around Taren. "Welcome home, bestie," she whispers in her ear.

She lets her go and walks back to the kitchen and each person steps up for a turn. We both get hugged and kissed more than we have in our entire lives. We didn't mind. Not in the least. Our home is filled with love, care, and the most important people in our lives. Food is stacked on our small table. People gathered around, filling plates, talking, and laughing. I walked with Taren over to the couch, already made up with a blanket and some pillows. They thought of everything. "You sit with Taren, Brock. I'll get you both some food," Ma says as she pats my shoulder. As I sit down next to my girl, I was gonna remind her that Taren needs to eat light, but then I thought, what the hell? She just got home, and I know she's starving. Mimi hurries over and bends down, putting her arms around Taren, whispering words of love and thankfulness in her ear. Those damn tears return in my eyes, but I'll save them for later, when we're alone. I look over and see Caylan sit down on the floor. He sets his plate heaped with food on the coffee table across from us and smiles. Seems like he's joined our family and rightly so.

"Caylan," Taren whispers. His eyes turn to her, his brows lower. "Thank you so much for saving Kane and Brock's lives. I'm sorry I haven't been able to tell you sooner. You'll never know how much it means to me." She takes my hand and squeezes. "To us."

He swallows hard, wetness developing in his eyes. He clears his throat, nods, and smiles. "Anytime. Was glad to do it." He and Taren stare at each other. I'm not jealous. Not at all. I'm truly thankful.

After a couple of hours of fun, family, and friends, Taren starts yawning and I know we both need to rest. Everyone says their goodbyes with hugs, kisses, and promises of stopping by again and helping out. I couldn't feel more loved. Ma, Mimi, and Mrs. Mills stay behind to clean up as I help Taren to our bedroom. I get her tucked in, kiss her forehead, and tell her I'll be back in a few minutes. Before I even close our door, she's sound asleep. I walk back to the kitchen and sit down in a chair at the table, too tired to help clean. I feel bad but I'm told not to worry, that I need to heal too.

As they all bustle around me, Mrs. Mills pulls out a chair and sits down beside me. "Brock," she begins. "I have a great idea and would like your blessing." *Huh?* I lean back and listen with the greatest of attention. "I'd like to have a house built for you and Taren. I'm going to look into buying the land where your shack was as well as the land leading to it from the road. I think after you all built it, the pond, and surrounding land should be yours. It would make for a wonderful house and an out of the way place to bring up your baby. Don't you?"

To say I'm shocked and stunned doesn't cover what I'm feeling. "Mrs. Mills," I start but she reaches over and puts her hand on my arm.

"Betty, please. We are family," she says proudly.

I smile. "Betty. That sounds more than amazing but it would be too expensive. I couldn't let…."

"Nonsense!" she says, pulling her hand back and waving. "With Tom gone..,." Her face fills with sadness but then changes back quickly. "I have more money than I know what to do with. Let me help you and Taren. Let me make your lives easier and my grandchild's. Please. I want to do this." Her eyes widen as she looks at me hopeful.

My brows lower. It's not that I don't want to take her up on her offer, and it would be a dream come true, but I'm feeling like this would be too much. I look into her eyes and smile. "Let me talk to Taren first. Okay?"

"Deal!" she says and leans back in the chair. Something tells me she's gonna get her way. But would that be so bad? I'm the bread winner, the man of the house, and I want to do everything for my family myself but wouldn't it be a dream come true to have a house there? In our special place. Sigh. I don't know what to do.

"Oh, honey. That is fantastic. You really should take her up on this. Pop and Kane said they would help you design the plans for the house and format the land. You and his crew could build it," Ma says in one breath. *Hmmm. They all know about this?*

I turn in my chair and give her a look. "So. You're all in on this? What the hell, Ma?"

She brushes by me, putting dirty dishes into the dishwasher. "My grandchild...." She turns her head and smiles at Betty. "*Our* grandchild needs a good place to grow up. What better place than where their parents grew up." True. She has a point.

"I get that and would love it. I'm just not so keen to taking such an expense from someone." I turn to Betty. "Don't get me wrong, I really love the idea and I'm so grateful. Really. I just wanted us to make it on our own, ya know?"

"So stubborn. Such a man. Take it and live a happy life, Brock." Ma smirks at me.

I feel a hand on my shoulder and look back at Betty. "I understand, Brock. I really do. I want to do this for you and my daughter. I want you all to have the happiest life. I know you already have the love and support. Let me do this for you."

I put my hand over hers. "You know what? Let's do it!" Her smile is wide, and she seems to bounce and when I look at Betty, she's bouncing in her chair. "But let's make it a surprise for Taren." They both nodd, smiles plastered on their faces. I swallow the lump in my throat, and something tells me swallowing your pride every once in a while is the right thing to do.

Chapter Seventeen

Taren

I awaken from the best nap in the arms of my love. I'm sore and my stitches itch, but I've never felt more content. Walking in and having our family and friends here, welcoming us home, was overwhelming but in a good way. Our small apartment was filled with laughter and great food. I ate more than I probably should have. At the time, I didn't care. I was starved! My stomach seemed to handle it okay. However, it made me even more tired and ready to crash. Everyone understood when the time came for them all to leave. I just about fell asleep on the couch. Brock helped me to our bedroom and into bed. I barely remember him kissing me on my forehead before I was out like a light. Now I hear his light breathing, his warm breath hitting my neck. I need to pee in the worst way, and I hate disturbing him. I think some have forgotten that he was injured too and needs his rest as much as I do.

I slide to the edge of the bed, my stitches pulling with my movement, and I wince. I lay my hand on the nightstand, helping me to stand. He stirs and my head whips around, holding my breath so I don't wake him. When I'm sure he's still asleep, I creep, as much as my body will allow, to the bathroom and close the door. After flipping on the light, I catch my reflection in the mirror. I've really avoided it because I'm afraid I'll look as bad as I feel. I'm a little relieved when I see myself. There are dark circles under my eyes, not to mention the bandage on the top of my forehead as well as the bruising that's now turning that ugly yellow-green on my cheek. All in all, I look like I was hit by a truck, but I could look worse. After relieving myself, I try to run my brush through my hair and gave up after a few tries. Even that tired me out, and now I'm hungry again and ready for another nap. Soon it will be nighttime so a nap might be out of the question.

As I walk out of the room I look over at him and sigh. He's moved onto his back, his t-shirt has ridden up above his waist. I can count the ridges of his tight abs, the ones I've explored with my fingers and tongue so many times. Damn. Now I'm horny. I walk out of the room, closing the door quietly. When I walk from the hallway into the living room, I see Mom sitting at the kitchen table. She looks up and smiles as I approach. I sit down across from her and smile back. "What are you doing here? I though everyone left."

She has her laptop on the table and pulls her reading glasses from her face as she looks into my eyes. "Well, honey. We all decided to take shifts, so to speak. We want to make sure you two don't overdo it." I sigh but deep down, I'm glad they decided this. Ever since we left the hospital, I've been worried about just that. I know Brock would do anything and everything to make sure I do nothing. I'm afraid he would hurt himself trying to take care of me, and I couldn't live with that. "Take the help, sweetheart. We're only thinking of you and Brock."

I give her a big smile. "I know, Mom. Thank you." I look down at her laptop and then back at her. "So what are you doing?"

She opens her mouth to speak but nothing comes out then she tilts her head and looks down at the screen. "Oh, just a little research. Something Barb and I are working on together." *Okay, that's really strange. Not so much that she's become friends with Brock's mom but that they have become good enough friends to "work on something together". Maybe it's everything that's happened that pulled them closer. Still seems odd though.* "Would you like something to eat? Drink?" She stands and as I start to peer over she quickly grabs the mouse and clicks then the screen goes dark. *Hmmm.*

"Do we have any of that casserole left, and oh, how about those rolls and some butter? Maybe a glass of diet Coke? Please?" I smile as she nods and walks to the fridge. She may regret helping after I ask her for more when I'm done and another diet Coke but she tells me she's just glad that I'm alive and I can have anything I wish. That might be scary for me. Right now, I feel like I haven't eaten in days when it's only been a few hours that I gorged myself. I'm halfway through my second plate of food when I hear a noise and turn my head towards the hallway. My sleepy man approaches. He puts his arm over his stomach as he bends and kisses the top of my head then walks to the chair beside me and sits. He looks down at my plate and smiles at me.

"Babe. You need to eat more than that." I put my hand that's holding a buttered roll over my mouth so my food doesn't spew.

"This is ma secon pwate," I mumble.

He laughs, and it's the most awesome sound in the world.

The next few days are full of eating and lazing around watching movies. The next few days after that I spent quality time throwing up everything I've ever eaten in my life. Both Brock and I are still getting around a little slow but getting better every day. Well, except for me losing my appetite because every time I eat – I lose it. Pregnancy. Mom, Barb, and Mimi have been so concerned, they took me to see mom's OB/GYN. I'm officially six weeks pregnant and Brock and I get to hear the baby's heartbeat at the next appointment. The doctor did say the baby has a really strong heartbeat when they checked during my surgery so that's makes me feel better. She also gave me a prescription for vitamins as well as something that will help with the nausea. Thank God!

Now, I'm in Brock's truck, out for a little ride. He thought it would be a good idea for us both to get out since he's feeling up to driving now. I didn't argue. I'm sick of being cooped up in our small apartment. When I first moved in with him, I thought it was great, still do – at least the part about living with him. But now that we're gonna have a baby, the second bedroom is so small. Hell, the entire apartment is really small. For now, I'm good with the two of us there. It's cozy. Quaint. The familiar scenery starts making me feel anxious and a little queasy. As we drive down the road we have driven so many times, my hand grabs the door handle and squeezes until my knuckles are white. "Uh, baby? Where are we going? I don't think…."

I look down when I feel his hand take mine. "Hey, it's okay. I have a big surprise." I suck my lower lip into my mouth and lower my brows at him. "Trust me?" I take a deep breath, hoping my stomach will quiet down.

"With my life," I whisper.

He pulls our hands up together and kisses the top of mine. We come to the turn off that takes us in the wooded area, and my grip tightens around the door handle. Suddenly, I'm nervous to see the place where Dad was killed. Where Brock and I almost lost our lives. And this is gonna kill my stomach. Even though the stitches have been removed it's still sore and tender not to mention the nausea I still have from the pregnancy. What is he thinking bringing us out here today? I mean – I love him, but even he's still trying to heal. We both aren't one hundred percent yet.

As he turns off, I close my eyes, waiting for the bumps and grinds of the rough terrain. I wait. And I wait. Still feeling a smooth ride. Confused I open one eye and see that we're on a dirt road. Okay, this might be freaking me out a bit. I'm more and more confused as I open my other eye and look all around. A bunch of the trees are gone, and as we get closer to that slippery rock creek, I gasp. A bridge was built over it large enough for a car to drive over. "Brock?" My eyes shift to him. He's watching the road, but a huge smile is on his beautiful face. I've never been very patient when it comes to surprises. This is even worse. So much work has gone into this and he kept it to himself. I'm so gonna punch him, right after I smother him with kisses and other things. We turn the corner several feet after the bridge and he stops the truck. My heart stops and I blink rapidly. "What? What's all this?"

He turns in his seat, but I can't stop looking at what's before me. "Surprise!" He squeezes my hand and I feel the tingles move up my arm, something that always happens with his touch. Finally, I turn to face him, tears clouding his gorgeous face. "It's been really hard not to tell you about this. Taren. Your mom bought the land, clear from the main road all the way to the pond. She bought all the area where the shack was too. It's all ours, baby. She's gonna have it all signed over to us."

I grab our hands and squeeze. Probably a little too tightly. "Oh, my God, Brock. I…."

He laughs but then turns serious. I blink a few more times and notice there are tears in his eyes as well. "Both my parents, your mom, and Mimi want us to build a house and have this land. They now understand how special it is to us, how much we love each other. Pop has a crew gonna work on it starting next week. I have plans tucked away at home but want you to see them, give input on how you want things. This is gonna be ours, baby. Our new home."

I think I'm in shock. Knots form in my stomach along with excitement, awe, and love. I rip my hand out from his, open the door and start losing the contents of my stomach. I feel him grab my hair, pulling it back. Such a gentleman. I'm so tired of losing my cookies and what a special time to be doing it. When I think I'm finally done, I sit back up, turn to him, and smile. He leans over me and opens the glove compartment, taking out a small container of tissues and hands it to me. I smile and take almost all of them out of it and wipe them over my face, mouth, and stick my tongue out, rubbing them over it. I hear him chuckle and watch him pull out a pack of Tic Tac's. *Lucky Tic Tac's.* And I'm horny again. Sigh. I pop a few in my mouth and as soon as I think my breath is minty enough, I lean towards him and kiss him hard.

"This is amazing! I can't believe it! Our own house!" His lips turn up into a smile, my mouth still pressed to his. "But it's so much and…." His mouth is replaced with a finger, which I kiss too.

"That's what I said but your mom is a stubborn woman. Kinda like her daughter."

I laugh against his finger and then he moves it away and kisses me back. Hard.

Brock

The look on her face – beautiful. Her opening the door and throwing up her guts —pregnancy. Our kissing afterwards – priceless. Totally worth it. I drove her up closer to where everything was lined out for the construction to begin. I can't wait to show her the plans. I'm sure there some things she'll want to change or even add on to and I'm okay with that. We're in this together.

"Wow! It looks so different with the tall grass and rocks gone," she says as I stand behind her, leaning against my truck, with my arms around her slim waist. I really think between the surgery and the pregnancy, she's lost too much weight. If she ever stops throwing up, I'll have to just fatten her up.

"I thought so too, when I first came out here, but now I envision the house, miles of green grass out front and around the sides, and a huge backyard." I point to where I'm talking about and then move my arm to the right. "Then there'll be a stone path, straight to our beach and pond. Can't you just imagine our children growing up here? I'll build them a playhouse in the backyard. A swing set and anything else they want."

Her hand rubs over my arm that's around her stomach. Her touch makes my breath hitch. She leans her head back against my shoulder and her eyes move around the area, imagining. I bring my other arm around her on top of the other. Her more than ample breasts feel like they've already grown from the pregnancy, laying down against the top of my skin. Damn, I'm so freaking horny. We haven't really made love since that night, when our lives changed.

Oh, we've gotten pretty close, but then we realized we both needed to heal more, not having much energy, and figured we have plenty of time. But shit. I am a man. A man who loves his woman more than his life. I have needs. Wants. Desires.

I feel her breath on my skin and look at down. She'd turned her head and her mouth is close to my ear. "Take me home and make love to me," she whispers.

She doesn't need to ask me more than once. I grab her hand and hear her giggles as I pull her, almost roughly, to the door. Once she's settled in, I run around the back, doing a fist pump in the air, and run to my side. I think it was the fastest ride back to our apartment I've ever done. By the time we get inside the building, I'm struggling to unlock our door as my mouth is on hers. My arm is around her waist as she does some amazing things with her tongue. Finally, I get the door open, and we grope each other as we manage to get inside. I keep moving my foot around, trying to find the door. I kick it shut and reach around her, blindly searching for the lock. Turning it closed, I put my hand underneath her long hair and move it up until it's around the back of her neck. She moans into my mouth, guttural and deep. I can actually feel it in her chest. My cock is so hard I feel like I could combust as we make our way back to our bedroom.

We begin undressing each other, frantically, breaking our kissing long enough to pull each other's shirts over our heads. I push down the waistband of her yoga pants. She unbuttons my jeans, and then pulls down the zipper. We laugh as we knock our heads when we try pushing each other's pants down at the same time and then by the time we get them down, our arms are back around each other. We look at each other and grow serious, hungry in our desire. Our mouths smash together and I start to walk backwards. We go down in a rush as I trip over my jeans. We land with an "Omph!" and then burst out in laughter.

I get concerned and start scanning all over her, my hands moving over her arms, her neck, and her face. Her eyes grow serious but there's no pain in them. Only lust and love. Her hands cup both sides of my face, and her lips press against mine, so hard, so needy. Our naked bodies molded together. I grab her hip with one hand and my cock with the other. She lifts and I thrust into her, trying to be gentle, trying not to hurt her, but I've longed for her for so long I can't seem to fight the strain. I grab her other hip as she pulls up to straddle me. She begins to rock, and I know I'm not gonna last long. Her mouth leaves mine and she starts kissing down my jaw, my neck, and sucks the skin on my shoulder. Her long hair falls, shrouding us. A moan leaves me, loud in the small area but her hips rock harder at the sound. In turn, that spurs me on even more and our rhythm becomes faster.

"Brock. I...." Another moan leaves her sweet lips, but then she does something that not only touches me but causes my climax to hit me hard. She leans down and kisses the scar on my chest, where the bullet went into me, reminding me how I almost lost her. I cry out her name, my hands digging into her hips. I feel her clamp around my now deflating cock, and then she yells my name, collapsing on top of me. I envelope her in my arms. Our bodies are slick with sweat and our heavy panting now the only sounds in the room.

"God, I love you so much. So much," I whisper in her ear. My body shudders as hers shivers with her own release, and I hold her even tighter. We lay there and enjoy each other's love for a few minutes more. I move my hands up to the sides of her face, lifting it so I can see her eyes. "Are you okay? Did I hurt you?" She doesn't speak. She searches my eyes with hers. "Taren, I'm sorry if…." Her mouth is on mine, not frantic, not hard. Just gentle with her love.

She smiles against my lips and then raises up just a breath away. "I'm perfect. You're perfect." I smile in relief and raise my head, kissing her again. I lay my head back down, and she lets out a deep breath. "God, I needed that." We both start laughing, and I roll us over. I don't know how long we laid there, laughing, our pants down at our ankles. All I know is I have everything I need. Everything I've ever wanted, right here in my arms.

When I awaken the next morning, all I think about is how we made love again on the floor in the living room last night and then again once when we finally managed to make it to our bed. I reach around, feeling cold without her warmth snuggled up against me and find the other side of the bed cool to my touch. I open my eyes and look around, the sun brightening up the room and wonder what time it is. The clock on the nightstand shows eight in the morning. Wow! I haven't slept this late in a long time. Curious to where my girl is, I climb out of bed, hurry to relieve myself and brush my teeth. Forgoing a shower, I put on a pair of jeans and go in search of her. I stop short when I start to walk into the living room. She's sitting at the kitchen table. I lean against the doorway and watch her studying the floor plans that I'd left on the table yesterday. I notice she has a glass of orange juice beside them and a piece of half eaten toast. I hope her stomach is feeling better today. I start walking towards the kitchen, her face deep in concentration. She doesn't notice me as I reach her and lean down to kiss her neck. "Morning," I say after I nip at her beautiful skin.

She doesn't take her eyes off the plans. "Morning."

I walk over to the counter and notice the pot of coffee. Even though she's sworn off coffee until after the baby comes, she still makes it for me every morning, telling me she's living off the fumes for now. I chuckle as I grab a cup from the cabinet, fill it up then take it over and sit down in the chair beside her. "So. Do you like what you see?"

Her eyes snap to my waist, over the bare skin of my stomach and chest, then slowly make their way up to my eyes. "Mmmhmm," she hums.

I laugh. "I mean the plans, silly girl."

She blinks, twice. "Oh. Oh! The plans. Yes! I love them." I shake my head and laugh again. She's just too cute.

"Anything you'd change?"

She looks at my body again and stares. "Not a damn thing."

I growl. "Taren. I'm about ready to pick you up and throw you over my shoulder."

She looks up quickly and smiles. "Sorry. Hormones. Or sexiness. Yes. Both." I begin to rise and she sits up straight. "Okay! Okay. But um, after." I sit back down, trying to slow my heartbeat. I was ready to grab her. So ready. "There's only a couple of things I'm thinking about. Here." She points to the kitchen. "And here." Our bedroom.

We spend the next two hours going over the plans, excitement filling the room. She has some great ideas, and I swear she could be an interior designer. Hmmm, gives me an idea. After we're done, we ended up on the couch, sex filling the room. We took a lazy bath together and rested. All the excitement and physical activity wore us both out. Shit, I can't wait until we're both healed completely. We may never come up for air.

Once I woke up from my nap, I let her sleep. I couldn't help staring at her, all spread out on our bed. The sheet pulled down, barely covering her waist. My eyes scan up her flat stomach, soon to be full with our child. Nothing sexier than that. Her full breasts that are always perfect, visions of their weight in my hands, and then her long slender neck, one I love to nibble on. Her hair is splayed out across the pillow, dark, long and slightly wavy. Her face is that of a goddess. Creamy porcelain skin. I miss her blue eyes when they're closed but can imagine their radiance in my mind.

I sigh and leave the room knowing if I don't get out, I'll never get anything done. I walk over to the couch, sit down, and call Mom. "Hey, I have a plan."

Next week comes quickly but the excitement of breaking ground at our new house creates mayhem and havoc. Taren is busy with Mom, Mimi, Irish, and Betty picking out and ordering all things needed once it's finished. Appliances, blinds, tiles, furniture – her mom told us the skies the limit. We'll never be able to pay her back, but Taren said that from her inheritance from her dad's death, she can cover some too. I'm feeling more than uncomfortable about it all yet she just kisses me and tells me that since I'm actually helping to build everything, that's more than enough. I guess she's right but still I feel weird about it. What she doesn't know is the plan I have once the house is done. In about a month, give or take, my plan will be set in motion.

The days are long but the night's make up for it. We're both healed now and with my sex drive and love for her and her hormones that have well kicked in, we make love like it's our last night together. Sometimes it's slow and sweet while other times it's frantic and hurried. Each time it's full of love, sensual, full of desire, want, and need. We'll never get enough of each other. Never.

By the next week, we're over halfway done building and just finished the roof today. Now it's smooth sailing as we can start on the inside, storms be damned. Taren's driving me crazy because I won't let her go look. "It's gonna be an epic surprise," I'd tell her. She'd roll her eyes, reminding me how much she hates surprises. She's gonna love this one. I know she'll be excited about the extra little things I've incorporated into the layout, she won't be mad. I hope. Pop called in a couple more crews, the owner's friends of his. He told them he needs to get this finished soon for his son and soon to be daughter in law. After everything that happened, he and Betty have gotten close and put the past behind them. I wish things could have been different. That our families would have seen our love from the beginning. Things would have turned out differently. Her dad would still be alive. I guess everything happens for a reason, but I still feel so bad for Taren. Her dad saw it too late, but at least he attempted to make it right, in the end.

* * * *

"But if I close my eyes then I can't see," she whines as I lead her out of the truck, holding on to her tight. I chuckle with her moaning and groaning, although her sounds are going straight to my cock. In my mind, I'm telling it to calm down, that they'll be plenty of time for that once her surprise is unveiled. "Brock. This is silly. Just uncover my eyes already." She never was good at surprises.

I don't answer. I just let her continue to whine as I walk her over to the spot that will show everything. My heart is beating so fast, I can feel it thumping against my chest. We'd finished the house two days ago. I have to say I'm pretty proud. I couldn't have asked for a better one. It's perfect. Just like she is. We added the finishing touches last night then I went home and made love to her like I never had before. I guess it was the adrenaline that kicked in from getting done and the excitement of showing it to her tonight that did it. Well that and I'm always horny and wanting her.

"Brock! Quit stalling already!"

I chuckle again but suddenly my heart feels like it's lodged in my throat. I look at her and then around and nod to everyone. I know they're just as excited as I am and they should be. They all worked so hard to make this happen whether it be helping to build it, helping Taren pick out and plan everything inside, or just cooking up all the great food for tonight. We couldn't have a better family or friends. Even Caylan looks over and winks at me. He's become part of the family so fast except Irish is always so stand offish around him. But then again – it's Irish. 'Nuff' said.

My hands have become sweaty, covering her eyes. "You ready, my love?" She lets out a huff, and I chuckle. I start to uncover her eyes. "Welcome home." She lets out a scream, covering her mouth with her shaky hands. Her legs almost buckle so I wrap my arms around her waist and rest my chin on her shoulder. "What do you think, baby?" Her head turns all around as she takes it all in.

She's speechless, so unusual for her. My heart feels like it's about to choke me as I wait for her to say something. Anything.

"Oh, my God, Brock," she finally whispers. "It's more than I ever dreamed."

I relax as I look around at our accomplishment. I'd waited until dusk to bring her here, to get the full effect. A beautiful log cabin, two stories. Full wrap around porch that starts on the left side of the front then moves all around the right side of the cabin. Thick wooden beams in a few places jetting out from the floor of the porch extending up to the upper deck off our bedroom. Trees surround the right side and back, giving it that woodsy feeling. Off the porch to the right is an opening, a wooden walkway that leads straight to our beach, our pond. Lights adorn the small railings of the porch, all the way around as well as the walkway. There's also tier lights in the yard in front. A small fountain in the middle with a statue of Romeo and Juliet. Perfect. To the left is a concrete drive, wide enough for our vehicles. A garage made from the same wood creating the look of another cabin attached to the house. All the lights are on inside, in every room.

I lean in and kiss the side of her face, her head lulls back against my chest. "I…. I don't know what to say. I just can't believe it. It's beautiful."

I smile huge. So proud and so excited. "Wait until you see the inside." Her head turns, her blue eyes wide in wonderment. "Come on, baby. Come see." I walk around and take her hand, threading my fingers through hers. Everyone is smiling, yelling their congratulations as we walk up the porch steps. I stop and open the front door, but she doesn't move. I turn and look into her tear filled eyes. "Are you okay? Are you gonna throw up?"

Her eyes find mine and she smiles, shaking her head. "No. It's just so much. So beautiful. I just want to take it all in. Slowly." I understand how she feels. When we got the last piece of furniture put in its place, I just stood there and couldn't stop looking at everything. Only with my explanation, my thoughts of what it would look like, she'd picked out the perfect furniture, appliances, and everything else needed to decorate. Unknowingly, she'd made this look like a home. Feel like it. She squeezes my hand and takes a few steps inside. I look around as she does, taking in the vast living room. The stones for the fireplace give it that earthly feel, with the wide wood mantel. Betty had brought pictures of the two of us and some of her family to set on top. Ma gave me some pictures of my family too, making it complete. In the corner between two large windows sets a wide screen TV. The antique rocker with padded seat, the big recliner, covered in an earth-toned throw, the large coffee table, and the L-shaped couch gives the room a lived in look already. Homey. To the left are double wide wooden steps that lead upstairs.

Her eyes land on the mantel and her hand leaves mine as she walks over to it slowly. She raises her delicate hand and runs it across the pictures until it lands on one of her and Bast. She picks it up and turns her head to me, tears streaming down her beautiful face. "This is perfect," she whispers. I give her time to look at the pictures and when she sees the one of her with her mom and dad, she lets out a sob. I take my cue and walk over to her, wrapping my arms around her slim waist. "I miss him." She lets out another sob, her body shaking slightly.

"I know, baby." I have no more words. What can you say to someone whose Dad gave up his life to save his daughter?

"I'm gonna go get out all the food and get it ready." I hear Mimi say behind us, telling me everyone has made their way inside.

Taren's stomach takes it cue to growl, hearing the word "food". I can't help but chuckle into her back, my mouth pressed against it. "Come on. Let's get you something to eat. Plenty of time to see the rest of the house." She giggles, setting down the picture, and I lead her through the room but stop short when she doesn't move as we enter the kitchen.

"Oh, my God!"

My eyes move around the room, proud of our handy work. The left wall consists of cabinets above and below a granite wood counter and lights underneath the above cabinets. Then a doorway that leads to a half bathroom. To the right is a long pantry and built in two door refrigerator with another long cabinet on the other side. Another small doorway rests beside it, leading to a small entry with wooden steps that go upstairs. Along the wall to the right of that is another counter with the same cabinets. The huge stove/oven is beside it, encased with the same stone as the fireplace. That same stone is the back splash under all the cabinets throughout the kitchen, tying everything together. To the right of the stove is more counter space, more cabinets winding around to a long L-shaped breakfast bar. The outside of that is filled with the same stone. Between the breakfast bar and the wall with the fridge rests a huge island complete with cabinets and the same countertop as the rest.

"It's magnificent. Perfect. A cook's dream." She walks in and I let her go, watching her walk around, opening cabinets, and gasping every time. My heart is full of love and joy. I couldn't be more proud of our work. She turns around, wide eyed, when she sees the opening between the breakfast bar and looks at the smaller one with three padded stools. She's right. It is freaking huge. But with all the children I have planned for us, we'll need the room. We've talked, over the years, both of us wanting a large family. We've always said that we'd give our children everything we can, show them that it doesn't matter where you come from, that's love is love, and that's okay. You can't always help who you fall in love with. We plan to show them that when it's right, it's right. Sure we know there'll be knocks and bumps along the way, but a family's love and support will always be there for them.

The night is full of food, laughter, and the best of times. Mimi outdid herself, cooking more food then we could ever eat in a lifetime. We'll have plenty of leftovers. And with what I have in mind, we'll need them. Two hours move by quickly and we say our goodbyes to everyone, thanking them for everything. I couldn't have done this without them With full stomachs, I lock up and take my girl around the house, showing her the rest of the rooms. She's full of excitement and awe as we walk around. When we get to the baby's room, I put my arms around her waist and explain that we left it bare and that she should start picking out the furnishings and decorate it however she wants. She turns in my arms and kisses me hard.

"Where's our bedroom?" she whispers. Her voice filled with desire. I bend down and she giggles as I lift her into my arms. Her mouth instantly presses against mine as I carry her down the hall and into our room. She doesn't look at it, her mouth never leaving mine. I lay her down on our new bed, the mattress high and comfy. Her hair lays out all around, and my cock pulsates in need and want. I lean over her, pulling up her t-shirt and press kisses on her stomach, up her abs, and nuzzle her bra. I reach under her and unclasp it then find a nipple, sucking it into my mouth greedily. She moans and arches her back, pushing her nipple into my mouth even more. I release it with a loud wet pop and place kisses across her chest until I reach the other peak, nipping at it with my teeth. "God! Brock! Need. You!" She screams, digging her fingernails into the skin of my shoulders.

I make quick time getting rid of our clothes then plunging into her. I grab her hands and move them, setting them on the bed on either side of her head. Threading my fingers through hers, we begin moving slow but pick up speed quickly. The urgency in our love, being in our new home, on our new bed, reminding us of everything we've been through, heats so fast that I know we're both not gonna last too long. We both call out each other's names as we reach our climaxes together.

Our bodies are slick with sweat so I do what any other man would do. I pick her body up in my arms, kiss her all the way into our bathroom, and set her down on the counter. Instead of flipping on the lights, I strike a match from the box laying on the small table. I light the candles around her on the counter and the ones that outline the huge Jacuzzi bathtub.

When I turn around, her eyes are wide, and her face glows in the warm low lighting. I lean over and turn the knobs, holding my hand underneath the spray of water waiting for the right temperature. I smell her before I feel her arms move around my waist. Her body smells of sex and *her*. My cock is already hardening as she begins to place kisses all along my back. I pull up on the stopper, letting the water fill then turn around and capture her swollen lips. My hands rub her back as our tongues play a game of chase. I don't know how long we stand there, kissing and groping. Soon I turn my head and the water in the tub is almost to the top. I release her reluctantly and turn it off then lift her into my arms and step in. The water sloshes over the top as I sit down, her legs straddling me immediately. The scent of the candles fill my nose, along with the scent of her hair as I nuzzle into her neck. Our bodies move as one, my fingers digging into her hips as hers bury into my shoulders.

"Brock," her cry muffled as her mouth presses against my arm. Her body shakes as mine shudders with my own release. We don't move for the longest time, just holding each other. My day is complete.

Once dried and dressed in our sleeping attire, I carry her to our bed, and cover us up. She snuggles into my chest, like she always does, and places her leg in between mine. As I listen to her light breathing, all I can think about is that now we'll be together forever, with nothing and no one trying to stop us. I nuzzle my nose in her hair and breathe her in. "I'm gonna marry you," I whisper. "Soon."

Epilogue

Caylan

My life's been full of lustful women, too easy and always giving it up to me. I've never minded but I always lose interest. I've been a love 'em and leave 'em kinda guy, only 'cos I haven't found the one woman who I want a relationship with, yet. However, I never once led them on. Always told them from the beginning there were no strings attached and this was only a one night thing. They didn't seem to mind. In fact, that's all they really wanted me and my body for anyway. What can I say? I'm always on the prowl. I have a healthy appetite. Some call me stubborn, hard headed, and possibly a neat freak. I can't help the way I am, although I have a hard time dealing with anxiety, at times. I'm the kind of man who always wants everyone around me to be happy, to the point of my own unhappiness. Guess that's the worrier in me, which causes the anxiety and small bouts of depression sometimes. Why? I guess it's the way I was raised. I was taught to help others, treat women like they're all ladies, even though some are far from it. I always open doors for them, never walk in front of them or walk ahead. They're always the first to sit down and the first to take a bite of their food. I make sure of it. Gentleman through my core.

I sigh, thinking of the term "neat freak" as I straighten my towel on the rack. Okay, yeah, that could be a good name for it. Hey, at least I'm not the *Sleeping with the Enemy* kind. My can goods do not have all the labels turned around facing the front. Well, not all of them anyway. That reminds me. I need to pick up all my discarded clothes off the floor from last night and get some laundry started.

Since moving here, there's a new abundance of women to be had. After having a great time at Brock and Taren's new house last night, I ended up at Pops Bar and had a couple of drinks. I don't drink much but I like the occasional light beer. Of course, Pop wouldn't let me pay for anything, saying he owed me after helping to save his sons. I only did what I was compelled to do. I like them. Kane gave me a job when I first got into town without knowing anything about me. I pay back what's due but even without that, I would have done it anyway. Just the kind of guy I am. The sense of pride was swelling in me when Brock showed Taren their new house for the first time. To think I had a hand in building it and how it turned out made me feel so good. Probably the most proud I've been on a construction project. The sight of Taren's face when Brock brought her home was something to behold. She was more than surprised and the house – it's like a work of art. Knowing I had a hand in it fills my heart. Someday. Someday I'll have what they have. Their love is strong, the house magnificent. And they have a baby on the way too. Some day.

My pocket vibrates, reminding me I forgot to take my phone off vibrate last night. Guess I was too preoccupied. I look at the phone and sigh then bring it up to my ear. "Amanda. How are you?"

"Great, Caylan. And you?" Her voice sounds like normal, too chipper. I cringe, shivers running through me.

"I'm good. Look, kinda busy. What can I do for you?" I hated to ask knowing she never calls unless she has something she needs or wants me to do.

"Good. Hey, there's a book signing at *The Ritz* next Saturday. Can you attend with me? I'll have some posters for you to sell and sign. You can make a little extra money. I need you there on Friday night and stay until Sunday morning. I'll pay for your room and food. Please?" She sounds so hopeful but she knows I'd never tell her no. She's really done a lot for me.

I walk into the kitchen, open the drawer, and pull out the small pad of paper and grab a pen. "Sure. What time do you need me to be there and what's the address?" I scribble on the pad as she excitedly gives me the information.

"Thanks, Caylan. You're the best! See you next Friday." Click. Well, okay then. Guess I'll be going to a book signing. Hmmm. Book signing. Readers. Women readers. Maybe this won't be so bad after all.

I start to head back to my bedroom to get the clothes to start laundry when a knock sounds on my front door. Damn, never gonna get my clothes washed. I walk quickly to the door and open it.

"Well, I'll be." Irish is standing there, looking everywhere but at me. I've been intoxicated with her ever since we first met but she won't have anything to do with me which makes me wonder why she's here. And how did she know where I live?

Her hand reaches up and in it she's holding my jeans jacket. "You left this at Pops last night," she says like she's totally put out that she had to bring it to me. Her eyes finally find mine, and I have to press my lips together to try not to smile when one of her eyebrows raises high up into her forehead as she smirks.

I take it from her and put my hand in the front pocket, pulling out my wallet. So that's how she knew where I lived. "Thanks, doll." She turns and starts to walk to the front steps. I step out of the door and turn. "Ya know. If you wanted to know where I lived, you could have just asked. I would have figured out eventually that I left it there and would have gone to get it myself." I can't help but smile trying to look all suave and confident but truth be told – inside my stomach is in knots, and my cock is harder than a rock.

She turns around in a huff, her hand lands on her cocked hip and a sneer graces her mouth. "Ha. Funny. First of all, the name isn't "doll". Second, I could have cared less where you live. Just thought I'd do you the favor since I was on my way to the gym. Don't worry. I won't bother again." She throws her head back, her dark brown haired ponytail whips around her as she storms down the steps. I normally go for women with blonde hair. Long so I can wrap it around my hand as we…. Well, you get the picture. But something about her dark hair and eyes that match the color is hitting me hard. Maybe it's also her snarky attitude and the fact that she doesn't want me like all the rest.

I lean back against the door frame and watch her walk quickly to her truck. She's a feisty one, that's for sure. One thing I love -- a woman who's as stubborn as me. Confident. A woman who will make me work for it and not just want to be with me for sex and my fit body. Someone who's not only gorgeous on the outside but inside as well. A *real* woman. One that I'd take home to meet my family. She seems to be all that and more. Now. What can I do to get her attention? Maybe I need some inside help. Taren is her best friend, and I know Brock has known her most of his life as well. I may just have to find out what I can from them. In a nonchalant kind of way of course. Looks like I have my work cut out for me. Suddenly, I feel the urge to work out. Forgetting all about laundry, I go back inside, slamming the door behind me and walk to my bedroom. I hurriedly change into my gym clothes and brush my teeth. Can't have too fresh of breath. I grab my truck keys from the small dish on the table by the door, walk outside, and lock up.

As soon as I'm in my monster truck, my phone vibrates. "Hey, Taren!" I speak as I pull out of my parking space. "What's up? Everything okay?" I look both ways and pull out onto the road.

"Hi, Caylan! Yes. Everything's fine. Brock and I were just wondering if you'd like to come to dinner tonight."

Perfect opportunity to get some information. "I'd love to. What time?" I couldn't have planned this better myself. It's like she read my mind.

"How about seven?" She sounds like she has a smile in her voice.

"Perfect! I'm just heading over to the gym now to workout. That'll give me time to get a shower before I head over. Can I bring anything?"

"Nah. Just bring yourself. Oh! Irish will be there too. Thought you might wanna know that. See you later."

I laugh and hang up, putting my phone back in my pocket. Taren is a sly one and smart. She definitely knows I have feelings for Irish or something. I think I could trust her though, tell her how I feel about Irish. Maybe that would be a good thing. I don't trust easily. Too many people have taken advantage of my good nature. Still, if someone needed something and I could do it for them, I would. Cue anxiety. That's just how I am. One thing is for certain. Taren and Brock are good people. They've never done anything but treat me well. Respect me.

I pull into the gym parking lot and lock up my truck. When I walk in the front door, the girl at the front counter waves and smiles at me. She's pretty young, just seventeen. She works here on the weekends and some evenings after school. She has a major crush on me. I give her a wave and head to the men's locker room. Since I've been working here part time as a personal trainer, I have my own locker. I stow my wallet and keys then head upstairs and look around. I spot her immediately in the room that has mats, fitness balls, and a couple of punching bags. I stand there staring as she hops back and forth, her hands looking larger in the gloves. She punches then bounces. My heart rate increases as I start walking towards the room. Why am I sweating? I've never felt so scared in all my life. I walk into the room until I'm just a few feet away from her then cross my arms.

Irish

"You're doing it wrong."

His voice sends chills through me. Which is weird since I'm hotter than hell and sweating up a storm. I grab the bag, stopping it from hitting me, and look at him, giving him a smirk. He's standing only a few feet away, his beefy arms crossed over his large chest. I think I might hyperventilate. I've always had a thing for red heads. Especially dark haired red heads. Broad chest. Slim waist. And those tight abs. Can you say -- large six pack? Definitely gonna hyperventilate. He has the biggest shoulders I've ever seen. Images enter my mind. My small hands hanging on to those large shoulders as we....

"You okay there?" My eyes focus back to his face. "You look a little.... flushed."

I try to cross my arms over my chest but the gloves on my hands prevent it so they drop to my side. "I'm fine," I all but growl. "And I'm doing just fine by myself." I turn and start punching the bag, this time in anger.

He chuckles, low and rough. *Dammit.* "I could show you the right way. Don't want you to hurt yourself." *What the fuck?*

I push against the bag, stopping its swing, and decide to try to be nice. Well, nice for me. "Look. I know you're all that…." My eyes scan down his body then back up slowly until they reach his. "But. I've been working out for a few years now. No one finds anything wrong with this body." Those shivers return as his eyes take their turn scanning over me. When he reaches my eyes, I swear I'm about to combust.

He turns and heads over to the other bag. "Suit yourself, doll." Those feelings of desire and lust. Yeah, they just turned into anger. *Doll.* I'm still holding onto the bag as I watch him walk over to the shelves and put on some gloves. His muscles flex not only in his arms but with that wifebeater on, I can see the muscles ripple in his huge back as well. *Damn, him.* The chills have returned. He turns, still fixing one of the gloves as he walks to the bag. I pretend to punch my bag but watch him from the corner of my eye. I have to say, he has great eye and feet coordination. He's swift and sure like he's taking the bag down. I have a lot to learn.

"If you have good foot work, that's half the battle." He hits again and I look down at his feet. Large feet. *You know what they say. Okay, that's not always true.* "Don't jump around but move keeping low to the ground." His hits the bag, twice. "Don't punch the bag. Snap. A good snap." He hits it a few more times, moving around it slowly, staying bent, low. "Good flow." I continue to watch, aimlessly hitting my bag. "Don't continually do hard shots. Instead do a constant flow and punches, snapping the bag then you can put in a few hard shots here and there." I stop and hold my bag. My eyes are zoned into his form. He moves with grace and ease. He does some snapping punches, continuing low and around the bag, then does a few hard shots. "It's all about power and speed." I'm mesmerized by him. He seems to be floating, and his hard shots hit with a force. "Irish?"

My eyes snap to him. I can feel the heat of my embarrassment. "Yeah. That's pretty good." His mouth clamps shut, like he's trying not to laugh. "Good to know." I start taking my gloves off and walk passed him to the shelves. I struggle getting off the first glove. They're so big and encumbering.

"Here. Let me," his voice is right beside me, and I freeze. His large hands are gloveless. *How the hell did he get his off so fast?* He unfastens my glove and pulls it off easily then the other. I try not to look up into his eyes. I really try hard but it's like mine are just magnetized right to his. Hazel green. A fucking red head with hazel green eyes. I take a stuttering breath until I realize he's staring directly into my eyes. I pull back and take a few steps back then turn quickly and start power walking to the doorway.

"Thanks," I yell over my shoulder and run like hell, hearing his low chuckles behind me and I think I heard "doll" in there somewhere. Ugh!

I practically run out of the gym and into my truck. As I start it up, I look over and see his mammoth truck. *What is it with big guys and big trucks?* After getting home and taking a much needed shower, I get dressed in my black yoga pants, a silky white tank top, and my favorite black flip flops with the glittering rhinestones that lace the straps. I'm anxious to get over to Taren and Brock's new house. I didn't really get a chance to take a good tour last night. It's the most beautiful house I've ever seen, and I'm so happy for them. They truly deserve it and a lifetime of happiness. Of course, I'm ecstatic that I'm gonna be an aunt. Okay, not by blood but I'm her best friend so of course I'll be their baby's aunt.

The drive up to the house is beautiful. They've added some more outside lights along the road and the railing on either side of the bridge. Magical. I pull into their driveway and park behind Brock's truck. His truck isn't HUGE like someone else's. I roll my eyes and get out then walk up the porch steps and knock on the door. It opens quickly, and I'm in Taren's firm hold. "'Bout time you got here." I struggle and choke until she releases me, and I stumble inside. She puts her arm through mine and leads me to the kitchen.

"Well, I worked out. Didn't want me to come over stinky, did you?" She laughs as I sit down on a barstool. I watch her walk to the fridge, bringing me back a cold beer. I twist off the cap and pick up the bottle, taking a huge drink. "Damn. I needed that." She grabs her bottled water and leans on the counter in front of me.

"So working out, huh? And how is the new job going? I feel bad. With everything that's been going on, I haven't even asked." Her smile is big and waiting for all the details. She's the bestest friend I've ever had. Okay, she's the only "real" friend I've ever had. 'Cept for the guys but they don't count.

"I love it! I'm learning so much." I take another drink and swallow hard. "Only. They want to send me to this convention next weekend. You know how I am with crowds and there'll be other tech companies there. Ugh! I can see the guys hitting on me now. You know that makes me crazy." I take another drink. I may have to have a lot of these at the convention. "And there's a party of sorts that first night too." Sigh.

"So, it's all weekend?" She asks anxious to hear.

"Yes. I have to be there Friday night and stay until Sunday morning. Hey, at least it's all paid by them though. That's a plus I guess." I take another big gulp. I get up and throw away the empty bottle and get another one from the fridge, twisting off the cap and dunking it in the trash can. I return to my seat and take another big swig.

"That is a plus. Uh, you can stay the night in one of the guest bedrooms, if you want." She smiles sweetly.

"Nah, I'm good."

"Hey, look who's here," Brock's voice sounds excited behind me. Wonder who…

"Hey, doll. Fancy meeting you here," his voice sends those chills down my spine. With my bottle up to my lips, I turn my head. Caylan is standing there, big grin, beefy arms across his beefy chest, and those hazel eyes lit up like a Christmas tree.

Fuck. My. Life.

The End

Falling For Love (Beyond Love series #2)

Love can be deceiving,
Love can be unkind,
Love comes when you least expect it,
If you're lucky, love will find you

Caylan Dorn drives himself hard to make something out of his life. He holds multiple jobs; construction worker, fitness trainer and model. He's already been on two book covers and has been asked to attend a book signing with the author. A month before the signing, he decides to move to the town where it will be held to begin a new life and has no trouble finding jobs in what he excels. The signing is located in a plush hotel, but little does he realize what awaits for him there.

Irish Hadley has worked at Pops Bar most of her young life and loves her extended family there. However, she's tired of constantly being hit on by all the guys. She wants something more so she accepts a full time job at a large tech company, while continuing to help out at the bar on weekends. She's been instructed to attend a convention at one of the ritzy hotels nearby but dreads being around all the mayhem. She soon finds there's another event being held there and her curiosity is piqued.

What else will she find there? A hot and sexy redhead that won't take no for an answer.

About the Author

Vicki Green grew up in Overland Park, Kansas and currently resides in Olathe, Kansas. Along with her husband and two teenage boys, she shares her home with her cocker spaniel's Shadow and Mocha. She has been working full time at the same company for 35 years. Her life has been filled with the most loving and caring parents, who are both gone now but are still in her heart and mind daily.

Vicki enjoys reading Romance books which is what inspired her to begin writing this book. She has always admired Author's dedication and hard work. She had a dream that played out for over a year, came home one day after work and decided to put it on a word document to see how it read and that became 'My Savior Forever', the beginning of her Forever Series, and that's where it all began.

Website: http://www.vickigreenauthor.com/

Facebook page: https://www.facebook.com/VickiGreenAuthor

Twitter: @rileyks3

Goodreads Author:

https://www.goodreads.com/author/show/7112966.Vicki_

Green

Made in the USA
San Bernardino, CA
28 March 2015